Man of
All Passions

MAN OF ALL PASSIONS

THE CONFLICTING DRIVES AND COMPLEX DESIRES OF A MAN OF GOD

ROBERT HICKS

NAVPRESS

BRINGING TRUTH TO LIFE

NavPress Publishing Group

P.O. Box 35001, Colorado Springs, Colorado 80935

The Navigators is an international Christian organization. Jesus
Christ gave His followers the Great Commission to go and make
disciples (Matthew 28:19). The aim of The Navigators is to help
fulfill that commission by multiplying laborers for Christ in every
nation.

NavPress is the publishing ministry of The Navigators. NavPress
publications are tools to help Christians grow. Although publications alone cannot make disciples or change lives, they can help
believers learn biblical discipleship, and apply what they learn to
their lives and ministries.

Unless otherwise identified, all Scripture quotations in this publica-
tion are taken from the *New American Standard Bible* (NASB), ©
The Lockman Foundation 1960, 1962, 1963, 1968, 1971, 1972,
1973, 1975, 1977. Other versions used include the *HOLY BIBLE:
NEW INTERNATIONAL VERSION* ® (NIV®). Copyright © 1973,
1978, 1984 by International Bible Society. Used by permission of
Zondervan Publishing House. All rights reserved.

Hicks, Robert, 1945-
        Man of all passions : the conflicting drives and complex
    desires of a man of God / Robert Hicks.
            p.   cm.
        Includes bibliographical references.
        ISBN 0-89109-791-0
        1. David, King of Israel—Fiction. 2. Bible. O.T.—His-
    tory of Biblical events—Fiction. 3. Israel—Kings and
    rulers—Fiction. I. Title.
        PS3558.I26M36   1995
        813'.54—dc20   95-22513
                                                        CIP

Printed in the United States of America

1 2 3 4 5 6 7 8 9 10 11 12 13 14 15 / 00 99 98 97 96 95

Contents

To Carol Seitz
Wife, Mother of two,
Educator, Violist, Performer,
Conductor and Psalmist in your own right.
A Muse Par Excellance.
A Sister worthy of her praise.

To Jacqueline Dillon-Krass
Wife, Mother of hundreds of students,
Clinician, Cellist, Performer,
Music Educator and Author.
A Mentor beyond the Pale.
A Sister to be praised as well.

—Lechavod Hamashiach

CHAPTER ONE

A Man of All Passions

"A HEART WHOLLY DEVOTED"

As Ari reached the tel's flattened apex, a blast of hot, dry wind greeted him. These furnacelike blasts called "Hamsins" often come up from Saudi Arabia during the summer months. Swirls of dust created by the wind looked like small tornadoes, emerging across the Negev. Though the temperature exceeded 100 degrees, Ari loved the dry heat.

The height of the tel not only provided an excellent view of the land, but also represented the history of his people back to Abraham. Here he felt a deep religious—almost mystical—connection to his people, mixed with a certain longing for something more. A missing kinship perhaps.

As commander of a crack Sayeret Giva'ati unit called "Samson's Foxes," he was well acquainted with the terrain, the climate, and the region's history. But on this occasion he moved his six-foot frame to the top of ancient Tel Beersheba, not only to gain a reconnaissance position overlooking the Negev, but also to do some rare personal reflection.

Removing his distinctive purple beret, he brushed back the wavy brown hair from his face and tucked the beret under the epaulet of his olive drab fatigue uniform. Ari (short for Ariel) took his canteen and poured the last measure of water over his head. Israelis often joke about the reality of the dry desert heat. It is said that when this canteen exercise is accomplished, no water ever hits the ground! That is how fast moisture evaporates during a Hamsin.

Ari leaned back on a large rock, probably the remains of an ancient Israelite threshing wheel, and placed his face directly into the sun. For a few moments he closed his green eyes and let the sun's dry heat beat upon his well-tanned face. With the sleeve of his uniform he wiped off the remains of moisture running off his chiseled jaw, which was shadowed by several days of stubble.

At this ancient locale overlooking the Negev, his thoughts naturally gravitated to the past—both recent and distant. He thought of how Abraham had wandered to this place almost four thousand years before and dug a well. He wondered if the well discovered on this very mound was the one dug by Abraham's hands.

Of course, in the modern city of Beersheba is a restaurant called Abraham's Well, which is built over an ancient well. Here tourist buses stop for lunch, picture taking, and the historical spiel.

Even though Ari was skeptical about these "religious tours," he also realized this site still might be accurate. Of course, in this ancient land, something historical happened at every site! *Beersheba* means "seven wells." So this could be one of the ancient Abrahamic wells. No one really is certain. But Ari preferred the rugged, rocky antiquity of this site over the more comfortable commercial site. He preferred it for yet another reason: Tel Beersheba was a favorite spot of Ari's father.

The afternoon heat beat down on Ari's lean, sinewy body. He unbuttoned his fatigue and allowed the wind to ventilate his warm body. His exposed chest did not reflect the body of a middle-aged man. The many forced marches across the desert and the rigorous physical exercise special-forces units face had kept Ari "lean and mean" at a slim 185 pounds. His broad chest was still muscular and his belly rippled. As Ari ran his hand over his stomach, he thought, *Not bad for a forty-seven-year-old, graying-at-the-temples kind of man!*

Ariel's father had fought in some of the fiercest battles around Beersheba during the war for Israel's independence, and distinguished himself as a heroic, risk-taking warrior against both Egyptian and Jordanian troops. Often, in those battles, the lack of modern military weaponry and formal military training forced the Jewish fighters to do the unthinkable and sometimes the impossible. They all become *davidkas*, "little Davids," taking on superior forces with limited means and turning around the attacking Arab forces through stealth, bravery, and pure Jewish panache.

Ari's father, Jacob Rabinowitz, a Polish Jew, had fled for his life as a teenager when the Nazis invaded his homeland. Jacob's parents were among the few who believed the reports that Hitler would invade Poland. They secretly sneaked Jacob, their only son, out of the country. He left first by train and then was passed from friend to friend throughout Europe until he found his way to a kibbutz in Israel. He never saw his parents again. The fires of the Holocaust consumed not only his parents but the secure environment in which he was raised.

The agricultural community located on the Sea of Galilee's southern shore provided Jacob his first experience in farming. It also covertly provided training in firearms and military operations. Always surrounded by enemies, every kibbutz member became acquainted with the use of arms. First, in defense of Arab attacks upon the communities, and then after the war with Hitler, against their supposed allies, the British. It was there on the sands of the land-locked "sea" that Jacob Rabinowitz took a Hebrew name and joined the Haganah, the Jewish military underground.

At his swearing in, he took the name Yakov Ammud—"Yakov," the Hebrew form of Jacob, and "Ammud," the Hebrew word for "foundation" or "platform." It was a name appropriately chosen for him by the Haganah leaders, since his chief desire was to forge a new foundation for both himself and the Jewish people. His life would be a platform upon which those who followed would build. Ariel ben David Ammud, his son, was one of those.

Ari was born in 1949, four years after the Allied forces had defeated the Axis powers in World War II, and one year after the Jewish War of Independence. Ariel's earliest memories were of warfare or expected warfare. With Ariel and the rest of the kibbutz children safely placed underground in the middle of the kibbutz compound, all the kibbutz adults became soldiers and defended the fronts during the War of Independence. With seven Arab nations simultaneously attacking this small, struggling country, every Jew who could fire a gun became a soldier.

Jordanian shells fell all around the Galilee kibbutz. Ariel's dad had been here in this area of Beersheba, while his mother, a striking

British beauty, was in Tel Aviv tending to the wounded in makeshift hospitals. As a British citizen, she had served as a nurse in Israel with the British forces during World War II. Half-Jewish (on her mother's side, making her Jewish by later Israeli law), Karen Powers stayed after the war and committed several years to helping rebuild the country. She never left.

One summer she volunteered to help harvest the crops and serve as a kibbutz nurse. Yakov Ammud was the handsome young man who drove the tractor near her during the day. At night he trained her in the use of firearms. After lessons in lethal weapons, they took long walks. The walks soon turned to love, and they were married by the local rabbi in Tiberias.

Ari would learn later that his life during this time had been protected and defended by many women—mothers and teenagers—who were all Haganah trained. They were trained by his father, Yakov Ammud, a man he knew very little about as an adult.

One of the midwives came with more hot water. Abinadab asked, "Any news yet?"

"No, but it won't be long now. The head is already showing," the midwife answered.

Ozem looked at his father and said, "Well, Father, any feelings about this one? After seven sons and two daughters, you are a real expert at this."

"Oh, my son, feelings are of no regard in times like these. And besides, the only experts at such things are those inside. Your mother and the midwives are the real experts," replied Yishay (Hebrew for Jesse).

Their conversation was interrupted by the shrill sounds of a moaning woman and then by screaming. After a few seconds, the cry of a baby pierced the early morning silence.

"Hallelu Ya," Yishay proclaimed as he raised his eyes and hands toward the sky. The midwife opened the door and motioned to Yishay. He peeked into the dimly lit room and saw his beloved wife with babe in arms.

The midwife took a towel and wet basin and washed the baby in salt water, removing the birth fluids around the head and body. She wrapped the child in cloths and brought the small bundle to the anxious father.

Placing the baby into Jesse's arms, she said simply, "It's another boy. How blessed are you, Yishay."

Yishay looked up to heaven and prayed, "Blessed are Thou, O Lord God, who brings forth the fruit of the womb."

He moved over to where his wife reclined, kissed her, and placed a blessing upon her womb. He then walked outside to the waiting group of friends and children. He held the child over his head and said, "The Lord gives to the house of Yishay another son. May His name be great in Israel!"

Ariel heard footsteps behind him. Instinctively grabbing his Galil assault rifle, he swung around to see who was coming up the incline.

"Shalom, Major," greeted Sergeant Eyal as he approached.

"Shalom, Sergeant Eyal," Ari replied. "Is it time to go?"

"No, we still have a few minutes before we need to check into headquarters."

"I love this place. Give me a few more moments here, Sergeant Eyal."

"Beseder," Sergeant Eyal replied as he distanced himself from Ari.

Ari walked among the rubble and ruins and slid down the trench where archaeologists had cut a slice through the tel. He took an old potsherd and began digging. Suddenly he realized he was doing what his father always did. He could never resist the temptation to dig around the ancient biblical sites. *Like father, like son*, Ari thought.

Ari's father was not a religious man or a scholar; only a simple farmer and soldier. But he loved the history of the Jewish people and their land. Ari's finest memories were of being with his father when he took a true Sabbath. On those rare occasions, they always did the same thing. They would pile into the kibbutz truck and drive to an obscure place. Yakov would turn off the main roads, bouncing along rocky roads for several kilometers. Then together they would hike to a remote site. Ari thought they must have climbed every mountain and tel in Israel. He wondered how his father even knew about such places.

But it was during these times that Yakov's great love for the land

and the biblical stories came alive. His knowledge of the Bible always amazed Ari. Though he hated the religious orthodoxy of Judaism, Yakov's evening routine was almost as strict. After a day's hard work in the fields, he would shower, share the communal kibbutz meal, go for a walk with his wife, and then read the Bible before retiring. As far as Ari knew, although his father loved the Bible stories, he held no particular religious beliefs.

Ari remembered when someone once asked his father what his religion was. His quick answer was, "I'm not anything but Israeli." After losing his parents in the Holocaust, he blamed the Orthodox for being so piously weird in dress and behavior as to give Hitler an "excuse" for his atrocities against the Jews.

Having lost almost all living connection to his Polish family, it was very difficult for his father to believe in a God who supposedly was there to protect His people. Ari remembered him saying on several occasions that God would no longer fight for Israel—"We must defend ourselves."

But being at this place where his father made biblical stories come alive prompted Ari to think perhaps there was more to his father's faith than self-reliance. Yakov Ammud was a great admirer of King David.

To Yakov, David was not only Israel's greatest king, but its most astute warrior. Ari remembered well the lessons taught on this very site at the edge of the Negev.

"God protected King David because he knew where to hide," he could hear his father say. "David was a great warrior because he asked for God's help, and he was a good shot!" Ari laughed at his father's humor and insight.

Ari retrieved the beret from its shoulder placement and placed it snugly on the side of his head. Slinging his Galil over his shoulder, he took one last glance toward the northeast and a small ridge of hills. He thought about the kind of man King David must have been; how a young, last-born shepherd could become Israel's greatest king. And more importantly for Ari, how this ancient king had become such a model for his own father's life. In the Jewish scriptures, King David was the model man, the example for all later kings; the scale upon which all other leaders would be measured. Either they followed the ways of King David or pursued evil ways. *Why was this?* Ari wondered.

As he walked down the road toward where his Bedouin tracker

and Sergeant Eyal were waiting in the jeep, a word came to his mind. *Passion*, he thought. *That's it!*

Ari knew that the Hebrew language used two words to express that concept: *'ahavah*, "love," and *sa'arat*, "whirlwind" or "storm." While remembering his dad, it suddenly struck Ari as quite appropriate that the word *passion* carried the idea of a whirlwind. Watching the circles of windblown dust cross the Negev, he visualized the kind of passion he had seen in his father.

Yakov was a passionate, loving whirlwind. Whether in battle or conversation, viewing the land or telling Bible stories — whatever he did consumed him. So it must have been with King David, his historic mentor.

Men of passion are whirlwinds. Their passion for life consumes whatever they do. They are the lovers of life, and their loves encompass all they do, often in contradictory ways.

For good or ill, men of passion are men who feel deeply, act decisively, compete heroically, and err significantly. To an observer, their passions often seem paradoxical. But it is this conflict that makes them unique. King David was no dull, passive couch potato. He was a man with a full range of human, masculine passion. He was a man of all passions!

Sergeant Eyal hit the gas and the jeep jumped forward toward the main road. Ari again glanced toward the northeast and pondered that shepherd-turned-soldier who defeated the Philistine giant in the Valley of Elah just a few kilometers away. In one critical event, the young David tasted the reality of the warrior.

There is no way around it. The warrior's passion is a passion that includes — yes, may even demand — bloodshed. Being a man and a warrior, both in biblical times and contemporary times, is seldom a quiet, pastoral life. It is a life cluttered and clouded by images of warfare and bloodshed.

CHAPTER TWO

A Man of War:
Passion for Blood

"HE TRAINS MY HANDS FOR BATTLE"

I n Israel, all citizens are warriors. Even public rest rooms reflect that reality. On rest room doors, "Men" is *gibbor* ("warrior" or "soldier") and "Women" is *gibborot* ("female warriors").

According to Israel's 1959 Military Service Law, all eighteen-year-olds are conscripted into military service. This includes women. The only exemptions are married women, those who have criminal records, and those who have religious convictions against serving in the military (the ultra-Orthodox). Every Israeli serves at least three years and is held in the reserves until age fifty-five. The standard Israeli joke rings true that in Israel there are no civilians, only soldiers on leave for ten months every year!

In a country surrounded by enemies, the military takes on a more positive role than in most Western countries. The warrior is considered at the highest end of the social stratum in Israel. But to the rest of the world, the positive value of the warrior is sometimes lost. Soldiers, as warriors, exist to defend and secure a country's boundaries. True warriors do not fight battles for self-interest or self-advancement. Military organizations are not necessarily the "loose cannons" the media often portray them to be. More commonly, warriors serve the orders of superiors, who in turn serve in the interest of national security and defense. Everyone in the military community knows why an armed force exists. It exists to shed blood, kill, wound, and destroy. The reality of the warrior is blood—the willingness to risk his own and the willingness to shed another's. It's a nasty reality, but any country without warriors is in a precarious position. Ask the Kuwaitis!

That night Ari retrieved his father's copy of the Holy Scriptures from the musty trunk where he kept his father's military memorabilia. He found the story of David and Goliath and read,

> David said to Saul, "Your servant was tending his father's sheep. When a lion or a bear came and took a lamb from the flock, I went out after him and attacked him, and rescued it from his mouth; and when he rose up against me, I seized him by his beard and struck him and killed him. Your servant has killed both the lion and the bear; and this uncircumcised Philistine will be like one of them, since he has taunted the armies of the living God." (1 Samuel 17:34-36)

He read on,

> And David put his hand into his bag and took from it a stone and slung it, and struck the Philistine on his forehead. And the stone sank into his forehead, so that he fell on his face to the ground. . . . Then David ran and stood over the Philistine and took his sword and drew it out of its sheath and killed him, and cut off his head with it. . . . And the men of Israel and Judah arose and shouted and pursued the Philistines as far as the valley, and to the gates of Ekron. And the slain Philistines lay along the way to Shaaraim, even to Gath and Ekron. (verses 49-52)

Ariel closed the text and tried to visualize the event. He had driven and walked across this valley many times. He had spent nights on top of Tell Azeka overlooking the Valley of Elah and the little village below. He tried to visualize the thousands of slain bodies littering the valley from Azekah to Gath (about eight kilometers) and then up to Ekron (another ten kilos).

This event was David's first campaign, his first route, his first blood. The event established him as a courageous man of war and in response Saul gave him a warrior's reward. Young David was given command over other men of war (1 Samuel 18:5). David's victory spontaneously created musical celebrations of epic proportions. David very quickly achieved celebrity status simply because he had taken the life of another feared warrior (verse 6). A popular tune heard all over Israel went,

Saul has slain his thousands,

And David his ten thousands. (verse 7)

Ari had seen the same response after Israel's wars. Men of no reputation from insignificant towns and villages, through their heroism, quickly became celebrated soldiers, complete with dancing in the streets and songs honoring their bravery. But what struck Ari about this ancient text was not the victory but David's preparation as a warrior, which gave him his unique warrior perspective and tactics.

⌒

DAVID'S PREPARATION FOR BATTLE

It sounded like a rock moving and then falling. In the crisp night air, every sound is heightened and amplified. But still, every shepherd sleeps with one ear open. The young teenager was about to close his eyes, roll over, and go back to sleep when he heard movement in the sheep pen.

He reached for his staff and swung his sling over his shoulder. Then he heard the quick movement of a large animal and the squeal of one of his sheep. He rushed to the pen in time to see a large shadow leap over the rock wall and dart into the darkness.

Instinctively, David chased the animal. Running as fast as he could, he listened for sounds of movement or violence. Twice he stopped, but only long enough to look for signs of blood or paw prints in the moonlight. Discovering such, he was off again at his swift pace. As David came to the incline of a rocky climb, the moon cast enough light on the side of the mountain for him to make out the figure of a lion, a small lamb in its mouth, delicately picking its way through the craggy terrain.

David placed a stone in his sling and swung the leather pieces. Taking careful aim, David released the stone with all his skill and strength. The projectile struck the lion directly on its side. The lion dropped the lamb, turned, and let out a piercing roar.

David was out of breath and his heart was pounding. For several moments the two figures in the night stared at each other to see what the other's next move might be. David wrapped another stone into his sling and walked toward the lion. The lion would not be denied its prey. It let out another roar and moved toward the lamb, lying in a state of shock. The young shepherd released another stone, this time striking the side of the lion's head. David ran up the incline and, taking his knife, thrust it into the lion's neck, finishing off the violator.

David looked over the lamb and noticed several bloody fang marks. He laid the lamb on its side, took ointment out of his pouch, and rubbed the healing mixture into its wounds. Cradling the wounded animal in his arms, he returned to the encampment.

David's preparation for war had not been in war colleges or military academies. He had never undergone basic training or officer candidacy school. Rather, his preparation had been in the obscure routines of shepherd life.

Ari had certainly seen that kind of life, though he had no personal experience as a shepherd. His knowledge of sheep raising was more confined to the agricultural kibbutz in which he was raised, which had some sheep, than to the pastoral Bedouins, who move their sheep from place to place in the Arab countries surrounding Israel. However, Ari's knowledge about the Bedouin shepherds was personal and rich.

One of the little-known facts that rarely enters the Western press is that Israel has many Arab friends who serve in the IDF (Israeli Defense Forces). Two special units, the Sayeret Ha'Druzim and the Ha'Beduim, are remarkable reconnaissance units within the Israeli army. Ari's experience with both groups had been intensive.

While growing up he had played with Druze Muslims, many of which were his best childhood friends. Druze Muslims are citizens of Israel who have served and continue to serve in the military voluntarily. But the group from which Ari had learned most about desert life were his Bedouin trackers. The art of desert tracking is considered to be almost the exclusive knowledge of the Bedouins.

The army, from its earliest days, recognized this rare skill and employs Bedouin soldiers as expert scouts, trackers, and infiltration guards for Israel's borders. Should a terrorist cross Israel's borders, it is the task of these Bedouin trackers to follow the carefully concealed footprints of the intruder's movements until they can be traced directly to the attacker. Because of this, these special groups of warriors are often the first to engage terrorists head-on.

Ari's current tracker is Falah. Although Falah wears the IDF olive uniform, on his head he also wears the distinctive red-and-white checkered headdress, which represents his Bedouin tribe. The skills he uses in tracking the nearly invisible traces of human footprints are learned over centuries of tracking errant sheep. These skills, passed down from father to son and from older brother to younger brother, have been lost except to those who still live in the desert. (The reason Muslim Bedouins have more allegiance to Israel than to their fellow Muslim Arabs is simply because the Israelis have allowed them to keep their nomadic lifestyle, while the Arab nations have tried to transplant them into the cities!)

As Ari reminded himself of this Bedouin shepherd reality, it seemed to make sense. David had learned his warrior skills far more by being a shepherd than he could have as a student in any classroom. The Israeli army does not even try to teach these Bedouin skills to urban recruits. These skills can only be learned through years of complete immersion in the desert and absolute dependence upon it for survival. The Israelis simply recruit the Bedouins!

The shepherd's life consists primarily of being provider and protector of the flock. To the shepherd, the flock represents his food, covering, drink, and income from exporting the wool. His task is simple: find food and protect the flock from the elements and enemies. If a small lamb is attacked in the middle of the night, the shepherd himself must go after the enemy and snatch the young lamb from the enemy's jaws.

Such a counteroffensive tactic was used in the Valley of Elah. An uncircumcised Philistine had crossed the boundaries set by the living God and was threatening to destroy the people of Israel, God's property. Apparently, the men of Israel, including King Saul, did not have the shepherd instinct and were intimidated by the giant. All they saw was his well-armored size. But David responded out of his shepherd training and instinctively exploited the vulnerability of this enemy.

When Saul tried to fit his own armor on David, the young shepherd realized very quickly that these were articles for defense, not offense. If a lion or bear grabbed one of his sheep, his tactic was not to defend himself against the bear, but to *attack* the bear before it ate the lamb. David naturally thought offensively, whereas Saul was on the defensive.

Sizing up the situation, David realized Goliath had no bow. There was no danger of being hit at long range. But the arrows of Saul's army were useless against this well-armored giant. Besides, Goliath had a shield bearer who walked before him and was trained to ward off the enemy's arrows.

To get an unobstructed shot at Goliath, David would have to outwit this well-defended team before coming within range of the giant's sword. The shepherd's tool of trade was perfectly designed for this tactic. The sling, with its small piece of leather and two thin cords of flax attached to opposite edges, and a stone missile placed within, became the superior weapon.

The marksmanship of the shepherd was not determined by how well he could hit a stationary target. A shepherd chasing a carnivorous animal had to learn to use the sling while on the run. He had to load and release while running. This is exactly what David did. "David ran quickly toward the battle line to meet the Philistine" (1 Samuel 17:48).

Perhaps the shield bearer could not believe his eyes. There were no arrows or swords on this young lad. Nothing he could defend against. This strategy allowed David to get close enough to the giant for a clear shot at his most vulnerable place, the forehead.

The stone was released, striking deep into the skull of Goliath, either rendering him unconscious or killing him on impact. David was not about to allow this giant to violate his nation's boundaries.

Being a warrior is about protecting and defending boundaries. It is about the willingness to do what needs to be done even though it involves violence and bloodshed.

⌇

RELUCTANT WARRIORS

Ari put down the Bible and crawled into bed. Thoughts about what he had read kept interrupting his sleep. Ari often thought about his "first blood" and the men he had killed in the line of duty. He always considered himself a reluctant warrior—one who did not enjoy killing but did so as a necessary evil to ensure Israel's security. But he was never personally proud of taking another man's life.

In the Sinai campaign, as a young, right-out-of-basic-training tank driver, he still remembered the stench and horrible sights of Egyptian armor and soldiers burning. As their massive tank assault eventually pushed the Egyptian army back to the Suez Canal, their Centurion tanks firing on the run, all the young soldier could see was the black smoke and all he could smell was burning flesh.

There is no joy in the taking of life, nor is there a proud sense of accomplishment. If pride or celebration exists at such moments, it lies more in knowing that you did your job and none of your own crew members or buddies were killed.

But he still wondered about the men he killed. Did they have families? How many children were orphaned, and how many wives widowed? These silent, never-to-be-answered questions kept him awake at night and caused other warriors to drink too much in the evening.

As Ari drifted off to sleep, he found strange comfort in the military exploits of David. Ari could identify with this young shepherd who, at such an early age, was thrust into the realities of war. David, too, was a man of blood. But he was also a great king and leader of men. A full reading of his life reveals a passion for defending and expanding the borders of Israel. In every case, this meant being a man willing—even if reluctant—to shed blood.

With David having achieved epic status among King Saul's household, Saul's daughter apparently fell in love with the image of the young warrior. She let it be known that she was "in love" with David (1 Samuel 18:20). When the amorous fact reached the ears of the king, a royal arrangement seemed only appropriate.

David had already been Saul's armorbearer and court musician while looking after the family sheep business. Now that he had obtained hero status in the country, Saul had a flash of insight. It might be better politically to have David married to the king's daughter. So word was sent privately to David that it would please King Saul to have David take his daughter, Michal, in marriage.

David must have thought it was a joke, as his reply was, "I am a poor man and lightly esteemed" (1 Samuel 18:23). He was saying,

"I have no dowry to give." Being the youngest in the family and having the responsibility of caring for sheep while his brothers served in the army did not make for a large savings account. This was no problem for Saul. His concern was elsewhere. He had already recognized David as a potential threat to his regime.

It was the king's responsibility to guarantee the safety of Israel's boundaries. And there were more Philistines in the land. Saul planned to solve two problems at once. Therefore, the king answered back, "The king does not desire any dowry except a hundred foreskins of the Philistines, to take vengeance on the king's enemies" (1 Samuel 18:25). The text then adds, "Now Saul planned to make David fall by the hand of the Philistines."

Now this is an interesting response. Even though the demand for foreskins was a feigned way to get rid of David, these are the kinds of details from biblical stories that somehow are seldom taught in Hebrew Sabbath schools or church Sunday schools.

NO MORE RELUCTANCE—DAVID'S WARS
How does one obtain a hundred foreskins anyway? Apparently, this was no delicate, surgical incision such as the one performed on the eighth day in Hebrew homes. The Philistines were the enemies of both God and Israel, so it is reasonable to assume this was a very bloody event. David, just to prove a point and completely outdo the request, went out and took *two* hundred Philistine foreskins, put them in a bag, and dropped them before the feet of King Saul (1 Samuel 18:27). In keeping with the motif, it is entirely possible to conjecture that the entire male organ was cut off and given as a bloody dowry to the king.

Michal, the king's daughter, became the first wife of David, through the emasculation of two hundred Philistines. One hundred more than required by Saul! What is now unthinkable by modern moral standards became the dowry for David's bride. David was asked to do it, and he did it twofold! It was a marriage secured through bloodshed.

Taking foreskins to gain the hand of his bride was only the beginning of this warrior's exploits. Scripture reveals, "When there was war again, David went out and fought with the Philistines, and defeated [smote] them with great slaughter, so that they fled before him" (1 Samuel 19:8). While fleeing for his life from Saul, David heard that Keilah, a small village in Judah, was being plundered by the Philistines. Seeing that Israel's boundaries and that of his own tribe were being violated, David acted decisively and attacked them. The text says he "struck them with a great slaughter. Thus David delivered the inhabitants of Keilah" (23:5).

So territorial was David's thinking that he took upon himself the necessity of ridding Israel of all noncovenantal peoples who threatened the boundaries and the lives of God's people. He also raided the camps of the Geshurites, Girzites, and Amalekites simply because they had lived in the land of Israel since ancient times (1 Samuel 27:8).

In these raids, he left neither man nor woman alive. At least with the Amalekites, there could have been a long-term grudge because of the way they had treated the defenseless Israelites during their wilderness experience under Moses (Exodus 17:8). As for the other two tribes, it seems he merely wanted to remove them from the land promised to God's people. Even during times of self-survival, while fleeing for his life, David saw himself as God's warrior and continued to defend the boundaries set by God's promises.

On one occasion, while David was still on the run, the Amalekites raided Ziklag and took captive all women and children, including David's two wives, Ahinoam and Abigail (1 Samuel 30:1-5). After inquiring of the Lord about the matter, David took his six-hundred-man army of volunteers and made a surprise attack on the Amalekites while they were celebrating their victory.

A slaughter took place from sunrise to sunset, and David captured back his wives, the spoils, and other women and children who had been taken (1 Samuel 30:18-20). Again, since Ziklag was the city given to David by the Philistine king, Achish (27:6), and was located inside the territory given to the tribe of Judah (David's tribe), David acted as a shepherd going after one of his lost sheep, as if he were protecting and defending the property entrusted to him by his father and older brothers. Although he was not the commander of Israel's formal army or its king at this point, he took personal responsibility for what happened within the boundaries under his divine charge, unabashedly shedding the blood of violators.

After his coronation as king, David continued to function more as a Bedouin shepherd than as the usual, palace-oriented politico. When Saul's innocent son Ish-bosheth was murdered by two of Saul's former commanders, his murderers brought Ish-bosheth's head to David, thinking they would find favor for removing a rival, an heir to the throne (2 Samuel 4:8).

Most kings would have been pleased with fewer rivals in the land. But David's response was not "politically correct": "When wicked men have killed a righteous man in his own house on his bed, shall I not now require his blood from your hand, and destroy you from the earth?" (2 Samuel 4:11). David saw this act as the slaughter of an innocent man, and for such he must see the murderers' own blood shed. David responded the same way when told of Saul's death. The messenger thought he was bringing good news—and it cost him his life (verse 10).

These actions appear to be arbitrary, whimsical killings unless one understands the heart of David. A true warrior sheds blood to secure the national boundaries or punish wrongdoers. David was not a loose cannon, swinging his sword in vain or trying to gain selfishly motivated spoils. His motives were higher. His passion was anchored in principle, not power. His passion for blood was subservient to principle. He never took needless blood, but did not hesitate to shed the blood of those who had violated the boundaries of God.

David's first act as a newly anointed king was another act of bloodshed. The inhabitants of Jebus thought they were securely protected by mountains on every side, and said to David, "You shall not enter here" (1 Chronicles 11:5). David immediately took them up on their arrogant challenge and threw down his own warriorlike challenge. "Whoever strikes down a Jebusite first shall be chief and commander [of my army]" (verse 6).

Joab, jumping at the challenge, drew first blood and became David's army commander. David then mustered his army and took the city and established it as the capital city for his reign. The city of David, ironically renamed Jerusalem ("City of Peace"), was established through violence and bloodshed!

Once David established his reign, he returned the ark of the covenant to Jerusalem and himself to the task of securing and expanding Israel's boundaries. He broke the back of Philistine control by defeating them in several battles (2 Samuel 5:17-25). The text records that he finally subdued them and took control of their key city (8:1).

Furthermore, by defeating the Moabites and Syrians, David expanded Israel's boundaries and created a "protection zone." He also placed armed garrisons in Edom (2 Samuel 8:2-18). In these expansion wars, the kill list was enormous. David's army killed 22,000 Syrians and 18,000 Edomites. In other battles, 700 Syrian charioteers and 40,000 mounted cavalrymen were killed (10:18). At David's hand, the blood of enemies flowed.

Even in exile, David continued the slaughter against Absalom's army. In the final battle, in which his son Absalom was killed, 20,000 fellow Israelites died as a result of fighting in support of Absalom. Although David himself did not fight in the battle, he felt responsible for the slaughter and the death of his own son (2 Samuel 18:1-33). In his remorse, David desired his own death rather than his son's (2 Samuel 18:33).

The chronicler concludes that by the time David became king at Hebron, his war machine numbered about 339,000 men. They were called "a great army like the army of God" (1 Chronicles 12:22). Even by modern standards, this is a very sizable army.

Great warriors have always been driven by passions similar to David's. Alexander the Great, Napoleon, generals George Washington and George Patton—these men often distinguished themselves through war. When Robert E. Lee, the American Civil War general, watched his own Confederate guns cut to pieces the Union infantry at the Battle of Fredericksburg, he looked on the slaughter and said, "It is well that war is so horrible, else we should grow too fond of it."

THE WARRIOR AS HERO

The next morning Ari arose early and walked the streets of Beersheba before heading toward the offices of the Southern Command. Like most Israelis, Ari quickly grabbed a piece of cheese, fruit, and a boiled egg to start the day. Unlike most, however, he always added to that a heavy charge of Turkish coffee.

By the time he reached the offices, he knew what he wanted to check out. Even though manpower documents are highly classified, Ari knew he could at least get some estimates. The size of David's army he had read about the night before amazed this latter-day Israeli warrior. He wanted to compare David's army with the IDF's current statistics.

"Boqer tov, Ari," greeted the corporal seated at the desk by the front door of the command offices.

"Shalom," Ari replied. Finding the right office and obtaining permission, Ari pulled the documents out of a personnel drawer. He quickly computed figures of the current manpower in uniform. Ari was awestruck. He had never realized the heights to which David, the young shepherd boy, had risen.

Israel's combined forces of army, navy, and air force had no more than 190,000 men and women in uniform on any given day (140,000 conscripts and 50,000 professionals). If the reserves were called up, they could put an additional 410,000 into battle, making the figure an even 600,000. Ari recalled the recent war in the gulf, which put an estimated 500,000 combined forces up against the Iraqi army.

So, David's army at the time of his coronation was of remarkable size. David also had special forces, men of special accomplishment, who were housed in the "house of heroes" (1 Chronicles 11:10-47). Listed in this biblical hall of fame were the most decorated three, his valiant thirty, and the thirty-seven most honored (2 Samuel 23:8-39).

Reading the lists of heroic accomplishments in the biblical text was very much like reading many of the decoration requests Ari had written for his men over the years. In every battle are individuals who go beyond the call of duty and demonstrate extreme heroism at the risk of their own lives.

King David started his career with that kind of heroism against Goliath. When no one was willing to take on the Philistine giant, David looked at the situation with a different perspective. He saw through the eyes of a shepherd, but also with the eyes of a man who saw clearly the purposes of God for his nation. To David, Goliath was not a well-armored giant but an uncircumcised Philistine who defied the army of the living God.

This was a radically new thought for Ari. He, too, had been up against overwhelming odds, but emerged the hero. During the Yom Kippur War, Ari, then Lieutenant Ammud, was a tank commander in the Barak Armored Brigade defending the Golan Heights. When the Syrians raced five divisions across the purple line separating Israel from Syria, Israel was taken by surprise and immediately overrun.

For a while the Syrians retook portions of the Golan Heights, and it was up to the Seventh and 188th Armored Brigades to keep the advance from storming all the way into Galilee Valley. Within a matter of hours, the 188th was destroyed. It seemed that the Syrian advance was going to be unstoppable; that is, until a modern-day David appeared.

A lone Israeli Centurion tank appeared, waging a private, gutsy war. Firing at Syrian armor, always moving and hiding behind its own self-generated smoke, and then reappearing and firing again, it left in its wake a debris of burning tanks that significantly slowed the Syrian attack. This lone, maverick tank soon entered Israeli folklore as a "force tzvika" (little army) for keeping the Syrian armor at bay until the Israeli reservists could reach the front.

Who was this lone Centurion tank commander who made sure his crew and his 105-millimeter cannon kept firing against Israel's enemies? Lieutenant Ariel ben David Ammud. For his bravery during the height of Israel's most significant vulnerability, Ari was given Israel's highest military honors. Because of his achievements, he was considered one of Israel's most promising tank commanders who should be given opportunities to rise to senior leadership positions.

But by his own admission, Ari did not have King David's perspective while facing this goliath of the Syrian armor. At the time he was simply performing his duty to help keep the Galilean region from being overrun by this enemy. But now, some twenty years later, he wondered. *Was someone else a part of this? Was I fighting for more than Israel's survival as a nation? Was I fighting for the God of Israel, as David had?* Ari did not have an answer, but the questions bothered him deeply.

A PERPLEXING CONTRADICTION

What was this passion of David's that made him see human events through the lens of God's honor for Israel's boundaries? He was a man of great bloodshed, far more than Ari had ever had the opportunity to claim. Yet, David is called "a man after [God's] own heart," apparently by God Himself (1 Samuel 13:14)!

Ari was perplexed. How was he to reconcile those two concepts? Orthodox Jews did not believe in killing, unless of course one walked into Me'ah Shearim, their own community, on Sabbath. But because they took the Ten Commandments literally, they could not justify killing. They viewed it as an offense to God.

To the modern, secular Israeli, however, killing in warfare is the only means for protecting the nation. But most Israelis had no real belief in God anymore. They would fight for Israel and their own self-preservation. If their help came from above, it was from an F-16 fighter, not God! So Ari was greatly perplexed by his new insights into the military career of David. He could identify with the young warrior on the subject of territorial boundaries, but not on his perspective of God. The God factor seemed to confuse the issues of warfare and bloodshed.

That evening Ari and Sergeant Eyal took an evening walk to the Beersheba Mall. The anachronism always struck Ariel as a little humorous. Here in the middle of the desert, an American-type, air-conditioned mall existed almost side by side with the ancient Bedouin lifestyle.

Deep down, Ari hated these American additions to Israel. But since his daughter Dorit was turning seventeen, he wanted to find her a special birthday gift. Ari and his "chaver" (companion) mingled with all the Sabra teens, retired kibbutzniks, and Jewish American tourists. As they strolled through the mall, they stopped briefly to glance at store windows, looking for a suitable gift for Ari's soon-to-be-grown-up lady.

Out of the blue, Ari looked at his friend and said, "Youssef, how long have we known each other?"

"What kind of question is that, Ari? We've know each other most of our lives," Youssef replied.

"I know, I know, but what I was wondering was . . . I mean what I've been thinking about is . . . well, have you ever really read the Bible?" Ari asked.

Youssef looked a little surprised but honestly answered, "Oh, a little, but not since I was in primary school where we read it as history. Why do you ask?"

"I've been thinking a lot about my father recently. You see, King David was his model man, and I've been doing some reading to figure out why."

"That's easy," said Youssef. "He was a gutsy *gibbor*."

"Yes, I know, but he seems far more than that. David saw some connection between what he was doing in his own life and what God desired for the nation. Have you ever thought about that?"

"Are you kidding? Ari, I think it's time for a break. Let's stop here and grab a falafel and a Maccabee." After ordering, they spoke no more of Ari's thoughts about either David or his dad.

Ari selected a Bedouin-style necklace with matching earrings for his daughter. He had them wrapped in an attractive package and sent to Kibbutz Mahagan. After more shopping, these two modern warriors walked back to their respective apartments. "Laylah tov, Ari," bid Youssef.

"Lehitraot, my friend."

DAVID'S GREAT WARRIOR-SIN

Back in his bedroom, Ari reached for his father's Bible and turned to the account of the end of David's life. As he thought about the life of this great king, he remembered something about David committing a grievous sin late in his life. He found the section in the prophet Samuel and read:

> Now again the anger of the LORD burned against Israel, and it incited David against them to say, "Go, number Israel and Judah." And the king said to Joab the commander of the army who was with him, "Go about now through all the tribes of Israel, from Dan to Beersheba, and register [muster] the people, that I may know the number of the people."
> (2 Samuel 24:1-2)

What surprised Ari was Joab's response. "Joab said to the king, 'Now may the LORD your God add to the people a hundred times as many as they are, while the eyes of my lord the king still see; but why does my lord the king delight in this thing?'" (verse 3). A strange response for an army commander indeed. David's desire seemed very appropriate. As king of the nation and commander in chief, didn't he have the right to know how many people lived in his country?

But Joab gave in and numbered the people. But his final report to the king presented a different slant on the king's request: "Joab gave the number of the [muster] of the people to the king; and there were in Israel eight hundred thousand valiant men *who drew the sword*, and the men of Judah were five hundred thousand men" (2 Samuel 24:9, emphasis added).

Ari dropped the Bible into his lap and uttered, "This was not a population census, this was a military-strength report." These were the number of valiant men (strong men who bear the sword) who could defend the nation on any given day. What a number indeed— 1.3 million men in uniform! As soon as those numbers hit David's ears, he was troubled and responded, "I have sinned greatly in what I have done. . . . I have acted very foolishly" (2 Samuel 24:10).

Now Ari was completely perplexed about his reading of David. Any army commander knows that the most important piece of intelligence information one can have is troop strength, or the number of mission-capable tanks and airplanes. The number of men and women an army can mobilize on any given day is always a highly classified secret. It can clue the enemy as to one's true strength.

From Ari's perspective, what David did was what any king or commander should have done. It is crucial to know the available, healthy, and mission-capable resources one can go to war with on any given day. Why then did David consider this a great sin, and why did his own commander resist him regarding it? Ari seemed to be missing something here. Why was it apparently better not to know one's strength?

Before jumping into bed, Ari had a flash of insight. He was struck by the text from the night before: "I come to you [Goliath] in the name of the LORD of hosts. . . . This day the LORD will deliver you up into my hands" (1 Samuel 17:45-46), and "Thus David prevailed over the Philistine with a sling and a stone . . . but there was no sword in David's hand" (verse 50).

Ari considered the contrast between the two texts very striking. The young David, single-handedly, with sling and stone, leveled this professional Philistine soldier without using a sword. In this heroic act, he viewed the task purely from the perspective of God giving the Philistine into his hands. Later, as king of Israel with secured boundaries, David put on the field of battle an army of 1.3 million men wielding swords. Militarily, the king was in a far better position to wage warfare. But the act of gaining awareness of his own capability David viewed as iniquity. Sin!

THE PARADOX OF MISPLACED TRUST
IN WARRIOR STRENGTH

Could it be that David's real strength was in looking toward God as his ultimate Protector and Provider? Or, after knowing that a million-man army was at his disposal, would there be a greater tendency to develop trust merely in one's own military superiority?

Ari and most Israelis had experienced this wrongly placed confidence. Leading up to the Yom Kippur War, President Sadat of Egypt gave every indication that he was preparing for war. Even a week before the war, troop movements toward and around the Suez Canal zone were not treated seriously by Israeli intelligence. The leadership and intelligence community were so puffed up by their own sense of superiority that they merely looked at these threats and ground activities as Sadat "crying wolf."

Israel had so overpowered its Arab neighbors in every war, and had so prided itself in having the finest and most sophisticated army in the Middle East, that no one believed the Egyptians would attack. It was a misplaced trust. So Ari understood the downside of accurately knowing one's capabilities. Since the Yom Kippur War, Israelis have not felt quite so invincible; they have felt fallible, along with the rest of the human race.

When an armed robber breaks into a house and begins seizing property, superior strength is required to stand against the intruder. A man of war must have passion for his boundaries. Mature, adult men do not allow robbers, rioters, or looters to enter their boundaries and take whatever they will. Passion evokes a willingness to do the difficult, draw lines in the sand, defend moral and spiritual boundaries, and see blood shed.

There is a downside to strength and the shedding of blood. Bloodshed is always costly. One of the paradoxes of David's life was that, because of his fighting and killing the enemies of Israel, he ultimately had to face the price of having blood on his own hands.

As king of Israel, he was concerned that, unlike the other nations, there was no central sanctuary in which his God could be worshiped. He carried a passion to see in Jerusalem a house of God to which the people could come and honor the God of Israel. David gathered all the necessary artisans and materials to construct a magnificent and famous wonder of the world (1 Chronicles 22:1-5). But a word from God stopped him in his tracks. David confessed to his son Solomon that "the word of the LORD came to me, saying, 'You have shed much blood, and have waged great wars; you shall not build a house to My name, because you have shed so much blood on the earth before Me'" (verse 8).

Ari was disturbed by the paradox. The reason God had allowed His people to draft Saul as their first king was to ensure the deliverance of His people from the Philistines (1 Samuel 9:16). When Saul failed to be the king God wanted him to be, the prophet Samuel anointed David as his replacement (13:14). David was successful where Saul had failed. He secured the boundaries of Israel and delivered his people from constant violation by the Philistines. But he was then punished for doing what God desired!

Ultimately, the warrior's passion is not just a willingness to see blood shed, but a passion for the honor of God. In honoring the boundaries God had set, King David was honoring God.

As Ari fell off to sleep, he wondered, *Is this still true? Are these boundaries more than geographical boundaries? How could David be a man after God's own heart and shed so much blood, even in defense of God's boundaries?*

3

A Man of the Outdoors: Passion for the Fields

"LIKE AN OLIVE TREE, FLOURISHING IN THE HOUSE OF GOD"

Ari's demotion was not all that dramatic. In fact, the public knew nothing of a "demotion." Such treatment for a well-decorated war hero like Ariel ben David would give the high command a bad image. But Ari and everyone close to him knew he was indeed demoted.

He didn't get busted in rank, and there was no court-martial. He was simply taken off the fast track of upward mobility toward the high command. That meant he was passed over for key promotions for which he was well qualified. To add insult, he was given a field-command assignment, a lateral move. At first Ari was angered, which he expressed mostly in sullen and periodic depression. There is nothing worse for a man than realizing his career dreams have come to an end. Painfully, he accepted this reality as his deserved fate and, in some strange way, was happier.

The new assignment returned him to where his passions really lay—in the desert, being a foot soldier, and riding in a heavily armed jeep. Most Samson's Foxes rarely see a jeep, but even in the Israeli army, an army of equals, rank still has a few privileges. Riding border control in a jeep complete with a mounted machine gun and tank offensive weapons, with two other desert rats, was the kind of officer privilege Ari savored.

His unit, based in the Southern Command, was one of the old-est *and*, at the same time, newest units in the IDF. The Giva'ati Brigade had grown out of the Haganah Field Corps during the late 1930s. During the War of Independence, the unit was propelled into action and fought decisively against the Egyptians in the south. After the war, U.S. Army surplus jeeps were obtained, and the brigade was given its own indigenous reconnaissance company known as Shu'elel Shimshon, or Samson's Foxes. In 1983 the unit was recast as both a reconnaissance and commando unit, very much like the U.S. Marines.

To earn the coveted purple beret, each soldier had to survive a seven-day Hell Week. The week culminates with a 130-kilometer obstacle course at an undisclosed eastern Negev site. Each soldier competing for selection into the unit must negotiate the course with-out benefit of maps or buddy aid. The course takes them through gas attacks, sniper fire, cliff repelling, and running at top speed while firing their 5.56-millimeter assault rifles at various targets. And this takes place in desert heat, which sometimes reaches 110 degrees Fahrenheit.

For Ari to be given the command of this special-forces unit was a return to his roots. He was a man of the outdoors, and the demo-tion, though painful to his pride, returned him to the passion of his youth—the grand expanse of the outdoors. High command always confines its best operational commanders to paperwork and constant political considerations. Ari knew this, and would rather be outside.

ARI'S ROOTS
Though it was Sabbath, Ari took the day to drive to Tel Aviv. Impor-tant field commander meetings were scheduled to begin on Monday, and Ari wanted to arrive early enough to have a little time to him-self. The delight of "being alone" always surprised Ari.

Being a kibbutznik, where everything was communal, solitude was rare and negative to the basic principles of kibbutz life. Com-munity ownership of property, equality of all members, democratic decision making, communal responsibility for child care, and in the older days, communal meals and bathing, were all meant to empha-size the well-being of the group over the individual.

Ari didn't know if it was his own independent spirit that never fully submitted to kibbutz life, or because he had submitted so much to the communal requirements that he now enjoyed the degree of individualism he was allowed as a professional officer. However, Ari would be the first to argue for the benefits of kibbutz life.

Almost 70 percent of Israel's agricultural goods come from the combined efforts of kibbutzim and *moshavim*. (*Moshavim* are newer, less communal organizations that allow personal property ownership and the rearing of one's own children.) Besides, former kibbutzniks constitute a very disproportionate number of the officers, pilots, and special-forces members in the IDF. Kibbutzniks are usually well prepared for the discipline, sacrifice, and physical conditioning necessary for leadership in Israel's elite forces.

As Ari headed up the northern highway from Beersheba to Qir Gat (ancient Gath), he again reflected on the times he walked these sites with his father. Driving through the ancient Philistine plain and seeing direction signs for Ashqelon and Ashdod, he flashed back to the times when David passed through the same territory, either attacking the Philistines or fleeing from his enemies.

These "sea peoples," originally descendants of Mizraim (Egypt) and Ham (1 Chronicles 1:12 and Amos 9:7), settled in Canaan during the time of the Israelite judges. They formed a five-city league with each city ruled by a "lord." Gradually they moved inland, threatening Israel's security. The central shrine and capital that linked the confederacy was located at Ashdod, where the temple of Dagon (the Canaanite fish god) was erected.

As "sea peoples," the Philistines held the excellent military advantage of maintaining the sea lanes in and out of Israel. Ariel glanced at the Ashdod sign and chuckled to himself, "Ashdod is now one of our key naval bases!" But he quickly reminded himself that the Philistines still have Gaza! No Israeli would dare go to Gaza without military protection.

After entering the village of Qir Gat, instead of continuing north to Tel Aviv, Ari made a right turn and steered his vehicle toward the traditional site of the Adullum caves. Several decades earlier Ari and his dad had made this same departure from the main road, armed only with a couple of flashlights, falafels (fried falafel beans in pita bread), and canteens. Yakov loved to pack a light lunch and hike to some remote area. There he would eat his lunch, give his biblical speech, and then depart as quickly as he came.

Ari parked the car and walked to the entrance of the caves. It was

here that David, while running for his life from King Saul and having been turned away by the king of Gath, gathered with four hundred other outcasts of Israel (1 Samuel 22:1-3). The day Ari came
with his father had been a cold January afternoon. No sooner had
they arrived at the cave than it started to rain. Ari and his father went
into the cave, made a small fire to provide warmth, and ate their
falafels.

Ari remembered how, in the vast expanse of the cave, his father
explained that it would have been no problem for David to have hidden four hundred men. Its many interconnecting tunnels provided
excellent "checkpoints" to station guards while also providing many
avenues of escape. King Saul could very easily have come into the
area and not seen a sign of David or his comrades.

Ari also recounted how his father, a student of the psalms composed by David, developed the concept of "strongholds" as one of
the major themes in the Psalms. These *machsehs*, or refuges, were
central to David's understanding as places of protection. Yakov
attributed this emphasis to the one most important reality of the great
king. He was a vigilant shepherd! A shepherd must know his terrain, where the best pasture is, and the safe places for spending the
night. David, his formative years conditioned by the experience of
being a shepherd, knew all the nooks, caves, and crannies in Judah.
As Yakov often said, "David trusted in God, but he also knew where
to hide."

Ari saw these same instincts in his Bedouin trackers. They could
always see, hear, or smell things that eluded the average Israeli. Their
senses were completely in tune with the rhythm and movement of
the desert. As Ari looked into this Adullum cave, he reasoned that
David must have carried with him a mental map of the geographical
refuges. In the Shephelah, he had his strongholds in the caves of
Judah. When he needed a "high place," or *mishgav*, he retreated to
Engedi, off the Dead Sea valley (1 Samuel 23:29). This isolated and
protected spring was replete with a cave, a fresh flowing waterfall,
and a still pool of waters from which the easily frightened sheep
could drink.

It was in this cave that David so completely hid himself that he,
with considerable stealth, cut off a piece of King Saul's robe while
Saul relieved himself (1 Samuel 24:4).

As Ari climbed back into his car, he felt an affinity with this place and with the experiences of that distant, young warrior, David. They both loved the outdoors, the challenge of living off the land, and putting something over on their enemies!

IMAGES OF MORAL WISDOM: ARI'S DISCOMFORT

Ari checked into his quarters in Tel Aviv and walked to Steimatzy's bookstore. Though Ari didn't consider himself a scholar, he loved bookstores, especially Steimatzy's. It was the way he thought a bookstore should be: dusty shelves, books piled everywhere, and no visible signs of organization. Its manager knew immediately where to find any book or section. However, with Sabbath having just ended, Ari simply wanted to browse bookshelves and then enjoy the nightlife of Tel Aviv.

He looked at several new titles on Israel's Lebanon war and the current political situation with the Intifada. The book titles reflected the diversity of opinion for which Israel is noted. In Israel the saying goes, "Where there are two Jews, there are three opinions." Some books on the shelves even favored making peace with the Arabs and giving back all the occupied territories.

Every group of people who had been dispossessed of this land could make a legitimate, historical claim to it, including the Egyptians, Canaanites, Phoenicians, Syrians, Babylonians, Persians, Assyrians, Greeks, Romans, Byzantine crusaders, Ottoman Turks, French, British, and of course, whoever the Palestinians are! Rightwing extremists argue for ridding the entire land of the Palestinians and building Jewish settlements on Arab lands. Ari put the political books aside and began to leave.

As he exited the store, a book caught Ari's attention, *Images of Nature in the Psalter*. Picking up the volume, he perused the table of contents: "Agricultural Metaphors," "Animal Imagery," and "Impact of Terrain." Those concepts intrigued him. David, as author of most of the Psalter, was heavily influenced by the outdoor life. Consequently, when he put his feelings into words and music, he used the language of his surroundings to create vivid impressions. Ari took out his wallet, leafed through the various amounts of paper *sheqalim*, and purchased the book.

After mingling with other Israelis out for their after-Sabbath celebrations, he took a stroll, wondering what was going on within him. Why would a military officer, such as himself, purchase such a ridiculous book as *Images of Nature in the Psalter?* He thought, *My father would certainly turn over in his grave.* A second thought passed even more swiftly. *Maybe Yakov would be pleased.*

Ari found a sidewalk cafe and ordered a saucer of *hummus* (a spread made from chick peas) and pita bread to be followed with a lamb kebob. While waiting for his order, he took his newly purchased book and began to read. The subjects listed under "Agricultural Metaphors" were many: trees, chaff, grain, wine, olive trees, plowing, parched ground, and the planting of seeds. All were used by David in linking his thorough knowledge of outdoor, agricultural life with other, more hidden realities. The man who meditates upon God's law . . .

> is like a tree planted by streams of water,
>   which yields its fruit in season. (Psalm 1:3, NIV)

> The righteous will flourish like a palm tree,
>   they will grow like a cedar of Lebanon. (92:12, NIV)

Ari had seen how palm trees dotted the horizon across the Negev. They were signs to the traveler of water, rest, and shade. They flourished beside the hidden spring waters of desert oases. However, the cedars of Lebanon were long gone. They were cut down because of a "tree tax" imposed by certain Turkish rulers. Rather than pay the taxes as determined by how many trees were on one's property, the inhabitants of the land merely cut them all down, thus avoiding being taxed. This may explain why the topsoil of Israel and its surrounding territories has completely eroded down to the bedrock.

Ari read on,

> Not so the wicked!
>   They are like chaff
>   that the wind blows away. (1:4, NIV)

> May those who seek my life
>   be disgraced and put to shame; . . .
> May they be like chaff before the wind,
>   with the angel of the LORD driving them away.
>   (35:4-5, NIV)

Wow! Ariel thought. *This is heavy stuff! David was calling down fire from heaven upon his enemies.* Again, Ari had seen this metaphor in action. On the West Bank and around Arab villages, the ancient custom of winnowing is still practiced. Grain is thrown into the wind, thus separating the kernels from the chaff. The kernels fall back down upon a large sheet, while the chaff, or husks, are blown away. David likened his enemies to chaff—completely blown away!

David also expressed,

I am like an olive tree
  flourishing in the house of God;
I trust in God's unfailing love. (52:8, NIV)

But as for evil men,
  like the grass they will soon wither,
  like green plants they will soon die away. (37:2)

As for man, his days are like grass,
  he flourishes like a flower of the field;
the wind blows over it and it is gone,
  and its place remembers it no more.
But from everlasting to everlasting
  the LORD's love is with those who fear him.
    (103:15-17, NIV)

The waiter arrived with Ari's pita and *hummus*, and Ari put the book aside. Ari tore off a piece of the flat, rounded bread and dipped it in the *hummus*. Ari found the contrast in Psalm 103 striking. These were far more than agricultural metaphors; they were carriers of moral realities. Like most Israelis, Ari did not like to think about moral issues, at least over dinner during a Sabbath night celebration. But the contrast rolled over in his mind just the same. King David saw his own life as flourishing in the house of God, but the reality of evil men, those not in the house of God, is that they have a destiny with death and decomposition.

Obtrusive images of Ari's father buried at the military cemetery on Mount Herzel in Jerusalem flooded his mind. *I wonder if my father's body is totally decomposed yet? I wonder if he is some-where . . . where? Often, it seems as if he is still here, waiting for me to call him on the phone. A man flourishes for a while, then dies, and his bones and ashes are scattered as if by the wind. Is this all there really is?*

But David says, "From everlasting to everlasting is God's love to those who fear him."

How can this be? How can man, who is destined to die, experience God's everlasting love? Too much to handle at one setting, Ari thought.

MORE TENSION FOR ARI: DAVID'S VIEW OF THE SACRED

His meal arrived, and Ari picked up the book again and read as he ate. Two more concepts emerged from the Davidic agricultural passages.

Quoting his enemies, David says,

> They will say, "As one plows and breaks up the earth,
>> so our bones have been scattered at the mouth of the
>>> grave."
> But my eyes are fixed on you, O Sovereign LORD;
>> in you I take refuge—do not give me over to death.
>>> (Psalm 141:7-8, NIV)

The same tension struck Ari again. As is often the case in Israel when excavating or plowing, one encounters both animal and human bones. The Orthodox go crazy when this happens. They view life as so sacred that even human bones must be ceremonially picked up, transported, and placed in appropriate Jewish cemeteries by rabbinical authority. But here again was the contrast. The bones of David's enemies were plowed up, dumped, and set in opposition to David's making God the place of his refuge and focus. Ari summarized the section in his own mind. *David uses these agricultural metaphors to depict the contrast between men who are his enemies and his own relationship to God.*

As Ari finished his dinner, he overheard two young army recruits talking about their Masada "swearing-in." All new recruits in the IDF undergo the Masada climb as their "bonding" experience. This ancient fortress of King Herod, which became the last outpost of Jewish revolt against the Roman occupation, was the site of the enlistment.

Hearing those two warriors reminded Ari of his own trek up

Masada. It was one of the hottest, driest days of his life. The reminder gave Ari a special insight into the last Davidic metaphor:

> I spread out my hands to you;
> > my soul thirsts for you like a parched land.
> > > (Psalm 143:6, NIV)

> O God, . . .
> > earnestly I seek you;
> my soul thirsts for you,
> > my body longs for you,
> in a dry and weary land
> > where there is no water. (63:1, NIV)

That's exactly how Ari had felt both during his climb up the mountain and upon arriving at the top. His entire being thirsted, but not for God. It thirsted for a more human fundamental element— water! But David likened the reality of parched ground thirsting for water to his own "soulish" thirst for God. *Could it be*, Ari reasoned, *that as humans so thirst for water during times of extreme exertion and dehydration, so this is a glimpse of how human beings should thirst for God?* Apparently, it was for David. Ari would save the animal images for a later reading. He paid his bill, rejoined the sidewalk festivities, and walked back to his quarters.

Ari enjoyed a good night's sleep and spent most of Sunday in his room. After his morning Turkish, he left for the commanders' conference. Unlike the military formality of the American and NATO allies, Israeli conferences are informal, lacking in normal military protocol. Uniforms, rank, precision marching, spit and polish, saluting—all get downplayed in the IDF.

In Israel, all military activity gets reduced to pure functionality and getting the job done. Ari loved this professional army life, but the conference this day focused on the dark side of Israel's army. It was about the lessons learned in the Lebanon War, or as it was often called, "Sharon's War," after the mastermind of Operation Peace in Galilee, Defense Minister Ariel Sharon.

That war is considered by most Israelis a dark war. "Dark" because it was the first time the Israelis were truly on the offensive. Many noncombatants, including women and children, were innocently slaughtered. Hearing again the reports, evaluations, and mistakes of this war made Ari feel uncomfortable. If the Yom Kippur War was where his own heroic exploits placed him on the fast-career track, this Lebanon fiasco was where Ari's career came to a humiliating dead end. Ari could never articulate how he felt about this war, or what had happened to him and his men. But the emotions were so bottled up inside that at times he did not know if he could go on with his life. The wickedness and senseless violence and innocent loss of life that Ari had observed some ten years before still made him ill.

ARI'S REFLECTION AND REFUGE
Ari was relieved when the conference was over and he could return to the desert city he loved. Upon leaving Tel Aviv he took the coastal drive that winds around to the ancient city of Jaffa, biblical Joppa. Ari enjoyed nothing more than sitting at one of the sidewalk cafes and watching the mix of young Israeli couples walking hand in hand along with local artists and musicians and, of course, the ever-present tourists. After a while, Ari forgot the conference that for him was a personal confrontation with failure—his own!

Ari opened *Images of Nature* and began to read where he had marked his place several days before. In the chapter "Animal Images in the Psalter," he noted four distinct categories. The first leaped out at him as if there were a planned coincidence between the conference he had just attended and this chapter section: "Figures Used of the Ravenous Violence the Wicked Do to the Righteous."

Ari read some of King David's own prayers:

My deadly enemies, who surround me.
They have closed their unfeeling heart;
. . . they speak proudly.
They have now surrounded us in our steps; . . .
He is like a lion that is eager to tear,
And as a young lion lurking in hiding places. (Psalm 17:9-12)

Many bulls have surrounded me;
Strong bulls of Bashan have encircled me.
They open wide their mouth at me,
As a ravening and roaring lion. (22:12-13)

Ari could not believe his eyes! David likened his plight to the bulls in Bashan. Bashan was biblical Galilee and the Golan Heights, including sections of current Syria and Lebanon. The bulls of Bashan today are the 130-millimeter Syrian guns stationed just across the Israeli border in the Golan region.

King David likened the wicked to poisonous snakes and swarming bees.

> Rescue me, O LORD, from evil men;
> Preserve me from violent men. . . .
> They sharpen their tongues as a serpent;
> Poison of a viper is under their lips. (Psalm 140:1-3)

> All nations surrounded me. . . .
> They surrounded me like bees. (118:10-12)

An insight struck Ari as he read. David was putting his feelings into words, but the device he was using was *metaphor*.

The metaphors he used had their basis in his outdoors experiences. A shepherd must always be observing. David had watched lions attack and ravage their prey. Perhaps David was chased by wild bulls and swarmed by bees while trying to get honey for himself and his men.

Ari identified with David's feelings of being so overwhelmed by his enemies that he desired to flee like a bird. David prayed,

> Oh, that I had wings like a dove!
> I would fly away and be at rest.
> Behold, I would wander far away,
> I would lodge in the wilderness. (55:6-7)

Often Ari had wanted to flee the ridiculous plight of a country in continual turmoil and warfare. He had friends and relatives in both America and England, so relocating would not be difficult. But Ari prided himself in being a native-born Sabra. And besides, joining the ranks of the "jordanim" (those descending or leaving), the 370,000 Jews who have left the nation, would make him feel like he was betraying his country. But Ari identified with David's feelings of wanting to escape.

The second section of the chapter was entitled "Animal Images Expressing Feelings of Isolation and Loneliness." Again, this title hit Ari with irony. Here he was, reading this book all alone, having been divorced from his wife and separated from his children. Ari felt alone, even when surrounded by people and friends. David poured out his feelings of loneliness:

> I resemble a pelican of the wilderness;
> I have become like an owl of the waste places.
> I lie awake,
> I have become like a lonely bird on a housetop. (102:6-7)

Ari knew well those emotions. He had always valued his family, his career, and the kibbutz community in which he was raised. But now he felt as out of place as a pelican in the wilderness, and as a lonely owl hooting in the darkness. His family wanted nothing to do with him. His career had peaked, and the extended family of his kibbutz had for the most part rejected him for the humiliation he brought upon them. This great king of Israel, the hero of his father, had felt the same way. Ari was intrigued by both the existence and honesty of David's emotions and passions.

Ari ordered some shishlik (spicy roasted lamb) and another beverage while he pored over the animal images. The next section was more difficult to grasp: "Animal Images as Symbols of Joy, Celebration, and Renewal." What he read here seemed like confusing "God-talk."

> He [the LORD] makes Lebanon skip like a calf,
> And Sirion like a young wild ox. . . .
> The voice of the LORD makes the deer to calve. (29:5-6)

> Bless the LORD, . . .
> Who satisfies your years with good things,
> So that your youth is renewed like the eagle. (103:2,5)

The corner of Ari's mouth turned upward and formed a partial smile. *No one in Lebanon skips today—they all run for cover*, he thought.

But as he laughed, his empty, starved heart felt a strange yearning for the reality of the second passage. At this station of life, satisfaction with one's life was an alien thought for Ari. But still, his heart longed for it. To once again have a sense of youthfulness and satisfaction was for Ari about as likely as his being promoted to lieutenant colonel.

Not thoroughly understanding these animal images, Ari moved on to the last section: "Animal Images as Figures of God's Protection, Care, and Comfort." *Oh, no!* Ari thought, *here's where all the religious stuff comes in.* Ari pondered David's words,

> Be gracious to me, O God, be gracious to me,
> For my soul takes refuge in Thee;
> And in the shadow of Thy wings I will take refuge. (57:1)

He observed that this psalm was composed while David was fleeing from King Saul and hiding in the caves of Adullum. Ari had difficulty understanding David's words. With hundreds of men guarding all the entryways into the caves and having multiple escape routes, why was David praying to God and saying he was taking refuge in Him? His refuge seemed obviously in the caves and the protection of his men, not God.

Ari was acquainted with the historical concept of "trusting God," but it held no personal reality for him. He knew Moses had used that metaphor for describing how God had delivered Israel as a mother eagle saving her own chicks (Deuteronomy 32:11-12). But Ari could make no connection with finding a sense of personal comfort or refuge in God. His only image of such talk was what he had seen in the ultra-Orthodox Jewish community. For them, trust in God meant not recognizing the state of Israel as legitimate. They believe it is the Messiah who will gather His people and build a nation around faith in God. The modern state of Israel is seen as nothing more than an atheistic-secular state, founded by a Marxist-turned-Zionist, Theodor Herzl.

Those who seriously believe in God will not serve in the military, will refuse to bear arms, and want nothing to do with the secular, political state. On the other hand, most Israelis see their refuge in either making peace with their Arab neighbors or by completely subduing them. Ari had always positioned himself in the latter camp. Skeptical of any real peace accord, he was more in favor of keeping the occupied territories as buffer zones while upgrading the educational, medical, housing, and occupational opportunities for the Palestinians. Ari's refuge was in Israel's military strength and technological ingenuity.

ARI'S KINSHIP WITH DAVID
Ari's meal arrived. He put down his book and enjoyed the parade of passersby out for an evening stroll. Jaffa was the ancient port from which Jonah had tried to run away from his prophetic commission. It was also where Saint Peter received a heavenly vision to take the gospel to non-Jews. Although Jaffa still exists as a small fishing port, it is primarily filled with artist colonies, private and public galleries, cafes, nightclubs, and a museum. From the renovated old city houses one can either descend to the ancient harbor or climb to the archaeological excavations dating back to the Bronze Age.

As Ari consumed his meal, he leafed through the last chapter of his book: "Natural Surroundings in the Psalter." It was the longest chapter, and he didn't feel like serious reading. He merely paged through the main topic headings: (1) "All of Nature Reflects God's Handiwork"; (2) "Desert Represents Opposition to God's People"; (3) "Mountains Depict the Bond Between Heaven and Earth"; and (4) "Shepherds as Mediators Between the Desert and Mountain Realities."

Ari read,

Thou dost visit the earth, and cause it to overflow;
Thou dost greatly enrich it;
The stream of God is full of water. (Psalm 65:9)'

The heavens are telling of the glory of God;
And their expanse is declaring the work of His hands. (19:1)

Ari agreed with those passages from the first heading. His only times of spiritual reflection came while manning an observation point during the night. Looking up into the expanse with the starry hosts shining brightly, Ari believed that the world did not happen by accident, but rather was created by the hand of a superior being.

Ari also identified with the second topic. Throughout Israel's history, the desert had been the place of testing, extreme hostility, and opposition toward God's people. Desert realities are harsh and unfor-giving. As a unit commander, his main task was to prepare his men for the harsh realities they would face not only from fighting in the desert but from the desert itself.

As a shepherd, David understood those realities but saw the desert equally as a symbol of the anti-God forces in the world. As such, the desert is likened to a wasteland (Psalm 102:6) with scorch-ing summer heat (32:4, 37:6), hidden traps, nets, and pits (35:7-8, 119:85). When the rainy season arrives, the desert wadis (dry riverbeds) fill quickly with water and sweep away anything in their paths. David was relating to such an experience when he cried out,

Save me, O God,
For the waters have threatened my life.
I have sunk in deep mire, and there is no foothold;
I have come into deep waters, and a flood overflows me.
    (69:1-2)

Ari also had experienced several harrowing, near-death encoun-ters with such sudden rushing streams. A wadi is one of the best places to unroll a bedroll and spend the night. But unseen mountain rains can produce a freshet. Because the desert ground is so hardened by the dry summer heat, the rainwater has no place to go except to quickly fill the dry riverbeds. Should one be awakened in the night by a rumbling sound accompanied by a shaking of the ground, one needs to get out of the wadi as quickly as possible. Ari had seen men clinging to plants, rocks, and roots on the sides of canyon walls while these floods swept away all their provisions.

King David used this kind of imagery to describe his feelings toward those who were out to destroy him. In the Hebrew text, the imagery of the desert is that of spiritual opposition and oppression. From his book, Ari read this comment:

Graves, cisterns, prisons, pitfalls, ravines with suddenly
descending waters, parched deserts are regions from which
man can indeed be rescued by Yahweh's encompassing
power. But Yahweh is only marginally present in these

regions. They can therefore serve to represent the misery
which afflicts man in any godforsaken situation.

Ari felt a certain kinship with David at this point. Many of
the Davidic psalms were desert songs, apparently written while
David was literally running for his life. David expressed his feelings by using the imagery of his surroundings and linking them to
his own conflict. David was in battle, but with forces that tran-
scended the Philistines, Saul, and Absalom. Greater, hidden forces
were at work.

David was a man of the desert, a man with the paradoxical passion of loving the outdoors. He saw the desert realistically for its
deadly, harsh realities. If ever there was a time when he felt Godforsaken and abandoned, it was now. Knowing that David was a man
of similar passions strangely encouraged him and brought an unusual
calm to his spirit.

ARI'S RECOGNITION

The Jaffa passersby were beginning to clear out, but Ari remained
captivated by his book. Seated on the deck of an outdoor cafe, overlooking the Mediterranean, Ari felt the strange perspective that even
a little elevation grants. Being on higher ground, looking down on
what is below bestows a unique presence. It is no wonder the gods
throughout history have been worshiped on the high places. Hills and
mountains somehow bridge the chasm of the human and the divine.
All ancient societies had their holy hills that provided the link
between earthly life and the gods. David's choir director, in like fashion, sings,

> But [God] chose . . .
> Mount Zion which He loved.
> And He built His sanctuary like the heights.
> (Psalm 78:68-69)

The text in Ari's book commented that "the hill Zion is identified
with the primeval hill, paradise, the cosmic mountain and mountain
of the gods. But this identification depends less on Zion's relative
merits as a mountain than on its Holy Rock. The rock, with its solid-

ity and strength, constitutes the antipode to the bottomless, slimy, sluggish floods of Chaos."

It is toward this mountain that David enjoins worshipers to pilgrim:

> I was glad when they said to me,
> "Let us go to the house of the LORD." . . .
> Jerusalem, . . .
> To which the tribes go up, even the tribes of the LORD.
> (Psalm 122:1-4)

The Songs of Ascents (going-up songs) confess:

> I will lift up my eyes to the mountains;
> From whence shall my help come?
> My help comes from the LORD. (Psalm 121:1-2)

> Those who trust in the LORD
> Are as Mount Zion, which cannot be moved, but abides
> forever.
> As the mountains surround Jerusalem,
> So the LORD surrounds His people. (125:1-2)

After the ascending pilgrim arrives at the holy mount, David himself asks,

> Who may ascend into the hill of the LORD?
> And who may stand in His holy place?
> He who has clean hands and a pure heart,
> Who has not lifted up his soul to falsehood,
> And has not sworn deceitfully. (24:3-4)

Ari responded, "Oh, sure! What warrior, including David himself, has clean hands and pure heart? David's hands were always bloody, and he deceitfully had Bathsheba's husband killed and then tried to cover up his deeds." Still, Ari understood the essence of these texts. He always felt a mysterious presence on the high places of Israel. These high places today are dominated not by altars and temples to gods, but by Israeli observation and communication posts. Ari again smiled and thought, *Maybe these are our gods, the gods of military intelligence and technology.* All military strategy is based on controlling the high ground, whether it be the Golan Heights, Mount Hermon, or the cliffs of Arbel overlooking the Sea of Galilee.

Ari confessed to himself quietly, that as a semi-agnostic he did feel closer to God; that is, if there is a God on these mountains. A man of the outdoors, he could see more of God on these mountains than in any synagogue or church. But the Psalter uses one final image to connect desert realities with the mountains. David recognized the metaphor of shepherd as the prime mediator between God and His enemies.

As it is the shepherd's responsibility to move his flocks safely from the desert places in the winter to the summer pastures in the mountains, so David connects this task to his God:

> The Lord is *my* shepherd,
> I shall not want.
> He makes me lie down in green pastures;
> He leads me beside quiet waters.
>   (Psalm 23:1-2, emphasis added)

> Save Thy people, and bless Thine inheritance;
> Be their shepherd also, and carry them forever. (28:9)

The people of God are likened to the sheep of God's hand and the people of His pasture (95:7). As such, David asks that he might be led along level paths because of the presence of many enemies (27:11).

Many times Ari had watched Arab shepherds walking over rocky terrain with their flocks following close behind. He thought humorously how those sheep must have uttered the same kind of prayers to their shepherd. "Lead us along a little easier terrain, please." Under his breath Ari said the same words, and then wondered if that constituted a prayer. He paid for his meal and walked away from the cafe. As he rounded the corner, he heard music.

A Man of Music:
Passion for Celebration

"THE SWEET PSALMIST OF ISRAEL"

L ate afternoon winds brought a cold dampness that warned the young shepherd that the night was going to get colder. Gathering their collection of sheep, goats, and pack donkeys, he and his companion moved quickly to the leeward side of a small hill.

Finding the rocky sheepfold—a makeshift walled shelter of piled rocks covered with sharp thornbushes—the two young boys bedded down the flock for the night. David reached into his bag and retrieved a slab of cheese and a couple pieces of bread. He passed the bread and cheese to his friend.

Not much to eat on a cold winter night, but it still satisfies the appetite, David thought. He then lifted the goatskin flask over his head, unwound the tightly wrapped cords around the neck that keep the precious commodity fresh and safe, and handed the flask to his fellow shepherd.

"Tastes good," he responded, handing the water bag back to its owner. David drank deeply and then wiped his lips with the sleeve of his outer garment. Lying back and reaching into the donkey pack, David blurted out, "Now we can have some fun."

Unrolling several thicknesses of goat's-hair blankets, David pulled out his most prized possession, his lyre (*kinnor*). His friend reached into his pack and pulled out a dual-piped flute. The playing

53

of the lyre and flute relaxed the flocks. It was the recreation and enjoyment of those who played as well.

The youngest of eight brothers, David had been taught well by his older brothers how to shepherd. Most shepherds carried either the single- or dual-piped flutes. But David was unique. He preferred the multiple sounds he could produce on the stringed lyre. Most lyres had six or seven strings tuned in octaves or fourths attached to a rounded, wood frame. David's musical innovations were well known among the Bethlehemites. His talent was not by family training; it was pure gift.

David plucked the strings and the flute joined in. Then he burst into song—songs of the desert, songs about Israel, songs of praise about God's intervention into the lives of His people. In the crisp night air, the sounds of a passionate man cut through the still Bethlehem hills. Vocalized Hebraic lyrics accompanied by melodies of strings and pipes revealed the inner heart of a man of passion. A man with a passion for music and celebration.

⌒

ARI'S PASSION FOR THE STRINGS

As Ari rounded the corner and descended the steps from the Jaffa shops, he saw the street performers. These musicians were playing for fun and a few *sheqalim* from the passersby. Ari joined the small group of listeners. The simple trio of cello, flute, and clarinet blended well. With ease, the street musicians moved from contemporary Israeli tunes to Hasidic minor-key melodies and then to Bach. This was one aspect of Israeli life Ari especially enjoyed. In all his travels, the only country in the world that played classical music on its busses was Israel. It was another of the many paradoxical anachronisms that existed in Israel. Machine guns and violins both slung over the shoulders of soldiers, shopkeepers, and musicians!

As the trio finished a set of numbers, the listeners broke out in spontaneous applause. Ari dropped some shekels in their hat, smiled at the young lady playing the cello, and thanked her. She returned the smile, making Ari's evening. As he got back into his car, he began reminiscing about his own cello-playing days. One of the benefits of growing up on the southern shores of Galilee was the exposure to its rich culture, both in the kibbutz communities and at the annual En Gev music festivals held during the Passover celebrations. Ari's father was not much into music, but his mother played the piano and his older sister the violin. They would often spend an afternoon or evening gathered around the piano, playing everything from Mozart to Rubinstein. Ari always enjoyed listening, but it wasn't until he heard Pablo Casals perform with the En Gev Symphony that his sincere passion for music was born. Hearing the mellow bottom register played with such precision and passion set aflame in Ari a desire to learn how to play the instrument.

One of his father's trips took Yakov to Safed. On his return, he showed up with a three-quarter-size cello, a perfect fit for the young nine-year-old. The kibbutz music teacher got him started on the basic fingering and bowing techniques. Eventually he was playing in the small kibbutz orchestra, and finally in the very En Gev music festival where his passion was born. But when Ari joined the army, he left behind his cello.

Out of the blue Ari thought, *I wonder what happened to my cello? I tried to get the kids interested in it, but to no avail. Dorit was more into American pop rock, and my son, Benjamin, well, I have never quite known what he was into. Dorit was always very close with her mother, and they have gotten on fine without me.*

As Ari turned back onto the Tel Aviv–Beersheba highway and headed south, he again thought about his father and King David. Yakov once told him, "Ari, the insignificant things are the most significant. Just look at David. He had two skills he took from pasturing sheep to living in the presence of King Saul." Ari hadn't made the connection until hearing the mellow, haunting sounds of the cello that night. It is often the most insignificant of skills that puts one in high places. David just happened to be good with a sling and a lyre—the two very things King Saul needed!

THE PARADOX OF DAVID'S GIFTS

Ari had read the early history of David's life many times. Almost every Israeli knows the broad strokes of their greatest king's life. David is to Israelis what George Washington is to Americans. After the demise of King Saul, an evil spirit came upon Saul that so terrorized him that he became disoriented. Because most ancient Near Eastern societies viewed music with almost magical qualities, the servants in Saul's palace sought a musician who could soothe the extreme mental episodes that frequented Saul. Saul asked them to look for a "man who can play well" (1 Samuel 16:17). David's melodies in the night apparently had reached all the way to Gibeah, ten miles from Bethlehem. David's reputation of "knowing the *kinnor*" and playing well preceded his great military triumph over the Philistine giant. He was known foremost for his musical skills. Then one of the young men answered Saul and said, "Behold, I have seen a son of Jesse the Bethlehemite who is a skillful musician, a mighty man of valor, a warrior, one prudent in speech, and a handsome man; and the LORD is with him" (1 Samuel 16:18).

David was skilled at soothing animal and human restlessness. The years spent in anonymity and isolation with his flocks paid off for him. He had honed the very skills and attributes that would cause him to be noticed by those in high places. When the spirits played havoc with Saul's mind, David would take his rustic, wooden *kinnor* and pluck a melody to relieve Saul's mental anguish (1 Samuel 16:23).

How was it that an outwardly rough-and-tough warrior was a gentle appreciator of music? A warrior shouldn't love music. The passions required of the warrior are opposite those required of the musician. But are they?

Ari thought about the paradox. Perhaps, in some way, the passions are connected. Passion is passion whether shown with a sling or a lyre. David was both warrior and musician. Both talents had been developed around the same countryside. Some Bedouins still have primitive pipes, cymbals, and lyres with which they make music and dance in their tents at night. When David became king and established a central sanctuary in Jerusalem, he brought with him all the instrumental and vocal talent he could find to make hearty praise to God (1 Chronicles 25).

MUSIC IN DAVID'S HEBREW CULTURE
The Psalms alert us to how well-acquainted David was with the instrumental and vocal music of his day. The Psalter inventories a nearly complete list of the ancient instruments in use during the first millennium B.C. It mentions everything from percussion to wind to various string instruments. The Psalms picture young women beating and striking tambourines:

They have seen Thy procession, O God, . . .
In the midst of the maidens beating tambourines.
   (Psalm 68:24-25)

Sing for joy to God our strength. . . .
Raise a song, strike the timbrel. (81:1-2, see also 149:3)

We see the use of two kinds of brass cymbals as well:

Praise Him with loud cymbals;
Praise Him with resounding cymbals. (150:5)

The difference between the two probably lies in one being for loud, vigorous sounds, while the other is perhaps more restrained. This might argue for a variety in volume, depending upon the desired mood or emphasis of verbal meaning.

Three wind instruments predominate. The famous Jewish ram's horn, or shofar, was used as a signal trump to call the populace to the appointed time of worship: "Sound the ram's horn at the New Moon" (Psalm 81:3, NIV). But the long, silver, valveless trumpets are mentioned as well (1 Chronicles 13:8, 2 Kings 12:13). The psalmist encourages,

With trumpets and the sound of the horn
Shout joyfully before the King, the LORD. (Psalm 98:6)

The pipe, or flute, is only listed once in the Psalter (150:4), but was probably the most common instrument in use among the populace. As such, it was designed to be easily made, highly portable, and accessible to the masses. Early pipes crafted of bone and ivory have been found in Egyptian tombs. At the Megiddo dig, double flutes shaped as female demons were found in connection with Baal worship. Phoenician terra cotta pipes were dug up at Achzib on the northern Mediterranean coast of Israel. These apparently were used more in formal processions than at the central sanctuary in Jerusalem.

You will have songs as in the night when you keep the
   festival;

And gladness of heart as when one marches to the sound of
the flute. (Isaiah 30:29)

Then there was David's lyre. Some experts believe this to be the
oldest instrument. A beautifully carved lyre dating back to 2500–2300
B.C.—even before the time of Abraham—was found in a tomb of
the first dynasty period in Ur. The lyre was the basic instrument of
nomads because of its small, rounded shape and six or seven strings.
When God's people were asked by their Babylonian captors to sing
songs of Zion, they refused, saying they had hung up their *kinnorim*:

By the rivers of Babylon,
There we sat down and wept,
When we remembered Zion.
Upon the willows in the midst of it
We hung our harps [*kinnorim*]. . . .
How can we sing the LORD's song
In a foreign land? (Psalm 137:1-4)

Some musicologists have argued that it was during this period
that the minor key become dominant in Jewish music. The saddened
tones of the minor keys reflected a people in exile who could no
longer sing the jubilant songs of Zion. By contrast, today Israelis can
be seen celebrating Sabbath's end by dancing the hora (a circle
dance) and singing songs of Zion.

The Psalms also allude to the *nebel*, or harp. This instrument of
worship was probably larger than the common *kinnor* and was found
in court settings. The ten strings provided a wider variation in tones
and octaves. The *nebel* may have been plucked as a harp or struck
with a hammer, something likened to the hammer dulcimer. David
wrote,

I will sing a new song to Thee, O God;
Upon a harp [*nebel*] of ten strings I will sing praises to Thee.
    (Psalm 144:9)

Sing praises to Him with a harp [*nebel*] of ten strings. . . .
Play skillfully with a shout of joy. (33:2-3)

ARI'S SURPRISE: THE ROLE OF WORSHIP IN ISRAEL
Ari returned to his second-floor apartment, unpacked his clothes, and lay down on the sofa. Glancing at his dusty phonograph record collection, he realized how long it had been since he had played those now rare symbols of the past. Even though he embraced the latest technological equipment for military application, Ari was one of those who still lived in the dark ages of personal technology. Everyone he knew owned CD players, but he had never even purchased a cassette player.

His record collection and the absence of CDs and cassettes were not-so-subtle reminders of when his marriage had ceased. Ari could not stay reclined. He got up and dusted off a couple of records. Placing them on the turntable, he laid back down and allowed himself to be caught up in *La Bohème* played by Itzhak Perlman, the Israeli violinist. Ari remembered how much he missed the feeling of making a musical instrument a part of his being. That mystical communion of musician and instrument becoming one; when the passion of one is completely fused and expressed through the sound of the other. He thought perhaps he might find a cello while in Beersheba and regain that feeling. He pledged to remind himself to make contacts the next day.

Ari tried to sleep but was too restless. Getting up and pouring himself a soft drink, he again opened his father's Bible. He looked for the section that chronicled David's appointment of an entire musicians guild. He began reading, "And they carried the ark of God on a new cart from the house of Abinadab. . . . And David and all Israel were celebrating before God with all their might, even with songs and with lyres, harps, tambourines, cymbals, and with trumpets" (1 Chronicles 13:7-8). He continued reading,

> Now David built houses for himself in the city of David; and he prepared a place for the ark of God, and pitched a tent for it. . . . And David assembled all Israel at Jerusalem, to bring up the ark of the LORD to its place, which he had prepared for it. And David gathered together the sons of Aaron, and the Levites. . . . Then David spoke to the chiefs of the Levites to appoint their relatives the singers, with instruments of music, harps, lyres, loud-sounding cymbals, to raise sounds of joy. . . . So the singers, Heman, Asaph, and Ethan were

appointed to sound aloud cymbals of bronze. . . . And he
appointed some of the Levites as ministers before the ark of
the LORD, even to celebrate and to thank and praise the LORD
God of Israel: Asaph the chief. . . . Then on that day David
first assigned Asaph and his relatives to give thanks to the
LORD. (1 Chronicles 15:1,3-4,16,19; 16:4-5,7)

Ari knew "Asaph" as one of the more common Hebrew names
taken by modern Israelis, but he had no idea of the role Asaph played
in David's court. As a Levite, Asaph was first a minister to the Lord,
then a professional cymbal player, and finally the chief court musician responsible for all the praise to God in music around the central
sanctuary. Apparently, what David set up was a permanent guild
headed by Asaph. The school trained vocalists, choirs, and instru-
mentalists whose task it was to perform "sir ha'elohim's," songs for
God (1 Chronicles 16:41-42).

When Ari got to the chronicler's summary of the Davidic period,
he was stunned by what he read:

Moreover, David and the commanders of the army set apart
for the service some of the sons of Asaph and of Heman and
of Jeduthun, who were to prophesy with lyres, harps, and
cymbals. . . . All these were under the direction of their father
to sing in the house of the LORD, with cymbals, harps and
lyres, for the service of the house of God. (1 Chronicles
25:1,6)

What Ari couldn't believe was the role of the army commanders.
These commanders were involved in worship!

In normal Israeli categories, rabbis do the spiritual duties such
as pray, marry, bury, and perform synagogue services. Army commanders may go to a synagogue or the Wailing Wall to pray, but their
religious expressions have very little, if anything, to do with their
military tasks. Ari remembered being at an international conference
of mental health professionals at the Tel Aviv Hilton. Having had a
pivotal role in the Lebanon War, he sat on a panel with an Israeli
researcher and an IDF mental health officer. They briefed a group of
international therapists. Ari told of his experiences in Lebanon and
how combat fatigue affected his men, and discussed the longer-term,
post-traumatic effects still surfacing.

Following the panel discussion, an American Air Force officer asked him, "How do you, as a commander, utilize your chaplain?" Ari couldn't grasp what the American was asking.

Finally, one of the IDF mental health officers, a dark-haired female lieutenant, broke the silence. "He wants to know about the rabbi. What does the rabbi do?"

Ari answered, somewhat prickly, "He buries them," and walked off.

At the time, he thought the American's question was bizarre. Americans are always mixing their politics and religion, he thought. But now, as Ari read this section chronicling David's life, he thought differently. Israelis have so separated religion from life that the two rarely meet. God has nothing to do with everyday life, and the way Israelis live has very little to do with God.

But here, these army commanders were in the middle of commissioning, not officers, but musicians who would speak forth praises and prophecy in song. Functioning under their king and commander in chief, 4,000 musicians were appointed to the special tasks assigned to them out of the total 38,000 Levites. This number was divided into twenty-four orders of 12 each (1 Chronicles 15:16, 23:5). Another 288 were specially trained in vocal music (25:7). In addition, the chronicler recorded David's role as innovator and inventor of musical instruments: "4,000 were praising the LORD with the instruments which *David made* for giving praise" (23:5, emphasis added).

David was not an uninvolved monarch when it came to worship. He wrote lyrics, set them to music, brought in the whole range of instrumentation, appointed professionals, and even tinkered with creating different kinds of instruments. David's emotional life seemed to spill over into the realm of music. Some have suggested that David was the first to use music in a therapeutic way (with Saul), and process whatever feelings he himself was having, whether joy, sorrow, or anger. Through the medium of music, David gave expression to his passionate emotions.

As Ari turned out the light, he still felt somewhat uncomfortable about David. It was like he knew him very well and not at all. He could identify with much of David's life—his warrior instincts, his love of the outdoors, and even his appreciation of excellence in song and lyrics. But a piece of the puzzle was still missing. Ari couldn't put his finger on what it was. The difficulty bothered him.

≈

DAVID'S PASSION:
THE RECOGNITION OF GOD'S PRESENCE

David could barely contain the excitement within himself. After one attempt at returning the ark of the covenant to his royal city, the celebration had been preempted by a rather severe judgment. What appeared to David as a well-intentioned, innocent attempt by Uzzah to prevent the ark from falling off the ox-drawn cart, God apparently looked upon as irreverent. The action cost Uzzah his life. David was so angered by the event that it took him three months to get over it. They left the ark where the tragedy happened, only moving it inside the house of Obed-edom, to get it out of the elements. David perhaps had been so excited to return the ark that he forgot what it represented. This was no magical box dispensing mysterious powers, as King Saul had tried to use it. *It was a symbol of God's active intervention into the lives of His people.* David got the point. God was certainly able to keep His own ark from falling on the ground; He did not need the help of humans. All He wanted was a moment-by-moment recognition of His presence.

But now, David felt the same excitement building within that he had felt on the first attempt. Upon hearing the household of Obed-edom was being unusually prospered, David was ready to try it again.

This time David left the singers at a distance, while he and the ark-bearers approached the house. As they entered the house, his heart began to race. A mixture of excitement and fear shot through his being as he saw the ark where they had left it. Carefully picking it up, they walked about six steps, which placed them outside the door of the house.

David stopped the movement and brought out an ox and a fattened calf and, with his own hands, cut their throats. The action surprised everyone, but no one dared utter a word. After the blood was completely drained, he built a fire and placed the carcasses upon the hot stones he had erected. He lifted up his eyes toward heaven and asked God to be pleased with the sacrifice. When he was finished, he asked the Levite ark-bearers to proceed once again. They walked slowly and carefully at first, then sped up after a while. Finally, one of the Levites broke the silence by sounding the shofar. Then several singers joined it, soon followed by instruments. Excitement began to build as they approached the City of David. Everyone realized that God indeed had been pleased, and in response to God's favor toward them, they paused again and sacrificed seven bulls and rams.

By this time the news of the ark's movement toward Jerusalem had spread through the land. People began to come from all over Israel to join the procession. When the ark entered the royal city, the entire procession burst into song and celebration. Some just shouted for joy while others blew their horns and trumpets. Women joined in with their cymbals and tambourines, and the special Levites appointed by Asaph played their harps and lyres. David, at the front of the procession, was so overjoyed he would often just lift his hands toward heaven, grab a fellow Israelite, join hands, and dance for joy. Circling and whirling, sometimes jumping up and down, David had never experienced anything like this in his life. The celebrative joy he felt exploded into music, dance, and shouting. His emotions could not be contained.

⁓

ARI'S PASSION AWAKENS

The next morning Ari had a staff meeting. The IDF was planning a combined arms exercise in the Negev to test a new air-land doctrine. At an undisclosed location, Samson's Foxes, along with air support from the IAF (Israel Air Forces), would do a deep intervention strike against a mock terrorist base. Ari loved these exercises even though they were usually tougher than the real thing. The war planners prided themselves in their many scenarios, which created "glitches" that forced the units to think on their feet and improvise. These exercises are what made the Israelis the best in the world at terrorist intervention.

After a day of meetings and phone calls, Ari walked to one of his cello contacts. "Yonah's Musical Repair," the sign on the door read. It was just a little shop with instruments, parts, and tools lying everywhere. Ari quickly felt at home with the musty scent of rosin that permeated the shop. A little old man in a yarmulke and thick spectacles looked up and, seeing the two falafels (oak leaves) on the epaulet of his uniform, greeted him. "Shalom, Major," he said. "Ah, you're interested in the cello?"

"Yes," Ari replied.

"Tell me," said the old man, "what does an army major want with a cello? Is the IDF starting a symphony?"

Ari could detect an Eastern European Yiddish accent beneath his Hebrew words. Glancing down at what Yonah was working on, he noticed numbers on the man's wrist. As the man looked up, neither needed to say more. In Israel, these tattoos are ever present, though becoming fewer in number.

Ari finally explained. "Oh, I used to play, and I thought I might. . . ."

The shopkeeper smiled and said, "Let me see your hands. Ah, yes, these are the hands of a cellist. Wait right here." Ari looked around the shop at all the pieces of twisted brass—a tuba bell, violin bows, cases, and even a mandolin on the wall. Finally, Yonah emerged with a dusty, hard case in hand. After wiping it off, he opened it. Ari loved what he saw: a well-polished, full-sized, rosewood cello.

"May I?" Ari asked.

"Well, of course. Why do you think it is here?" the shopkeeper replied.

Ari remembered well how to tune it. He rubbed some rosin on the bow, sat down, and placed the cello between his legs. The first few notes were rough and skeeky, but soon the years of playing returned and his aging fingers more accurately remembered their correct positions. As Ari played the beginning of a Bach concerto, a tear came to his eye.

The shopkeeper responded, "I think we need coffee." The old man disappeared and returned with coffee and bagels. He emptied a chair of its pile of newspapers, sat down, and shared the evening snack with this man of passion.

As they ate, Ari felt a certain kinship with this fellow music lover. He couldn't believe he was telling a complete stranger about his recent discoveries about King David. Yonah was very knowledgeable of the Bible and far more polite than most Israelis about the subject.

Yonah said, "Perhaps I can provide you with what you think you are still missing about David." As the old man listened, he leaned back as if he had a flash of insight. He cut into Ari's discourse: "Ah, you don't know why you play! What is the purpose of music? Is it only to express the feelings and the passions of the performer?"

Yonah got up and reached over the counter. He pulled out a well-worn Hebrew Bible, opened it to the Psalter, and read, "Here is what our King David says, 'I will sing (*shir*), I will make melody (*zemar*) even with my own glory (*kevod*); so, awaken the harp (*nebel*) and lyre (*kinnor*), I will awaken the dawn! I will give thanks to Thee, O Lord, among the peoples; and I will make melody to Thee among the peoples' [Psalm 108:1-3].

"You, my friend, have had an awakening, but you don't know where to go with it. David says he will take all his significance and worth and express it in melodious passion. But it is all directed one way, to one Person, the Lord, blessed be His name. The reason for awakening the harp and the lyre is to give praise to this One. If you remember your biblical Hebrew, the word *praise* (*hallal*) can mean either the enthusiastic praise of a beautiful woman [Genesis 12:15, Song of Solomon 6:9] or the enthusiastic celebration and recognition of God [Psalm 113:1]. Our passions can seek to find satisfaction and expression in either place. It seems your musical passion has been awakened, but it is undirected and meaningless by itself. David's music was not undirected or misdirected. It was a jubilation so over-taking a man that his only means of expression was in the clapping of hands [47:1], dancing [30:11, 1 Samuel 18:6-7] with elaborate processions [Psalm 68:24-26], singing and making melody with polyphonic instrumentation."

Ari thanked Yonah for the coffee and for listening to him. He would think about the purchase of the cello, as it cost far more than Ari had at the moment. As he opened the door of the shop, he turned and looked at Yonah and said, "Yes, the missing piece. Thanks. Maybe that's it!"

As Ari walked the busy street, he contrasted two musical events in his mind. The first had been an experience with his daughter Dorit. She wanted to see one of her favorite rock groups perform at the ancient amphitheater in Caesarea. This ancient Roman theater, just a few hundred meters from the Mediterranean, had been turned into contemporary use for plays and concerts. The Israel Philharmonic Orchestra even does summer concerts there. For Ari, it seemed almost blasphemous to allow a rock band to perform on the same stage where some of the greatest drama and music in the ancient world had been performed. But since Dorit's mother refused to go

with her, and Ari had not seen his teenage daughter for some time, he
agreed to attend.

What struck Ari about this particular rock concert was that it was
mostly spectacle with no substance. "Noise without meaning" was
the way he summarized it. He felt such music paled in comparison
to the symphonies he had heard at En Gev. Now that was real music!
But as Ari maneuvered through the streets of Beersheba, he wondered if he had been mistaken about this also. *What is the purpose of
music anyway?* he thought.

Could it be that both this rock group and the finest of symphonies
could only be performing for their own enjoyment and musical pride?
If music is an artistic expression of the human heart, then music is but
a means to something else. But what is that something else? For King
David and Yonah, a Holocaust survivor, the something else was God.

CHAPTER FIVE

5

A Man Among Men:
Passion for His Friends
"YOUR LOVE TO ME WAS MORE BEAUTIFUL
THAN THE LOVE OF WOMEN"

The three spies returned from their mission. As they came into the vast entrance, shouts of joy echoed throughout the many tributaries of the cave. One by one, each man rose from his campfire and embraced the three. A few affectionately grasped the mens' beards and kissed them on the cheek. Uriah offered his old friends pieces of his freshly roasted lamb and bread and said, "Here, join me at my fire and rest from your journey."

Eleazar reported how he had seen the army of the Philistines camped around Bethlehem.

"Can you imagine that," Shammah broke in. "David's hometown! They have even taken over Jesse's house and made it their command quarters."

"Does David know?" Uriah asked.

"How could he? We have just arrived from the mountains overlooking the Valley of Rephaim where we saw the army. We asked a Judean shepherd boy about it, and he told us the Philistine commander had asked him where the son of Jesse's home was. He informed them that he didn't know, even though he did."

Josheb broke in. "Yes, we tried to recruit him as a spy, but he had sheep to get to pasture." Everyone around the fire chuckled.

Benaiah then got more serious and said, "Well, what are we going to do about this Philistine violation of the territory?"

David was awakened by the sounds of laughter and arose to find its source. His aide, Jehoiada, informed him of the arrival of the three famous warriors, Josheb, Eleazar, and Shammah. David increased his pace as he moved toward the entrance of the Adullum cave. As he rounded the corner, he saw the large group that had gathered around one particular fire.

"They came, my lord," said one of his men in passing.

As David approached, everyone jumped up, but he went directly to the three, embracing and kissing them. "Shalom, my friends, it's good to see you. I am honored that you have come. I am not worthy of your service."

Josheb quickly returned, "No, my lord, it is our great privilege to serve you, but we do have some bad news."

David sat down. "What's the bad news?"

Everyone looked at each other, but no one said anything. Finally Uriah broke the silence. "My lord, the Philistines have taken over Bethlehem."

"Even the house of Jesse," added Benaiah. "You were certainly wise to have sent your family away to Moab."

David hung his head. "Bethlehem, Bethlehem. Oh, Bethlehem. . . ." Then he got up and said, "I must go inquire of the Lord." With that he disappeared into the deep recesses of the stronghold.

With David's exit, the campfire became strangely hushed. No one spoke; most just looked down at the fire. But Eleazar looked at Josheb and Shammah. As their eyes met, a conniving smile simultaneously came to each of their faces, resulting in a silent nod of collusion. Without speaking, each knew what they were going to do.

≈

ARI'S SECRET MISSION

The purple-bereted brigade reclined beside the bare-base airstrip, leaning on their packs of carefully packed equipment. Each carried his basic fatigue uniform, a load-bearing web gear filled to capacity with ammunition (blanks on this occasion, although live ammunition is always nearby), grenades, medical equipment, canteens, individual rucksacks and, of course, the Kevlar ballistic helmet strapped to the chin. Besides those basic issue items, every one of Samson's Foxes carried a *pa'kal*, or squad support item. It might be a can of water, stretcher, field radio, mortar, a LAW (light antitank weapon), or antitank rifle grenades. And always near one's hand is the ever-present Galil assault rifle, or the CAR-15, a short-barreled version of the U.S. M-16, modified to carry the 40-millimeter grenade launcher. Officers generally preferred the CAR-15, while the squad members usually carried the Galil. Ari atypically preferred the Galil, since he started with it in basic training.

While waiting for the C-130s to appear on the horizon, most of the troops slept, read magazines, or readjusted their equipment. Ari noticed two women among the sea of men. One was a black-bereted tank instructor and the other a dark Sephardic *yahas*, or nurse. Ari smiled as he observed the nurse looking through a fashion magazine while the other painted her nails. *Even in an army of equals, men are still men and women still women*, Ari thought.

Women have always been involved in the defense of Israel since the earliest settlers arrived in the early years of Zionism (in the late 1800s). They were part of the armed pre-state underground and served as radio operators, intelligence officers, messengers, and even explosives experts. But in the war for Israel's independence, so many women were killed in defense of the country that the IDF vowed to never again place women in combat units. Therefore, the Israeli Women's Corps, called *chen*, the Hebrew word for "charm or grace," created after the war, has limited women to support roles. However, their basic training, though less rigorous than that of their male counterparts, does train every woman in the use of the Uzi submachine gun and the M-16. Upon finishing their training they are then integrated into their respective units. Since the Yom Kippur War, in 1973, which completely drained the nation's resources by taking all the tank instructors to the fronts, leaving the instructor ranks depleted, women have entered what is often considered the nonconventional role of armor instructors at the IDF Tank School, appropriately called "julis." The young lady painting her nails was a "juli" and was regarded as one of the finest tank instructors in the world. She was on the exercise as an observer.

Ari had been briefed on the exercise and the role of his reconnaissance unit. The war game had been given the label "Operation Hitgabber" (or Operation Overwhelm). It was a classic label for

Israel's philosophy of warfare: surprise interdiction with massive fire-power, ironically learned from the Germans (the Nazi blitzkrieg and Carl von Clausewitz, 1780–1831, a Prussian strategist). The C-130 cargo planes were to pick up the Giva'ati Brigade and fly them to an obscure destination in the desert. This would be the base camp for departure and pickup. By night, they would then hike to meet up with the Sayeret Tzanhanim ("Winged Snakes"), the famous red-bereted paratroopers.

Navy Commandos ("Batmen") were supposed to be coming ashore somewhere from someplace, but Ari had not been briefed on their secret role. He thought, *I hope they are not the mock terrorists we have to contend with, because they are a tough bunch. Upon finishing their Commandos of the Sea training, their gold batwings are literally pounded into their chests!*

The roar of the C-130s awakened everyone. Soon, on the horizon, two Herci-birds appeared, banking sharply and dropping their landing gear, and descended to the bare strip. These American Lockheed-built Hercules aircraft are the mainstay of the IAF. They are the workhorses and dirtbirds of the IDF as well. They can land on short dirt strips, reverse their engines, and back up as they did during the Israeli Entebbe raid. Each plane can hold about ninety passengers with equipment and some cargo. The C-130 can do assault landings and takeoffs on short runways and, as learned in Vietnam, take several rounds of antiaircraft fire and keep flying. Ari loved the plane because it was such a down-and-dirty warbird. It was made for the desert terrain Ari loved.

Once strapped in and airborne, Ari briefed his troops. They would be landing just after sundown and would immediately hike to their rendezvous point, meet up with the Tzanhanim, and get a couple hours of sleep before attacking at the crack of dawn.

Coming from another direction was a lone C-130. Lieutenant Colonel Baruk Levin, operation commander, stood up and briefed his crack unit. In the beginning, Israeli paratroopers were never envisioned as a counterterrorism force. But since the explosion of Intifada terrorism, whereby terrorist activities were planned outside of Israel to be carried out inside of Israel, these "winged snakes" were trained to jump behind the enemy lines and carry out their search-and-destroy missions. They specialized mostly in covert operations.

The yellow get-ready light came on, and the entire force got up and hooked their lines. The loadmaster opened the door. This was going to be a side jump, which makes paratroopers more nervous. Most love to go out the "back door," wherein the C-130's tail ramp is dropped down so that the men can literally run out the back door. But jumping out the side always looks like one is jumping right into the engines, though it is physically impossible.

"Green light," Colonel Levin shouted. "Follow me." And out the door he went. Within minutes all of the special-forces squad were on the ground safely. Pulling out his map and flashlight, the colonel aligned the map, took a compass heading, and said, "Let's move out. Put on your night glasses."

DAVID'S TRUSTED FRIEND

The palace attendant drew Jonathan's attention. He motioned to him, and they walked outside. The attendant told him a woman from the wilderness was waiting to see him. Walking down to the market area, Jonathan was fearing the worst. His first words were, "David . . . how is he?"

"He is fine. Well, I mean he is okay physically. But I fear his spirit has fallen," she answered. "Perhaps the exile from Saul is getting to him."

Jonathan thanked her and told the attendant to find her something to eat, and to provide her with enough for her return trip. He then returned to the palace and packed a few things in a pouch. He asked the attendant if he knew where his father was, but the attendant only replied, "He's chasing David."

"If my father returns before I do, tell him I have gone hunting with my bow," instructed Jonathan.

"Yes, my lord," he answered.

Jonathan quickly mounted his mule and took a back trail toward the wilderness of Ziph. It didn't take long for David's men, posted in the hill country, to see his familiar figure riding toward them. They sent messengers to David, announcing that Jonathan was coming. Upon hearing the news, David mounted a donkey along with a couple of his trusted warriors and proceeded to meet Jonathan. The reunion evidenced to David's escorts the deep affection the men carried for each other.

As they shared a meal together, Jonathan asked David for a favor. "My father knows of my allegiance to you, and it may cost me my life. Will you promise me something?"

David answered, "Of course. Name it, and it is yours."

"I know that you will be king one day, so what I ask is that you pledge to me to have regard for my family if I die. I do not want my name cut off forever."

David called over his trusted escorts and said, "I swear before the Lord God of Israel, and these witnesses, that I will protect and honor your offspring as long as I live." After further discussion, they finished their meal.

Jonathan then stood and said, "My friend, I must go, and return before my father gets back."

"I know," David replied. They embraced and set off in separate directions. As David rode, he looked back and gave one last wave to his friend.

ARI'S TRUSTED FRIEND

Sergeant Eyal crawled over to Ari and whispered, "Our perimeter guards have picked up movement to the southeast. Is that the 'snakes'?"

"Probably. They are right on time, but continue to monitor the movement with your night vision glasses, and keep your gun sights on them," Ari returned.

Ari continued to look at his watch with the red-lensed flashlight. Almost to the minute, the appropriate passwords were exchanged between the two forward recon point men, and the "snakes" and the "foxes" were united in the middle of a dark nowhere. The first recon member of the paratroopers to come through the perimeter was met by Ari.

"Shalom," Ari greeted, "where is your commander?"

"Over there," the young man with the red beret motioned. The dark figure of a man turned around to meet Ari. As they got closer and shined their muted lights on each other's face, they broke out in laughter. Even the lower-ranking personnel were surprised by the outburst and quickly told them to "cool it."

"Ari, is that really you?"

"Hen," Ari answered, pulling the lieutenant colonel down to the ground. "Baruk, I can't believe you would show up in the middle of this desert."

"I know, Ari, it's good to see you. It's been so long since we have been together. It's too bad we didn't pack some Maccabees. We could break one open and have a party," Baruk answered.

Sergeant Eyal motioned to Ari by pointing to his watch. "We have a war to fight, don't we?" Ari said, laughing.

"That's what NCOs are for, to keep officers on their toes," the colonel answered.

Ari gave Baruk another big hug and, keeping his arm around him, said, "Now, what are we going to do in this operation, kill some terrorists?" The two kneeled down, pulled out their respective maps and went over the operation details. Each then met with all their respective squad leaders to go over the same details. Finally, the two commanders called the entire force together. Both commanders gave a little esprit de corps talk and then told everyone to try to get exactly two hours of sleep. Ari set his watch alarm and laid down next to his old friend. He knew he wouldn't need the alarm. He was never able to sleep before any operation, real or contrived, but at least it was time off one's feet. The infamous Moshe Dayan was probably the only Israeli commander who could literally fall asleep in the midst of a battle!

Baruk rolled over and faced Ari. "How are things, Ari?"

"All is well," Ari simply answered.

"That's not what I've heard, my friend. You'd better tell me the truth. You know you could never kid me," Baruk replied.

"Oh, it's such a long story. I'm really not sure about what happened anymore," said Ari.

"Well, I know the story, Ari. I was there with you through most of it. But what I want to know is, how are you doing now?"

One of the paratroopers rolled over and looked up toward the direction of the conversation. Ari noticed the young man and suggested, "Want to go for a little walk, or would you like to sleep?"

"Well, since it's just an exercise, let's go talk. Who knows when we will get more time together." The two warriors walked a few meters into the darkness, found another spot, and sat down. "Too bad we can't light a fire and cook something," said Baruk.

"I know," answered Ari, "that would be just like old times in Galilee."

"And Lebanon," added Baruk. Both men laughed, though the laughter was based in deep-seated pain.

Out of nowhere Ari said, "I miss you, my friend."

Baruk nodded and muttered, "Me too."

"Not having any brothers, you are probably the only man alive who I would consider to be a brother. Oh, I had Hassan growing up, but you remember what happened to him," Ari explained.

"Yes, I remember," Baruk returned. "Irony of ironies, your best Arab friend, killed by an Arab mortar round."

"Yes, I really loved him," Ari added. "I still see his family from time to time, but things are obviously not the same."

"I know," Baruk acknowledged.

"What do you think makes for a good friendship?" Ari asked. "I mean, why have we remained close through all we have been through together?"

"I don't know. Perhaps conflict forges a sympathy of spirits," answered Baruk. "Look at most of your adult friends. Aren't they the ones you served with and almost were killed with?"

"I guess you're right," Ari replied.

"I've always considered good friendships to be modeled after David's relationship with Jonathan, the son of David's greatest enemy, Saul," Baruk offered.

"I can't believe you brought that up," returned Ari. "I have been reading, or rereading, about David's life recently. You know how he was my father's hero and model man?"

"Yes, I remember that," Baruk acknowledged.

Ari turned on his flashlight, glanced at his watch, and reported, "Another hour and a half to go."

"Good," said Baruk.

"Well, tell me how you see David's friendships; there seems to me to be an interesting mix of great loyalty and betrayal in his life," Ari added.

"Yes, like the IDF," retorted Baruk. Again, the two men laughed.

"Oh, it is good to be with you," confessed Ari. "Now tell me your thoughts about David."

DAVID AND JONATHAN'S TRAGIC FRIENDSHIP
Baruk leaned back a bit and propped up his head with his arm and began his discourse on David. "David was very much like you, Ari.

The youngest of the family. Apparently, his brothers didn't really like him, or at least they were upset when he showed up at the conflict with Goliath [1 Samuel 17:28]. On the whole, I think David was the kind of guy who made insecure men and women very uncomfortable. He was so gifted that he bred a lot of jealousy. He immediately found favor with everyone in Saul's household, except for Saul, of course. Jonathan immediately took to him, both of Saul's daughters were fighting for his attention. He won over all the palace servants. It seemed every time Saul came back to his own house, someone was praising David. It's no wonder Saul tried to spear him.

"Once Saul made his intentions clear that he wanted to kill David, it was his own son, Jonathan, who came to David's aid. He then interceded on David's behalf with his father to buy him some time [1 Samuel 19:2]. When David was running for his life from Saul, it was Jonathan who showed up to comfort and encourage David [1 Samuel 20:1-2]. David basically asked Jonathan to take his life, because he would rather have a friend kill him than King Saul. Jonathan, of course, refused, and then countered with his own proposal. Jonathan realized that his own life was on the line by protecting David, so he asked David to enter into a covenantal agreement with him. David pledged to not cut off the offspring of Jonathan's house, even when all of David's enemies have been removed [1 Samuel 20:14-16].

"It was a covenant born more of love than fear. Two friends pledging their commitment not only to each other, but to each other's house and progeny. The covenant was sealed with a *mitzpah* type of parting. Jonathan concluded, 'The LORD is between you and me forever' [1 Samuel 20:23]. In the same fashion Jacob and Laban had asked the Lord to be the watchman (*mitzpah*) between them [Genesis 31:49].

"Jonathan and David then devised a plan in which David could find out Saul's intentions toward him. It involved a fundamental lie about his whereabouts, and Jonathan more than obliged to carry out the test of his father's feelings. He set up the test, and laid the 'David in Bethlehem lie' before his father. He saw clearly Saul's intention to kill David. Saul picked up his spear and threw it at Jonathan for defending David. Jonathan then went out to the field to meet David to tell him the bad news.

"They kissed each other, wept, and again pledged their commitment to each other. Jonathan reminded David of their covenant by saying, 'The LORD will be between me and you, and between my descendants and your descendants forever' [1 Samuel 20:42].

"Once Saul began a serious search for fleeing David, Jonathan again risked his own life by going to David to both warn and encourage his friend [1 Samuel 23:16]. As I remember the text, it says, 'Jonathan strengthened David's hand' by telling him he would be king. They made another covenant with each other and then went their ways—David back to the wilderness and Jonathan back to his home. They never saw each other again. What an irony! David had to finally flee to the Philistines for protection from Saul. It was while he was living in Ziklag, a Philistine city, that the Philistines moved in on Saul's army and killed Jonathan [1 Samuel 31:1-2]. Can you believe it? David being protected by the Philistines while they were killing his best friend and his own King Saul!"

Baruk paused for a moment and asked, "How we doing on time?"

"We probably need to get back in another thirty minutes," Ari answered. He then interjected, "David must have been devastated."

"Yes, for both Saul and Jonathan, but for different reasons, I think. He wept for Saul because he was still the king of Israel. That his king was slain brought much sorrow to David. But for Jonathan it was much different. His grief was unbearable. David, in typical fashion, wrote a song to express his feelings, and asked that the song be taught to all the sons of Judah [2 Samuel 1:18]. He called the eulogy simply *Qashet*, or "the Warrior's Bow." Did you know that in the *Qashet*, David called Jonathan his *'achi*, or "brother" [2 Samuel 1:26]? Apparently, Jonathan was more of a brother to David than his own seven brothers."

Ari interrupted, saying, "Well, my friend, you can write my eulogy and call it 'The Galil'!"

Baruk returned, "You mean you are still carrying that old thing? You haven't moved up to the CAR-15?"

"No, I still carry my trusty Galil. It has been good to me and gotten me through a lot of tight situations."

"You and me both," Baruk countered. "Well, it's time. We need to get the men up. Let's go."

The terrorist exercise went reasonably well. The naval Batmen had rendered inoperative all the communication systems at the terrorist base, leaving the joint force of paratroopers and Samson's Foxes an open window for a complete surprise. The black-bereted female NCO observers tagged only four of the aggressors as "simulated kills." Three were paratroopers and one was one of Ari's men.

The entire action was over in about twenty minutes. Buddy-care was administered on the simulated wounded until two Huey choppers arrived to medivac the "downed" warriors to the base camp where the nurse had set up a temporary field hospital. An AH-64 Apache gunship hovered nearby providing air support for the entire operation. As quickly as they hit, they departed to reconnoiter at the point where the Hercules had dropped them off. Three birds were already waiting with engines running when the band of warriors arrived at the base camp. Since all were returning to the same destination outside Beersheba to debrief, Ari asked permission of Colonel Levin (he was still his superior and operation commander) to ride with the paratroopers and thus get in more talk time with his friend. The request was approved.

Ari put his brigade members on one ship, placing his second in command in charge, then quickly ran to the other plane. Ari and his friend buckled up on the web seats and sat speechless until they were airborne. Once in the air, Colonel Levin suggested they go back into the tail section. The two veteran commandos wove their way through men, equipment, and supplies to where the incline of the ramp provided a place to recline. Sitting down, the colonel said, "Now, where were we?"

ARI'S LESSON ON LOYALTY

Ari looked at Baruk and asked, "How's the family?"

"They are all fine," he answered. "By the way, did you know why we named our son Hushai?"

"No. Didn't he have something to do with David?"

"Just a little," Baruk replied humorously. "He was David's spy and the only individual called by the biblical text as 'David's friend' [2 Samuel 15:37, 16:16]. David finally called Jonathan his friend, but here Samuel acknowledges in every reference that Hushai is David's friend. When David was fleeing from Absalom and arrived at the Mount of Olives, Hushai was waiting for him [15:32]. Apparently, Hushai was going to leave with him. But David said, 'If you pass over with me, then you will be a burden to me.' It may have been that David just didn't want to lose any more friends or have the responsibility of a friend's blood on his hands. So he basically said to Hushai, 'If you are my friend, go back to the palace and say to Absalom, "As I have served David, so will I serve you."'

"David's intent was for Hushai to be the palace confidant and thwart any counsel not in his interest. Hushai did and saved David's life. I guess that's what real friends do. They are loyal to a fault. Both Jonathan and Hushai lied to protect their friends."

"They must have been Mossad trained," Ari jested.

"And we know about that, don't we?" Baruk added. "The way I see David is that he had these two long-term friends in Hushai and Jonathan. They were his close confidants. But he also had a collection of unlikely mercenaries and outcasts to whom he was very close and appreciative. Have you ever read through the list of his *gibborim?* They were all mercenaries. Look at the three of his inner circle—Josheb, a Tahchemonite; Eleazar, an Ahohite; and Shammah, a Hararite. They were all probably imported Assyrians. Josheb once killed three hundred men with a spear, and Eleazar and Shammah and David alone took on a whole band of Philistines to defend one plot of ground. Eleazar swung his sword for so long it appeared to be fused to his hand [2 Samuel 23:8-12, 1 Chronicles 11:11-14].

"These were gutsy, highly trained warriors of the Assyrian army who came to be the mainstay of David's house of heroes. When David desired to have a drink of water from the well at Bethlehem, these were the ones who immediately took off and went into the Philistine camp and brought back water to David. And this was no covert operation. The text reads that they 'split open or forced a breach' in the Philistine camp. In other words, they fought their way in and fought their way out to bring David his water. It's no wonder David was so overtaken by their courage. Rather than drink the water, he poured it out as an offering to the Lord [2 Samuel 23:16]."

"I've never thought about that aspect of David's friendships," Ari commented. "It seems friendship is about loyalty, incredible loyalty."

"Well, that's what's kept me hanging in there with you," Baruk replied with an affectionate smile on his face. "David forged some pretty solid relationships with those mercenaries. Almost the entire list of his heroes are foreigners [2 Samuel 23:24-39]. David was very loyal to his own people, but anyone who wanted to help defend the national boundaries of Israel, he was quick to bring into his circle of affection."

"Sounds like what the Saudis did with us when they couldn't get the terrorists out of their own mosque," Ari responded.

"Ari, you know that's classified information," Baruk quickly added.

Ari realized the paradoxical ironies that life throws at one. David, the defender of Israel, hired foreign mercenaries to help fight his battles and then made them his friends. Perhaps conflict does forge friendships.

Baruk stood up to use the questionable facilities located on the side of the tail section.

"It's certainly not El Al, is it?" Ari questioned.

"That's for sure."

Ari laid back his head and flashed back to the days of pranks, fights, and playing together with his Arab friend. Ari's relationship with Hassan Adib began with their two fathers. Hassan's father had been a policeman in Nazareth, a devout Muslim. But through a strange series of circumstances, Yakov ben Ammud's and Abu Adib's lives became intertwined. Ari never knew the whole story because even his mother did not like the relationship. As far as Ari could tell, as the result of something they went through together, they pledged to take care of each other's family for life. If one was ever in trouble or needed something, there was a blood oath between these two men to defend, provide for, and protect the other. After the death of Ari's father, Abu Adib, for the most part, adopted Ari as a son.

Since Hassan was roughly the same age, this Jewish Israeli and Muslim Arab become instant friends. The worst day of Ari's life was when he got the phone call informing him of the mortar round that landed right outside Hassan's home. Hassan, his wife, and three children were killed. Two of his children survived. Ari often wondered if Hassan was killed simply because of his friendship with an IDF officer. Ari was the only non-Arab at the funeral and was asked by Hassan's mother to give a eulogy. Following a reading of the Koran by the imam, Ari gave an emotional tribute to his best friend in life.

Ari had to wipe his eyes as he remembered the scene. As the sound of the four turboprop engines hummed, Ari closed his eyes and thought of the irony of that scene. An IDF officer in uniform weeping over the grave of his Arab friend in the middle of a Muslim cemetery while the rest of the world doesn't have a clue how to solve the Arab-Israeli conflict.

Baruk returned, stretched his arms out, yawned, and said, "It's really about loyalty, isn't it . . . about always having someone to protect your back, to cover for you, your kids, your property?" Ari nodded.

"Well, I left out the punch line to this discourse about David's friends," Baruk recalled.

"So what's the punch line?" Ari asked.

"Uriah," answered the colonel.

"Uriah?" questioned Ari.

"That's right, Uriah the Hittite. He's on the list of David's mercenaries [2 Samuel 23:39, 1 Chronicles 11:41]. Yes, this Syrian Hittite was in the circle of David's faithful *gibborim*. He must have been an accomplished soldier, but his own king did him in. That's the punch line. It seems David's whole life was centered around loyalty—loyalty to God, his nation, his men, his covenants, even to his enemies. But with Uriah we see the dark side of David's passions. Loyalty becomes betrayal and treachery. How would you like to have your commander in chief make you the point man in an operation and then have everyone else retreat from you?"

"Are you talking about my life now, my friend?" Ari interjected.

"Well, now that I think about it, I guess I am. But your commander didn't betray you for a woman," Baruk continued.

"That's right, but passion is passion, isn't it? A passion for self-interest and self-protection ends the same way, having an underling take the rap." With this, Ari's voice began to rise and his tone became increasingly angry.

"Then you understand the tragedy David brought on himself, his nation, and his own household when he didn't stay loyal to his friends and his men," Baruk added.

The sound of the landing gear dropping interrupted the two friends. They arose and gave each other a final embrace. Ari said, "Shalom, *'achi*, my brother."

Baruk answered, "Shalom, my friend. We'd better strap ourselves in."

Ari took one final look at his friend's eyes and uttered in amazement, "And he did it all for a woman?"

"That's right, all for a woman," Baruk answered.

A Man Among Women: Passion for Beautiful Women

"THE WOMAN WAS VERY BEAUTIFUL"

The palace was empty and quiet. David had trouble sleeping. Normally, during the night hours servants were still awake making preparations for the next day. The absolute quiet caused David to lie awake and ponder his life. He didn't know why he was feeling this way. The Lord had been good. The country was finally united, and gradually Israel's enemies had been either eliminated or defeated.

But David felt tired—tired of the warfare, the blood, the constant conflict, and the years spent running for his life. As he lay awake, he wondered if he had been right in sending Joab and the army out alone. Had he inquired of the Lord about the decision? Quickly he assured himself that as king his main task was to unify and rebuild the nation. Joab was a capable commander and could take care of the Ammonites without him. Finally, David thought, *This is ridiculous. My head is racing with all these questions. I might as well get up and do something more constructive.*

David closed the door to his inner chambers and walked down a long, stone hallway, hoping for someone to talk with. *Maybe Ahithophel, my trusted counselor, is awake, or maybe Asaph is up working on some new musical score.* He checked their quarters and found them asleep. David questioned why he had sent most of the servants away with Joab.

David opened the wooden door to the courtyard. Walking over to the stone wall, he looked down upon his city. "I wish Jonathan was still alive," he murmured. "He was such a good friend. My soul longs for his presence." David turned and looked up into the sky. A full moon illuminated the mountains surrounding the little city.

David thought, *As the mountains surround Jerusalem, so the Lord has surrounded His people*. David took in the splendor of the night and turned to place his face directly into the early morning breeze. He heard the distant sound of a door opening and then closing. David thought it strange that someone would be up so early. Then he noticed movement in the shadows below. His eyes fell on a dark figure of human form on the flat roof below him.

⌒

ARI'S CHALLENGE

All the commanders and first sergeants entered the conference room for the exercise debriefing. A table on the side of the room was loaded with olives, oranges, cheese, and sodas. Ari grabbed a plateful of the samplings and, along with Baruk, took his seat. Colonel Yigal Shalev entered the room and everyone stood.

"Be seated," the colonel said brusquely. "'Operation Hitgabber' was, for the most part, successful. But we did make some mistakes that would have been very costly had it been the real thing. We did some things well, but we still need improvement in some areas. I will turn over the rest of the briefing to our observer from the Kalman Magan Tank School, Captain Shalit."

"Captain," Ari muttered under his breath, somewhat choking on a piece of cheese. "I didn't know she was an officer. She had no rank on her uniform."

"By design, Ari, so no one else would know either," answered Baruk. Ari watched the young woman who had been painting her nails the day before step up to the lectern. Ari was so tired from the lack of sleep and the trek across the Negev that he didn't hear much of what she said. He hoped his friend was taking good notes. But Ari did observe *her* closely. Her shoulder-length brown hair cascaded down both sides of her face, framing her olive complexion. He hadn't noticed her hair before, because most of it had been tucked under her beret.

She talked tough, knew her facts, and spoke fast. She even corrected the colonel. But Ari sensed she had the true heart of a Sabra, the prickly cactus that draws blood quickly but when eaten is sweet to the taste.

Baruk read Ari's thoughts and said, "She's no pushover. She can tear down a Merkava [main battle tank of the IDF] and put it back together like no one at 'julis.' No one graduates from tank school without her approval."

Having begun his career in the tank corps, Ari understood Baruk. In typical male-to-male communication, Baruk was saying, "Stay away from her!"

The briefing was finally over and Baruk had to return with Colonel Shalev to Jerusalem in his staff car. Ari gave him one last embrace and said, "Next week in Jerusalem."

"Does that mean the Messiah is coming next week?" Baruk laughed.

"No, my friend, it was just so good to see you," Ari returned.

Baruk turned to leave and said, "Shalom."

"Lehitra'ot, Colonel," Ari uttered as he gave his friend a smart salute.

Ari went back to the food table and put a few more items on his paper plate.

"Shalom, Major," he heard from a pleasant female voice. Turning to his left, he noticed Captain Shalit standing next to him.

"Shalom, Captain, thank you for your briefing," Ari replied.

"Toda," she answered. Taking a bite out of an apple she said, "I've heard a lot about you, Major."

"And I you," Ari replied. "I hear no one gets their black berets without your approval."

"Then how did you get through?" she quickly shot back.

"Ouch, you're good. But how did you know I was a former tanker?"

"Oh, I have my sources," the captain said with a smile.

"I hope they are not in Aman," Ari returned, referring to the IDF intelligence service. They both laughed.

Suddenly, Ari no longer felt tired. He felt energized. He got up his courage, swallowed the piece of pita he was chewing, looked directly into her brown eyes, and said, "Would you like to go and get something real to eat?"

There was a side of Ari that hoped she would say no, but then there was another side that made his heart beat a little faster.

"I'd love to," she answered with a smile. They went to Ari's car and drove to a Yemenite restaurant. Over candlelight and the heady aroma of spices, they ate, talked, and tried to decide which Carmel wine went best with Yemenite food. They talked tanks, the exercise, the tank corps, and why she was not married. Ari talked about his divorce, his two children, his kibbutz upbringing, but carefully avoided "the Lebanon issue."

All through dinner Ari had a running conversation with himself. Looking into her deep, dark Sephardic eyes, he kept thinking, *Why am I sitting here? Why am I so attracted to her? Why did I invite her to dinner anyway?* and *What a stupid fellow I am!* Ari even found himself thinking, *Why would this young tank instructor even find me, a middle-aged, graying 'has-been,' interesting?* Then he would answer himself, *But she* is *a fellow army officer, and we're talking about the exercise we have just been on. She is one of the best tank instructors in the IDF. I should get to know her.* Then he wondered why he was even asking himself these questions. Why couldn't he simply enjoy the evening?

After dinner, he and Captain Shalit walked around several Beersheba city blocks, stopping occasionally to look in shop windows. By the time they returned to the car, Ari had reached down and taken her hand. She didn't resist. He drove back to the officers' quarters. She opened the door, looked back at Ari's penetrating, verdant eyes, and said, "Do you want to come in, Major? I *do* have a private room."

≋

A STEP TOWARD COMPROMISE

David moved along the wall of the roof to obtain a better vantage point. Looking down he saw the figure emerge from the darkness into the moonlit area of the roof. David observed quickly the form and dress of a woman. Wondering why a woman would be alone on her roof at this time of the night, David continued to observe her.

She carried a pitcher of water that she set on the edge of the wall. She then removed her outer garment, which was quickly followed by her inner undergarment. She reached for the pitcher and poured water over her face, arms, and legs. Taking a cloth in hand, she then began to wash her body. David was frozen. He wondered why she was bathing at such an unusual time, but he was captivated by her beauty. Although David had many women in his life (seven wives and at least ten concubines), none compared to the beautiful woman he saw in front of him. He felt a rush of passion permeate his soul.

As he returned to his room, he couldn't get the image of this dark-haired beauty from his mind. He determined to find out who she was.

The next day David made some carefully concealed inquiries to discover if anyone knew who owned the house where he had seen the beautiful woman. Finally, one passerby on the street told him it was the house of Uriah, the Hittite, and his wife, Bathsheba, the daughter of Eliam (2 Samuel 11:3).

David was shocked. Uriah was one of his most trusted and faithful men of war. One of the famous thirty-seven who had so distinguished themselves in battles (2 Samuel 23:39). *He is married to this extremely beautiful woman?* David thought. As David walked back to his palace, disappointment descended upon his inner disposition. Throughout the day, David returned to the rooftop hoping to catch a glimpse of Bathsheba in sunlight, but to no avail. She never emerged on the rooftop.

Looking down on the section of the roof where he had seen her the night before, he noticed that the pitcher was still there. Seeing that water vessel on the wall rekindled the feelings of immense passion he had experienced the night before.

David abruptly opened the door where dinner was being prepared. He told the servants there would be a special guest for dinner that night. Then David told his personal servant to go to the house of Uriah, one of his *gibborim*, and request the presence of Uriah's wife at dinner that night. He then added, "I wish to honor his wife for the courage and bravery of her husband." *After all*, David reasoned, *she is all alone, and it is only proper for the king to honor the heroism of his men.*

But in the more honest but dark recesses of David's soul, he wanted to get a closer look at this woman who had so captured his passion.

≈

ARI'S DETERMINATION, DAVID'S COMPROMISE

With the door still open, and the smiling captain still waiting for an answer, Ari paused and said, "I really enjoyed the dinner and the walk, but let's don't do something we both might regret tomorrow."

"Well, Major, I wouldn't regret it tomorrow, but I appreciate your concern. Good night." Captain Shalit closed the door and went in without looking back.

Ari put the car in gear and wondered if he had done the right thing. He would like nothing more than to make love to her. As Ari drove back to his apartment, he was surprised at what he was feeling. It was fear. *How could I feel so scared when I was so attracted to her?* Ari questioned himself. *Is it too much wine, or the fact that I haven't been with a woman for a while? Or is it simply having that nice feeling that someone is interested in me?*

Ari couldn't answer the questions his heart raised. But as he walked up the stairs, he knew it was about time he got honest with Baruk about the "other" details of the Lebanon fiasco. There was much more to Ari's career end than dereliction of duty. Baruk thought he knew everything, but he didn't. There was much more. *Besides, didn't he ask about my love life?*

Ari reported late the next day. The exercise had so worn out everyone that most were given permission to report in later. As Ari walked into his office, he noticed a dark case standing in the corner with a note attached to it. He immediately recognized it as the cello case from Yonah's music shop. Sure enough, the note was from his newly discovered friend. The note read, "You need this more than I do. Stop by and we'll work out a payment plan."

Ari sat at his desk and uttered, "I can't believe this." He called in Sergeant Eyal and asked if he knew about the cello.

Sergeant Eyal answered, "Oh, you can't believe what that did to the security folks downstairs. They were about to take it apart piece by piece, looking for a bomb, until someone recognized the little old man. He teaches instrumental music at Ben Gurion University and formerly played in the Israel Philharmonic. He's a well-known Holocaust survivor who has written several books."

"He never told me that," Ari added. "Of course, we really didn't talk about his life. We talked about me and King David."

Ari went back into his office and reminded himself to pay a visit to the generous musician. He also made a note to call Baruk that night.

Bathsheba was even more appealing up close than from a distance. David immediately was taken by her. David had put on some of his finest royal clothes and had the finest of meals prepared. During the afternoon he had appropriated a sizable gift of spices and perfumes for her. Over dinner he presented them to her in thanksgiving for the gallantry her husband had shown in battle. Throughout the dinner, every time David stared directly into her eyes, she either looked away or glanced downward. But by dinner's end, he could tell she was feeling more comfortable in his presence.

Finally, David confessed to seeing her on the rooftop that morning. She didn't blush or bat an eye, but replied, "Yes, I love bathing in the cool night air and, of course, one shouldn't do that during daylight!"

David then praised her beauty and expressed his feelings toward her. He explained that he had not been able to get her out of his mind.

Bathsheba interrupted his declaration and said, "So, having me here tonight has more to do with me than with my husband?"

David appreciated her directness. He stood up, took her by the hand, and said, "You are right. I am very desirous of you. Would you join me in my inner chamber?"

"Yes, my lord," she answered.

CONSEQUENCES OF COMPROMISE

Because Ari was scheduled for patrol duty for a couple of weeks, he wanted to talk to his friend before he left. Ari learned where Baruk was in meetings in Jerusalem. That night he called him at the historic King David Hotel. After some small talk, Ari launched into what was going on behind the scenes in the whole Lebanon inquiry.

"Are you sitting down, my friend?" Ari asked.

"Yes, I'm in bed," replied Baruk.

"Well, don't go to sleep on me," Ari pleaded.

"Oh, I won't. It sounds as if you're planning to lay something heavy on me. It's not classified, is it? This is not a secure line. I'm sure Aman monitors all traffic in and out of this place," Baruk added with serious concern in his voice.

"Don't worry. Everything I'm going to tell you the top officials in Aman, Mossad, and Shin Bet already know," Ari answered. "Well, here goes. . . . Let's go back to 16 September 1982. I was then the IDF liaison with my Phalange counterpart at the IDF divisional command overlooking Shatilla."

"How can I forget you and that great 'Christian' Eli Hobeika of the Phalange? Ari, how many times do you have to tell me about that?" Baruk asked.

"But there's much more, my brother. Please hear me out," Ari urged.

"Okay, I'll be quiet. Talk," Baruk replied.

"Well, you remember when Saguy asked me to go back with him and Sharon to attend Prime Minister Begin's cabinet meeting that night? He wanted me there to answer questions that might come up about Major Haddad's troop capabilities."

"I'm with you, Ari," Baruk assured.

"As you know, I felt deeply that my place was at the front, but Saguy was head of intelligence for the whole IDF. Even though I didn't report directly to him, I was required to get on the chopper with him and Sharon. Well, in the cabinet meeting Saguy kept falling asleep and, finally, the prime minister looked over at him sleeping, woke him up, and told him to go home to get some sleep. Saguy got up without saying anything, motioned to me to come with him, and we went outside. As we were leaving the building, Saguy told me he was going to sleep in and would catch a late-afternoon chopper back to the divisional HQ.

"He looked at me and said, 'You could be home in an hour or so. Why don't you go see your family? Who knows how long we'll be in Lebanon. You can even take my staff car. Just have it back here by four tomorrow.'"

"Is that it, Ari?" his friend questioned.

"No, that's just the beginning. You see, I didn't go to Galilee. I immediately drove to Tel Aviv."

"Tel Aviv? Why did you go there?" Baruk interjected.

"Why do you think?"

"I have no idea . . . to get a good falafel?"

"No, to see a woman," Ari confessed.

"So, what's the big deal? None of us are all that pure. Why, even Ben-Gurion and Dayan had their ladies hidden here and there. I wouldn't even put it past Begin, and certainly Sharon," Baruk said with a certain defensiveness.

"Boy, I hope this isn't being monitored!" Ari threw in and then continued. "But, you see, when the war escalated in Lebanon that night and early the next morning, I was nowhere to be found. Saguy called my home at the kibbutz, but my wife knew nothing of my whereabouts. No one knew where I was. When I returned driving in Saguy's car the next day, my fate had been sealed."

"Oh my, Ari. Now I understand," Baruk added.

Ari continued, "It stayed hidden with Saguy until four hundred thousand protesters showed up in Tel Aviv, protesting the Lebanon War and demanding to know what really happened at Shatilla. Prime Minister Begin was finally forced to appoint an independent commission to hear testimony about the matter. As it turned out, Saguy had to reveal where I had been, and to verify it they had to call the woman I was with. Can you imagine having your mistress called before the Kahan Commission and drilled about all the details of one evening by the Supreme Court Justice?" Ari asked.

"My worst fear," Baruk responded, and then added, "but thank God the hearings weren't public." Baruk paused and then spoke as if a light had just gone on. "But your father-in-law knew, didn't he?"

"Of course he knew. I never dreamed when I married Noam that her father would end up being deputy chief of staff for the IDF, under Eitan himself," Ari added.

"So that ended your marriage right there," Baruk concluded.

"Yes. By the time the commission was over, so was our marriage. Noam never could forgive me."

"I always assumed your career dead end was more connected to what happened in Lebanon," Baruk explained.

"Sure. That's what most believe, and I'm very comfortable keeping it that way. Noam might have been able to handle either the fiasco in Lebanon or the affair, but when they both happened at the same time, it was more than she could bear. It was just too humiliating for her, and she had every right to be humiliated.

"I've written letters trying explain myself and get her forgiveness, but she wants nothing to do with me. So that's the story, my friend. Do you still love me?" Ari asked.

"Of course," Baruk answered.

"Well, thanks for listening. I felt I needed to talk to someone about this. I've been gun-shy with women ever since."

"Like you were yesterday with that captain?" Baruk laughed.

"Well, we did end up going out last night, and had a great time. But I froze when we got to the door and she invited me in."

"You have to be kidding, Ari," Baruk responded.

"Well, when your entire life is destroyed in one day, you become more careful about consequences. If only I could get back that day and relive it," Ari concluded.

"Yes, you and King David. If David could have just gone to sleep that one night instead of wandering around the palace roof!" There was laughter on both ends of the phone line.

"Well, laylah tov, my friend."

"Laylah tov, Ari, lehitra'ot."

DEEP CONSEQUENCES, DEEPER COMPROMISE
The news hit David hard!

The words "I have conceived," scribbled on a piece of cloth and delivered by a neighbor. Signed, "Bathsheba."

David ran into the throne room and sat alone thinking about his options. *I could have her killed. That would take care of the problem quickly. But could I really have Bathsheba killed? Besides, she's carrying my child. I couldn't kill my own child.*

David had another flash of insight: *I know what I will do. I'll call for Uriah to come home so I can honor him personally for his valor. Having been away from Bathsheba for so long, he will certainly enjoy the pleasure of his wife before returning to the front.*

Uriah entered the palace and bowed before the king. "It's good to see you, Uriah. I know you are a mighty man of valor, and I desire to honor your commitment to Israel. I want to present you with a sword made especially for you. When the forgers finish it, I will have it delivered to your house. It is in appreciation for the valor and courage demonstrated to your king and your nation. Now go home and be with your wife."

David slept very well that night. He thanked God that he had shown enough restraint to spare Bathsheba. This way, Bathsheba could legitimately have the child and still be nearby. But the next morning, David found his plan had been thwarted. Uriah had slept at the door of the palace and had not gone home at all.

David was furious and called Uriah into his presence. He asked him directly, "Why did you not go down to your house?" (2 Samuel 11:10).

Uriah answered, "The ark and Israel and Judah are staying in temporary shelters, and my lord Joab and the servants of my lord are camping in the open field. Shall I then go to my house to eat and to drink and to lie with my wife? By your life and the life of your soul, I will not do this thing" (2 Samuel 11:11).

David didn't know what to do next. To buy some time he said, "Stay here today also, and tomorrow I will let you go." After Uriah left, David paced around his quarters wondering what he should do. Remembering that the right mixtures of wine can make a man amorous, David called his servant and asked for Uriah to join him for dinner that night. After several cups of wine, Uriah might be more motivated to go home and lay with his wife.

Over dinner David had Uriah's cup refilled after almost every sip. David asked Uriah, "How is it that a Syrian Hittite ended up marrying a beautiful Hebrew girl?"

Uriah explained, "I was recruited to be a mercenary for Saul's army to fight against the Philistines, but I soon became disenchanted with him as a leader. During that time I met a gallant Hebrew named Eliam. He was always talking about his beautiful, unmarried daughter. After some time, Eliam brought me home to meet his daughter, and the rest is history. We were married in the area of Gibeah, near Saul's residence. When I heard Saul was out to kill you, I left home to join your ranks in the wilderness. After you moved to Jerusalem from Hebron, we decided to move here as well to be closer to my lord, Joab, and the army commanders."

David offered him more wine and again encouraged him to go home to be with his wife. However, Uriah had drunk so much that he did not make it any farther than the outside of David's house. He lay down to sleep off his wine with David's household servants.

The next morning David wrote a letter to Joab, properly sealed it with the king's seal, and gave it to Uriah to take back to Joab at the front.

⌒

THE JUDGMENT OF GOD ON KING DAVID

Ari spent most of the next day getting all the equipment and in-field items needed for desert survival. It took most of the day, but Ari made sure he got to Yonah's shop before it closed. Fortunately, in Israel, most shops close in the afternoons and reopen for several more hours after dinner.

Ari parked his car in front of the shop and went in. Yonah was helping a customer with her violin. Ari took one look at her clothes, shoes, and makeup and knew instantly that she was an American.

Yonah looked up and a smile came to his face. "Did you get your surprise?"

"Yes, it overwhelmed me," Ari answered.

The American smiled at Ari and said, "Hello . . . oh, I mean shalom."

Ari smiled and returned, "Shalom."

Yonah broke in, "My, where are my manners? Major, this is Michele Anderson. Miss Anderson, this is Major Ammud."

"Please call me Ari," the major quickly replied. "So what brings an American to a music shop in Beersheba?"

Yonah answered for her. "She is on loan to us at the university."

"Yes, I'm on sabbatical from the University of Pennsylvania for a year. It's basically an exchange program. A professor from Ben Gurion and I trade places for a year."

"What a change," Ari responded. "From the Ivy League to the desert!"

"How did you know Penn was in the Ivy League?" Miss Anderson asked.

"Oh, I did some time at the war college at Carlisle Barracks, and we got into Philadelphia occasionally. In fact, I took in an Army-Navy football game while there."

"Unbelievable," she said in utter amazement. "What a coincidence!" Then she glanced at her watch and uttered, "I must go. I'm already late. When do you think it will be ready to play again?" she asked as she ran out the door.

"Tomorrow . . . late," Yonah replied.

"Oh, nice to meet you, Major. Perhaps we will meet again in this small town." Off she went.

"Americans," Ari smirked. "They let watches run their lives. Perhaps a year in Beersheba will take that out of her."

"But she *is* nice looking, is she not?" Yonah said, with a little gleam in his eye.

"You dirty old man!" Ari teased, "Anyway, what about the cello?"

"Well, pay me as you can. It is an Ernst Heinrich Roth. Once played, I believe, by the great Leonard Rose. I have the papers on it somewhere. It's probably worth ten thousand American dollars today, but I will sell it to you for what I have in it. If I can find the original bill, I'll figure it out."

"Ten thousand dollars? I'm not good enough to play a cello of that quality," Ari countered.

"Maybe the cello makes the man," Yonah added.

"Well, let me pay you something today." Ari wrote out a check and gave it to Yonah.

Ari started to leave, but abruptly turned around and walked back to the counter. "Yonah, you seem to be so well versed about King David. May I ask you a question?"

Looking very delighted, Yonah walked over to the shop window, pulled down the shade, and locked the door. He pulled up two chairs and asked, "Now, what is it this time?"

Ari jumped right in, saying, "David . . . he sort of failed when it came to women, didn't he?"

Yonah laughed and answered, "Having some love-life problems?"

Ari laughed as well and then countered, "But I'm serious. Tell me about David's relations with women."

"That's an easy one," Yonah answered directly. "Basically, he liked beautiful women, but didn't do too well with them. And, of course, he let Bathsheba so get to him that he was willing to sacrifice almost everything for a moment of pleasure.

"But the details are more instructive. His first wife was Michal, Saul's own daughter. It was probably a political marriage, but Michal started out genuinely loving David [1 Samuel 18:20,28]. When Saul tried to kill David in his own house, she protected him and helped get him out of the house. But when her father questioned her about David's escape, Michal blamed David, saying that if she hadn't let him go, he would have killed her [1 Samuel 19:11-17]. Of course, it was a lie, but she wasn't really committed to David at that point.

"While David was running from Saul's army, Saul gave her away to be the wife of another man [1 Samuel 25:44]. But as soon as Saul was dead, and David was established as king, he wanted Michal back and negotiated with Abner, Saul's general, to have her returned [2 Samuel 3:12-16]. David may have only seen her as his property, but I feel it was more than that. She was his wife, and he didn't want another man having her.

"Finally, at the height of David's joyous celebration, Michal botched it by telling David to his face that he made a fool of himself by dancing and celebrating in front of everyone while returning the ark to Jerusalem [2 Samuel 6:16-23].

"Apparently, Michal didn't think such behavior was very kingly, even though it is very Jewish!" Yonah commented in his Yiddish accent. "It's no wonder that she never had any children [2 Samuel 6:23]. Either God judged her with barrenness for her utter disregard and disrespect of her husband, or David never went near her again. I prefer the latter explanation. Who would want to be with such a woman?

"Is this boring you, Ari?" Yonah asked. "I can go on and on, so you stop me when you've had enough."

"No, please continue. This is fascinating and relevant," Ari answered.

"Then there was Abigail. Now Abigail is interesting. I hold to the view that this was basically a Levite marriage. Originally, Abigail had married Nabal [1 Samuel 25:42]. When Nabal refused to give provisions to David's men, David was ready to kill him and the entire male population in Maon [verse 22].

"The reason I believe David was so angered by this mistreatment was because he already knew Abigail and Nabal. Abigail was his half sister [2 Samuel 17:25, 1 Chronicles 2:16]. Thus, as a relative, he expected a generous family treatment for his men. Therefore, Abigail ran out to David and pleaded for Nabal's life [1 Samuel 25:23,28]. David recanted and instead blessed her for preventing the bloodshed. When Abigail finally told Nabal that he was on David's hit list, he suffered a heart attack ten days later and died [verses 36-38]. Perhaps David takes her as his wife, because as half sister, he must raise up seed to the family name.

"But the text adds a little highlight. It says, 'The woman was intelligent and beautiful in appearance' [1 Samuel 25:3]. I wonder why that is there? Would David have married her had she been ugly? Probably not. He liked good-looking women, and after his experience with Michal, he probably appreciated having someone who understood his passion for life. Apparently, Abigail had much more understanding than Michal!

"Now the rest of David's wives, except Bathsheba, we just don't know that much about. Ahinoam was from the Jezreel valley, and David married her after Michal was given away [1 Samuel 25:43]. Maacah was a Geshurite princess from the upper Jordan Valley in Syria [2 Samuel 3:3, 1 Chronicles 3:2]. Haggith we know little about except that she was the mother of Adonijah, who tried to make a play for the throne after David died [2 Samuel 3:4, 1 Kings 2:19-25].

"Likewise, we know nothing about Abital and Eglah, except for the sons they mothered by David [1 Chronicles 3:3]. My guess is some of those wives were political arrangements to help secure Israel's boundaries in the Jezreel valley, a key trade route, and Syria, a very strategic piece of property for Israel's security."

Ari interrupted, "You can say that again. It was there that I was so close to being killed by the Syrians."

"One thing we are sure about is David's concubines. We know he had at least ten of them because, when Absalom had sent him into exile, Absalom had intercourse with ten of them in public view in daylight [2 Samuel 15:16, 16:22]. Some believe David may have had more but took them with him in exile. That makes sense to me.

"Then, of course, there is Abishag. She is never called David's wife, but some scholars have thought perhaps she was a nonsexual wife for David while he was on his death bed. David was running a high temperature and could not keep warm. So his servants found a young virgin from Shunem to be his cook and nonsexual bed partner to keep him warm [1 Kings 1:1-2].

"Now it is interesting that the text adds, 'The girl was very beautiful' [1 Kings 1:4]. Why would David's servants search the countryside for such a beautiful virgin? Apparently they knew what he liked and what encouraged his spirits. There seems to be a common denominator with this great king.

"I left Bathsheba to the last because she is the one who revealed David's weakness and became his nemesis. Shall I continue?" Yonah asked.

"Of course, you can't leave out Bathsheba," Ari replied.

"Who knows why David did not go out with the army, or why he couldn't sleep that night. The text simply states, 'He saw a woman bathing; and the woman was very beautiful in appearance' [2 Samuel 11:2]. Again, the language suggests she had a good physical shape! David liked what he saw. And you know the rest of the story. David tried to cover up the deed by bringing Uriah home to his wife, but Uriah didn't cooperate. So David got him drunk. When that didn't work, David wanted him killed. Imagine that! David first committed adultery with one of his men's wives, then has Uriah killed. All Uriah wanted was to be a faithful servant to his king! But judgments are always after their kind. This is the part of the story that rarely gets told.

"When Nathan the prophet finally came to David and exposed his sin, he, speaking for God, placed a judgment on David, saying, 'The sword shall never depart from your house, because you have despised Me and have taken the wife of Uriah the Hittite to be your wife.' Thus says the LORD, 'Behold, I will raise up evil against you from your own household; I will even take your wives [women] before your eyes, and give them to your companion, and he shall lie with your wives [women] in broad daylight' [2 Samuel 12:10-11].

"What is interesting is how this judgment gets carried out. When Absalom usurps the throne and runs his father out of town, he calls for David's counselor, Ahithophel, and brings him in from Giloh [2 Samuel 15:12]. Ahithophel apparently had 'retired' from being David's counsel and was now living in Giloh, near Hebron. The question is, why would Ahithophel, who was David's long-term, private counsel, suddenly turn against his friend?

"It was said of Ahithophel that his counsel to David was as the oracle of God [2 Samuel 16:23]. When Absalom asked his advice, he counseled, 'Go in to your father's concubines, whom he has left to keep the house; then all Israel will hear that you have made yourself odious to your father' [2 Samuel 16:21].

"Now why would Ahithophel turn against his friend? Because he was Bathsheba's grandfather! Eliam was the son of Ahithophel [2 Samuel 23:34] and Eliam was the father of Bathsheba [11:3]. This old man got sweet revenge on David, who had killed his granddaughter's husband. As David had violated Bathsheba sexually, so Ahithophel counseled Absalom to sexually violate David's concubines publicly on the roof of David's own house. To add more grief to David's house, David's other son, Amnon, raped his own sister Tamar. Why? Because she was beautiful! [2 Samuel 13:1-14].

"So, my friend, David's nemesis was the power of a beautiful woman. Because of his failure, the sword fell on his own household. David's sons followed in their father's footsteps, violating women sexually," Yonah concluded.

"That's scary. But that is true in my own life," Ari confessed.

"I'm very sorry to hear that, Major," Yonah responded.

As Ari got up from the chair, he said, "Well, I am indebted to you for much more than the cello. I appreciate your wisdom on these matters, but it *is* very complicated to me. I'm a common man who keeps getting caught in uncommon situations. I'll be glad to return to the desert where I can clear my mind and sort out these things. I'll be gone about two weeks. Try to find the papers and the bill on the cello. I'll check back with you when I return."

As Yonah got up and unlocked the door, he said, "And what about the American beauty? I know she is divorced, and I *do* have her telephone number."

"I can't think about that now. But please hang on to her number just the same," Ari responded.

"Shalom."

CHAPTER SEVEN

A Man of the People: Passion for the Common

"RIDE ON THE KING'S MULE"

Abishag entered Bathsheba's chambers. "The king is not responding to my care. I'm afraid his time is not long with us," she explained.

Bathsheba looked horrified. When Abishag asked why her countenance was so fallen, Bathsheba answered, "Nathan the prophet was just here and informed me of Adonijah's preparations for taking the throne after David is gone. Is the king conscious and able to speak?"

"Yes," Abishag answered, "but he has trouble recognizing people. You must get very close to him and speak directly into his ear."

"The king must know what his son Adonijah is doing," Bathsheba uttered. Abishag agreed and left the room.

Bathsheba spoke with Nathan again, and they agreed to see the king. Nathan stayed outside the king's chambers while Bathsheba entered. She pulled back the veil covering the king's bed and looked upon the man she loved.

His thin body was very warm and wet. She placed her hand on his brow and felt the fever that was ravaging David's body. She silently bowed her head and prayed that the Lord would be gracious toward her husband.

As she prayed, David opened his eyes and recognized the beauty for which he had sacrificed so much. Bathsheba's eyes met his. She reverently bowed and said, "My king."

David took her hand and spoke. "What is it, my love?" He could tell Bathsheba was concerned about something, even though the fever was causing his mind to fail. He still managed to force a smile for his beloved wife.

"My lord, do you remember your pledge to me by the Lord God that Solomon, my son, would be king after you?"

"Yes, of course, this is true by the living God," David responded in very soft tones.

"Well," Bathsheba continued, "your son Adonijah has declared himself king, and Joab, your commander, along with Abiathar, the priest, have joined him. As we speak, they are making sacrifices at En-rogel. In addition, all the king's sons, except Solomon, are there along with many of the king's servants. Even some from your own tribe of Judah have gathered with Adonijah."

"Traitors!" David shouted. "They start making their political moves before my body is cold and in the ground. What about my *gibborim*, my mighty men? Have they also betrayed me?" David asked.

"No, my lord. They are all outside the palace awaiting your next order. Nathan is outside your bedroom door. In fact, here he is now. So I will take leave." With that Bathsheba left the king's quarters.

"Nathan, my friend and good counselor, are these things true?" David asked as he sat upright and looked Nathan in the eye.

Nathan returned, "Yes, my friend, it is all true. He has even taken your chariots and horses, and has at least fifty private guards running before him" (see 1 Kings 1:5). An inappropriate smile came to David's face as he burst into a laugh.

"I should have known not to bring home those chariots from Mesopotamia [2 Samuel 8:4]! At the time they looked like such innocent spoils of war. Absalom used them against me [2 Samuel 15:1], and now another son has taken them from me to buttress his own army. Now I know why the Lord had Moses write that it was not for kings to multiply horses for themselves [Deuteronomy 17:16]. Your own sons end up using them against you!"

Nathan chuckled, though he knew this was no laughing matter.

He was pleased the king was in good enough spirits to be his normal, humorous self again.

David then asked Nathan to call Bathsheba back into the room. When she arrived, he again pledged, "Solomon shall be king after me, and I will make him king today."

David arose, looked at Nathan, and said, "Call Zadok the priest, and Benaiah, my second in command, and get my mule" (see 1 Kings 1:32-33).

A NATION OF EQUALS

Modern Israel is a nation founded on the common. The first settlements were communal arrangements in which all property, farm equipment, and finances were held in common. Sometimes criticized as being "communistic," the communal aspects are internal and voluntary. People are always free to leave the kibbutz.

The government inside the community is highly democratic, with rotating, elected kibbutz presidents. Kibbutz products are sold for profit on the open markets around the world. The profits are then used to upgrade the standard of kibbutz lifestyle.

Usually, the older the kibbutz, the more wealthy and modern the conveniences. The kibbutz has become the premier celebration of the common man. It is a place where all—doctors, craftsmen, teachers, soldiers, farmers, and engineers—have equal status.

In theory, Israel is a classless society. In practice, of course, this is not true. But it comes closer to being classless than most Western countries.

Since the IDF grew out from the early Haganah militia, largely kibbutzniks, the army still reflects the common, classless society of the kibbutz. The IDF has no officers who have not come up through the ranks. Compared to her Western counterparts, where the officer corps is made up of college graduates (United States) or an elite aristocracy (Great Britain), in Israel every officer was once a private.

This makes for closer relationships between the enlisted troops (privates through sergeants) and the officers. Whereas "fraternization" is a dirty concept in the United States and England, it is what the IDF is all about. All soldiers are on equal common ground because they have all had shared experiences in the military.

Ari was shocked at the tradition in the United States, where the enlisted personnel could not dine with officers in each other's respective clubs. Ari enjoyed the common ground of the military camaraderie among his men.

Sergeant Eyal was Major Ammud's right-hand man. As a non-commissioned officer, he had great responsibility and the wartime experience to match it. Over the years, Ari and Uri Eyal had become a team. Though different in rank and background, an unmistakable commonness existed between them.

Sergeant Eyal made the final preparations for their two-week border patrol. He took the jeep to the supply depot and obtained the necessary supplies: rations, medical kits, water, ammunition, maps, and the latest reports generated through Aman, the IDF intelligence branch.

Upon returning to headquarters, he found a newly bereted Sayeret waiting for him. The new graduate was to join them on their patrol, and it was the sergeant's duty to "break him in."

Sergeant Eyal responded by saying, "Oh, no, they have done it again. They've given us a new recruit to train."

It's not that the sergeant minded. It was always an additional responsibility and adjustment to have a new recruit attached to an already cohesive team. But Uri reminded himself that he was once in the same position, and that it had been some other NCO who hadn't been happy to see him!

Uri introduced himself, exchanged greetings, and sat down with the young soldier. His name was Haim Yishai.

Haim, Uri thought. *I hope he can bring a little "life" to our tour of the desert.*

Haim is the Hebrew word for "life." Uri liked Haim in an instant, without knowing anything else about him. But Uri knew that by the end of two weeks, they would have covered almost everything about each other's lives and would know more about each other than either really cared to know.

Uri was pulling out the maps of the Negev and Sinai when Ari walked in. "Shalom, Major. This is our new graduate from Sayeret Giva'ati training. He will be accompanying us on the patrol," Sergeant Eyal explained.

"Shalom and congratulations," Ari returned.

They quickly exchanged handshakes and looks, and then both

looked down at the maps Sergeant Eyal had arranged. Looking at Ari, the sergeant said, "We will be taking the Beersheba-Hebron road and then turning off toward Arad and the Dead Sea. We will receive a current 'intell' briefing at En Boqeq, and then follow the fence all the way down to Qetura. That's a good one hundred and twenty kilometers, so we have quite a distance to cover before reaching civilization again.

"From Qetura we will continue on south till we arrive at Elat. There we can take a couple of days of R and R before making the return trip and retracing our path.

"I have all our equipment packed, and the jeep is fully gassed and serviced. So I think we are ready," the sergeant finished.

Ari looked at the two men and replied, "Beseder. We will meet here at 0600 tomorrow." With that brisk pronouncement, Ari left the room and went home.

Uri looked at Haim, "Well, how about something to eat? We can go over the rest of the details over dinner."

"Great," Haim answered.

As the two downed falafels and tabule salad, Haim asked about the major. "What is the major like?" asked the private.

〜

A KING FOR THE COMMON PEOPLE
David heard the sound of flutes and a large procession moving through the streets toward the Gihon spring. Though feeling feeble, he asked Abishag to get two house servants to help him get to the roof.

Bathsheba joined her husband as they worked their way slowly up the stone stairs. Arriving at the roof, David took Bathsheba's hand and looked down upon the royal procession. It was just as David had ordered. Zadok the priest led the procession and was followed by Benaiah, the newly appointed commander of the army, followed by the delegation of the Cherethites and Pelethites, David's personal bodyguards (2 Samuel 8:18, 15:18, 23:23).

The bodyguards were reassigned to protect their next king, Solomon. Finally, Solomon appeared dressed in his finest royal attire and riding David's trusted mule. Bathsheba looked up at David and said, "Thank you, my lord."

She added, "Solomon, my son, shall reign in your place. But why does he ride on your mule?"

"Horses," David muttered, "are what the Philistines ride. And, of course, my other sons rode them as well.

"Absalom and Adonijah were always infatuated with the power, speed, and agility of horses. They liked running them across the plains and fastening them to my chariots, parading around the countryside and impressing the young girls. Finally, they used them against their own father.

"But mules are for common folk, for mountain people, for farmers in the hill country, and for shepherds looking for their lost sheep in craggy rocks. Mules have the unique combination of a horse's strength and a donkey's steady footing.

"The Egyptians and Philistines brought the horses to Canaan and, because of that, have always ruled the coastal plains. Horses are made for running on flat, soft ground and pulling chariots on dry, solid roads. But once they reach the hill country, they are useless. The noble horse with thick mane and highly held head cannot function well in the difficult terrain around the mountains of Zion.

"No, the mule is a more fitting symbol for the house of David. It is not at all majestic. Its legs are muscular with tipped hooves that are small and as hard as iron. They negotiate steep slopes without faltering, and when they step on smooth boulders, they rarely stumble.

"Our hill country around Gilead, Galilee, Shechem, Hebron, and Jerusalem deserves a king who can reach the common people on a mule.

'The king is not saved by a mighty army;
A warrior is not delivered by great strength.
A horse is a false hope for victory;
Nor does it deliver anyone by its great strength.'
    [Psalm 33:16-17]

"I believe the strength the Lord gives to His people is seen more in the common mule than the majestic horse.

"Ah, here comes Nathan with the anointing oil. Tell the servants to begin blowing their trumpets as soon as the oil is placed upon Solomon's head."

David motioned to the two servants to leave his side. Bathsheba moved a little closer and took their place by holding on to David's arm. Suddenly, shouts of joy were heard throughout the streets of the City of David.

"Long live King Solomon! Long live the king!" they proclaimed.

David pushed back tears as the trumpets began to sound. Shofars and brass trumpets echoed off the mountains surrounding Jerusalem. "King Solomon, my son," David uttered rather quietly.

Bathsheba looked up at the deep brown eyes she first saw over their first dinner. She smiled affectionately and added, "Our son, my lord."

David returned her smile and said, "I can go to my fathers in peace now. I do hope Solomon keeps riding my mule!"

ARI'S RESPECT FOR THE COMMON

"I have known Ari for most of my adult life," Sergeant Eyal answered. "He's a kibbutznik raised in the Galilee area, but was best friends with an Arab boy growing up. Even Ari's father was good friends with Hassan's father. But Hassan was killed by Arab terrorists. Ari never knew if his death was an accident or because Hassan was Ari's friend.

"The death of his best friend affected him greatly. He's never really gotten over it. I guess I've filled part of the hole left in Ari's life since Hassan's death.

"Ari used to be a good friend of Lieutenant Colonel Baruk Levin, but since the colonel and Ari have gone different directions, they don't see each other as often.

"One thing about Ari. He is a good soldier, no matter what you may hear about him. There is no one I would rather have leading me into battle than Ari. His fairness and dedication are two of his strong attributes. And he is loyal to our Bedouin trackers. I have even seen him offer extreme kindness to captured Syrian soldiers and PLO prisoners.

"In the midst of battle, he is courageous and willing to do whatever it takes to get the job done. I would not want to be on the other end of his Galil rifle.

"I think his philosophy of life has been influenced by the country we will be driving through tomorrow," Sergeant Eyal continued.

"The desert simplifies everything. In the Negev and Sinai, the desert is the enemy, and all humans are brothers. It is man against the desert. The desert has a way of making human beings equals by forcing them to share their common resources for survival. The oasis is the place where even enemies sit down together and share the cool spring water. At other times and places, warring tribes may be killing each other, but here they are brothers.

"The law of the desert is to be hospitable to every stranger in the night and sojourner at the oasis. Anyone is welcome at one's camp-fire and desert tent. That is, except the PLO!

"Ari ben David is a man molded by the commonness of kibbutz life and the sense of comradeship that the desert creates. Tomorrow you will see firsthand. Now we had better get some sleep. We leave early in the morning."

Four sleepy-eyed men climbed into the jeep at exactly 0600. Sergeant Eyal took the wheel, as always, with Major Ammud next to him. In the back seats were their Bedouin tracker, Falah, and their new addition, Haim Yishai. Sergeant Eyal sped northward toward Hebron until they reached the east-west connector road leading to En Boqeq. The three passengers slept as best they could as Uri drove. As they passed Tell Arad, Ari woke up. Seeing where they were, he noticed that his new team member was also awake.

"Ever been over there?" Ari questioned.

"No, sir," Haim answered.

"My father and I used to walk around the tel and watch the archaeologists digging. Did you know that the bottom layer of the tel reveals a civilization older than the time of Abraham?" Ari added.

"No, sir, I didn't realize that," the young private replied.

"Say, let's get something straight right now," Ari said. "I appre-ciate the respect you are giving me as an officer, but out here we are all equals. You can leave that officer respect stuff back in special-forces training. If I don't earn your respect in battle and out here on the desert, there's no use in addressing me 'Sir.'"

"Yes, sir," Haim snapped.

Ari shook his head, and then both men laughed.

Ari looked at the northern hill country they were passing and continued his tourist-type spiel. "The road we are now taking was perhaps the way King David took when he was trying to secure Israel's southern boundaries."

"Nothing has changed in three thousand years, has it?" Haim commented.

"You're right. We are still trying to secure the same boundaries. David moved his army from the region of Beersheba toward the southeast and the Valley of Salt [1 Chronicles 18:11-13], which culminated in his subduing the Moabites, Edomites, and Amalekites. With his southern boundary protected, he then worked on building a nation free from enemy insurgencies.

"When we reach En Boqeq, we will follow the same Valley of Salt where David fought those battles. Only now we keep these southern boundaries secure from any Jordanian or PLO terrorist that tries to sneak across the border."

Sergeant Eyal broke into the discussion. "What has always amazed me about David is how he was able to have respect and acceptance, even among his enemies. He was the chief killer of the Philistines; he knocked off all their top warriors. But when he ran for his life, where did he flee? To the Philistines! How do you explain that?"

Ari answered quickly, "A good soldier must always have respect for his enemy. A Philistine king even gave him a whole city and allowed him to be a part of his army [1 Samuel 27:6, 28:2, 29:2]."

Uri commented, "Well, that's the conflicting passion I see in David's life, and I must say, I see it in my own life as well."

The jeep suddenly hit a rough spot in the road and bounced Falah over into Haim's lap. Sergeant Eyal quickly apologized for hitting the washed-out section of pavement.

Falah, who had been fast asleep, was awakened and quite surprised. Looking at Haim he said, "Bet you never thought you'd have a Bedouin Arab sitting on your lap."

Haim didn't quite know how to respond, and finally managed to mumble out, "I guess not."

Ari readjusted his seat belt, glanced at Uri, and said, "Nice driving!"

He then turned around to Falah. "Tell me, my friend, does the Koran have anything to say about David?"

Falah thought for a few moments and said, "I am not a very good Koran reader, but I can't remember anything about David in it. I do know we share many of your prophets and apostles such as Moses, Elias, Jonah, and Lot."

"Lot?" Sergeant Eyal questioned. "He was a prophet?"

"We may see his wife real soon when we get to the Salt Sea (Dead Sea)," Ari added laughingly.

"Anyway," he continued, "to answer your question about David and the Philistines, that's one of the many areas of his life I cannot put together. When David fled from King Saul, he took refuge with Achish, king of Gath. Of course, he just happened to have on his person Goliath's sword as a not-so-subtle reminder of who he was and what he had done [1 Samuel 21:9-10]. Once there, he must have realized that, being all alone, he was very unprotected. So, of all things, he feigned insanity [1 Samuel 21:13]."

"Now that's a novel tactic," Uri butted in. "We'll have to try that the next time we get captured by the PLO!"

Ari again shook his head at Uri's sick humor and continued, "Well, apparently Achish didn't quite know what to do about this strange behavior. Finally, Achish, believing he already had enough madmen in his court, humorously sent David on his way [1 Samuel 21:15].

"Later, after David rallied his fellow Judeans and mercenaries to his side, he once more fled to Achish with his family and ended up living in the king's city [1 Samuel 27:3]. David, as a typical Jewish boy, had enough 'hutzphah' to go to the king and ask for his own city. So King Achish gave him the southern city of Ziklag, where David and his men could do him a favor by protecting the king's southern Philistine flank [verse 6].

"Now get the picture. We have David, the anointed king-to-be of Israel, serving in the Philistine army as one of their city lords. An irony to say the least! It would be like Shimon Peres taking refuge in Iraq and Saddam Hussein making him mayor of Baghdad!"

Sergeant Eyal interrupted: "I'm sure some in the Knesset might vote for that."

"You're such a cynic, Uri," the major returned.

"That's right. I'm Israeli," Uri added.

"I'm about to finish here," said Ari. "Finally, all the Philistine lords gathered their armies to make one final unified assault on Israel's king Saul. Now imagine the picture in your mind's eye. The man God had revealed, through the prophet Samuel, as Israel's future king is now riding with the Philistine army on his way to kill Israel's king [1 Samuel 28:1].

"This is the same man who, on two other occasions, when he had the opportunity to kill Saul, said he could not touch the Lord's anointed king [1 Samuel 24:10, 26:9]. He even felt guilty for cutting off a piece of Saul's garment [1 Samuel 24:5]."

"He was lucky David didn't cut off his head," Haim injected.

"I cannot understand how this man could do both things," Ari continued. "He is certainly a man of contrary passions."

Falah interrupted, "So did he end up killing Israel's king?"

"No," Ari explained. "Before they got to the battle in the Jezreel valley, the Philistine commanders began to have reservations about having David and his men in the battle with them [1 Samuel 29:3].

"Achish, the king, even defended David's reputation and argued for his loyalty against his own commanders [1 Samuel 29:3]. But the commanders were suspicious, fearful that, in the heat of battle, David and his men might turn against them and attack them from behind. So David was reluctantly sent back by Achish to Philistine territory [1 Samuel 29:8-11]. As a result, David was spared from seeing his own king die on the battlefield.

"Though I don't understand David's heart in all this, I do see David as a man who could relate equally to kings and to the common outcasts of Israel. Achish's tribute to David is amazing. I was reading it the other night. 'As the LORD lives, you have been upright, and your going out and your coming in with me in the army are pleasing in my sight; for I have not found evil in you' [1 Samuel 29:6]. He also called David an 'angel of God' [verse 9].

"Imagine that—an angel! Believe me, as I read the text, he was no angel. Most of his time in Philistine territory was spent telling Achish lies! [1 Samuel 27:8-12]. But he must have been quite a man to pull off such intelligent deception.

"David equally attracted the commoners and outcasts," Ari continued. "Apparently his reputation was so widespread that when the news got around that David was in his stronghold at Adullam, all those who were suffering oppression from unjust foreign rulers [1 Samuel 22:2], those who had lost their financial fortune, and those bitter-hearted from life all came to David and 'kibbutzed' around him [1 Samuel 22:1-2]. There must have been something very appealing about this man that gave him favor with both kings and commoners," Ari concluded.

KING DAVID LISTENS TO THE COMMONER

Shimei had been seething with resentment since the death of his king, Saul. The tribe of Benjamin, located at the key north-south and east-west intersections of Israel, had seen much bloodshed. Having settled at an intersection of valleys leading toward Jerusalem, the tribe was perfectly located for warfare. Hence they had become skillful in things military. They were a tribe of ambidextrous warriors, a real military advantage (Judges 20:16). They were able to handle the sling and bow with either hand (1 Chronicles 8:40). Ehud was a left-handed Benjaminite judge (Judges 3:15).

It stands to reason, then, that when the house of Benjamin fell to the Philistines, it was a severe blow to the tribe. The house of Saul no longer ruled in Israel. In Saul's place, a lowly shepherd from the tribe of Judah now ruled.

Shimei had been devoted to his king and his tribe and, therefore, when he heard the news of Absalom's revolt against David, he rejoiced. Little did he realize David's retreat would parade through his own village of Bahurim. The procession of David's six hundred men left the city of Jerusalem in great humiliation. Rather than resort to violence in an attempt to regain the throne, David decided to merely go into exile.

David walked barefoot with his head covered as a sign of the humiliation he felt. The surrounding crowds gathered on both sides of the Jericho road and wept as David passed by. One by one, in like fashion, they covered their own heads.

When Shimei heard the procession coming, he climbed up to one of the ridges overlooking the road to Jericho. There he waited. Midway through the procession he saw the object of his vengeance. Shimei could no longer restrain what he felt. In the midst of weeping, with a dejected army slowly moving along the dusty road, his shouts of anger and resentment broke through the lament.

"Cursed be the house of David! Cursed be the house of David!" Shimei yelled. David ignored the jeers coming from the ridge above and kept walking. He had not walked barefoot since he was a boy, so walking was not an easy task on the stony ground.

The procession could not make good time this way, but David felt it was important to leave his capital city this way as a symbol of the utter humiliation he felt in having his own son usurp the throne. The sound of cursing did not go away.

"You are a man of bloodshed. A man of bloodshed is David," was heard again.

As David kept walking, he thought to himself, *He is right, I have been a man of bloodshed. Most of my life has been spent in shedding the blood of my enemies. I always felt it is what the Lord would have me to do, but maybe he is right.*

Again David heard, "Killer of the house of Saul! Killer of the house of Saul! You have gotten what you deserve." Shimei continued, walking along the ridge, keeping pace with the slow procession.

Again, David said nothing, but some of his guards were becoming disturbed by Shimei. As Shimei moved along the ridge opposite the side of the Mount of Olives, he saw loose stones on the ground. He picked up one and hurled it at David. It missed. He then picked up others and hurled them one at a time at the king.

David's personal guards, the Cherethites, Pelethites, and Gittites, gathered closer around David and placed their shields above their heads, creating a protective canopy for their king. As they exited the village, more rocks descended upon the men, bouncing off their shields.

Finally, David's nephew and the brother of army commander Joab, Abishai, looked up and saw Shimei cursing David as he threw the stones. Abishai wheeled his horse around and rode over to David. "Why should this dead dog curse my lord the king? Let me go over now, and cut off his head" (2 Samuel 16:9), he shouted to David.

David shook his head in dismay and said, "We are men of bloodshed. How long will we chop off the heads of our enemies? Besides, this Benjaminite has every right to feel the way he does. If my own son has rejected me, why not these Benjaminites?"

David stopped the procession and wove his way through his defenders to Abishai. Looking at his faithful soldier, David answered, "Abishai, you have been with me a long time, and have been very loyal as one of my *gibborim*. But this is not a time for bloodshed. You wanted to kill Saul while he slept [1 Samuel 26:6-9], and you and your brother committed a murderous act in killing Asahel without my permission [2 Samuel 2:18, 24; 3:30]. Now you want to kill this solitary, common Benjaminite. Perhaps God wants him to curse me this day. He is no warrior, and does us no real harm. Let him be."

≈⟩

ARI CONSIDERS KING DAVID'S HEART

As the four soldiers pulled up to the shore of the Dead Sea, they stopped for a moment to take in the sight. The "Salt Sea" is impressive no matter how many times one has seen it.

Its concentration of salts and other minerals are such that a person can float as if he or she had on a life jacket. The sensation is strange, going against all of one's experience in water. In fact, one has to work very hard to drown in the Dead Sea! Emerging from the azure-colored sea are characteristic pillars of concentrated salt. From a distance, these resemble modern, high-rise buildings or the skyline of a city. Up close they appear eerie and strange.

"We're almost to our checkpoint hut. There we can get something cool to drink," Ari said.

When they pulled into En Boqeq, they refreshed themselves, obtained their intelligence report on activities in the area, and then drove to one of the more popular tourist restaurants for dinner. Ari and Uri liked to dine where they could get ice with their drinks. Ice in Israel is a real luxury, and very few restaurants have refrigeration comparable to Western standards.

After dinner the four men sat in the jeep and watched the last few rays of sun reflect off the changing colors of the Dead Sea before it slipped behind the mountains that separated the Rift Valley from the Shephelah. Ari got out of the jeep and savored the scene.

"It's hard to believe that our forefathers, nearly four thousand years ago, came to this country and crossed into this land from Jordan," he commented, looking across the sea to the Jordanian territory on the other side. "David sent his family to the plains of Moab for protection when Saul was chasing him [1 Samuel 22:3]."

"I wonder if they would welcome Ari ben David today?" Uri asked.

"Well, at least not in uniform," Ari replied. Still looking across to Jordan (formerly Moab), Ari continued, "David always had ties with Moab because his lineage through Ruth was Moabite. When David fled from Absalom, he went north to the Transjordan area near Mahanaim. Another seemingly common man, Barzillai, the Gileadite, supplied provisions for David and his six hundred men [2 Samuel 17:31-39]."

"Now that was a significant outlay of shekels," said Sergeant Eyal. "But most unbelievable is the fact that David's army in exile consisted almost entirely of Philistines from Gath! [2 Samuel 15:18]."

"Wherever David went, he was able to make friends with the people of the land," Ari suggested.

"You have certainly not done as well with the Palestinians, have you?" Falah probed the major.

Private Yishai answered, "Maybe we don't have the same heart as David."

"We probably don't," Ari returned.

On the drive back to En Boqeq, Sergeant Eyal pulled over to the opposite side of the road to avoid hitting a boy riding a horse in the middle of the driving lane. As the jeep passed by, Ari noticed it was an Arab boy, no older than about ten, riding bareback. What he originally thought was a horse was not a horse at all, but a mule.

Ari waved at the boy and spoke, "Salem aleichem."

"Aleichem Salem," the boy returned with a smile on his face. As the jeep accelerated, Ari thought, *We, as modern Israelis, do not have David's heart. We are very far from it.*

Ari loved mules. The kibbutz where he grew up always had two or three that he and Hassan rode to the top of the cliffs of Arbel overlooking the Sea of Galilee. Maybe he wasn't that far from the heart of his namesake. Besides, the jeep is the modern mule of the IDF.

As Ari lay on his cot that night, he again thought about the mixed messages in David's life. In spite of his shortcomings, David is called "a man after God's own heart."

As Ari pondered these things, he found a sense of hope flooding his long despondent spirit. *If David's failures were so blatant, and he was still considered a man of God, maybe there is hope for me. Maybe the God that David knew had a vastly different standard for righteousness than that of the pious, religious Orthodox.* Ari wondered if this God was still there, and if so, was He still the same?

A slight cool breeze blew through Ari's tent door and cooled his weathered face. It felt good. It was good to again be sleeping at the edge of the wilderness. He slept well, comforted by his new thoughts and the gentle sound of the Salt Sea waves lapping against the rocks along the shoreline.

CHAPTER EIGHT

A Man of Many Trespasses: Passion in the Wrong Direction

"I HAVE SINNED GREATLY"

David asked his Ammonite benefactor Shobi (2 Samuel 17:27) for papyrus tablets upon which to write. David knew it was an unusual request, especially since his friend from the Jabbok River valley had provided so much for him and his men. David never quite understood the Ammonites' generosity during this time. These unlikely friends supplied beds; pottery in which to cook; basins for washing; the basic provisions of barley, flour, beans, and honey; and sheep for clothing and meals (2 Samuel 17:27-29). David thought, *I am well cared for, even in exile!*

It took several weeks for Shobi to obtain the tablets David desired. But one afternoon he came riding in with a smile on his face. Unwrapping a blanket from around his prized acquisition, Shobi unrolled a beautiful, freshly made papyrus tablet. David was like a little boy with a new toy. He thanked his friend and immediately gathered his things for a hike up the river valley to a place he had already prepared for himself. Looking down over the Jabbok River, which runs from the Transjordan side of Israel and empties into the Jordan River, David reclined upon the special rock he used for meditation and reflection.

His recent experience with his son Absalom had caught him by surprise. All the signs were there, but he had missed them. It was one of those moments when an entire segment of one's life is seen as a vivid replay.

David was suddenly horrified. As he reflected on how Absalom had so rejected him, the pain and anguish of his failure as a father rushed through his soul. The pain was so overwhelming that David began to sob.

The flashback was all too clear now. Nathan had told him a sword would fall on his family because of his sin with Bathsheba (2 Samuel 12:10). But he never translated this "sword" in terms of the humiliation his son would bring him. The humiliation and grief were worse than death.

At times David longed to be reunited with his forefathers. Even as he cried, he looked down upon the dark valley below and thought, *This may be the valley of the shadow of death . . . but I will fear no evil, because Thou are still with me* (Psalm 23:4). "But confidence in God does not take away the pain felt toward one's own children," David murmured to himself.

David had been shocked by the incest that took place in his house. *How could Amnon, my own son, rape Tamar, his own half sister, in my own household*, David thought (2 Samuel 13:1-14). He could still feel the anger he carried toward Amnon, although it had been displaced somewhat by his anger toward Absalom for having plotted revenge toward his brother and having Amnon killed. Also, David had seen the scars left on Tamar, who was never the same after that.

David admitted that he didn't quite know how to properly deal with those sinful acts. Had the violators been anyone else, there would have been swift justice. David was good at handling the sword, but not with regard to his own children. He remembered weeping over the situation and being so immobilized by it that he could do nothing but retreat from most of his kingly responsibilities. "But I had to banish Absalom for the ruthless action he took against his brother," David tried to convince himself (2 Samuel 13:37-39, 14:13).

But at this moment, his self-talk was not working. He agonized over Absalom's absence during the time he was exiled to the king of Geshur and unable to return home. At the time, David felt it was justifiable, but upon reflection, he saw it differently. "Perhaps I was wrong. Did I sin against my own son by sending him away?" David questioned.

David reminded himself that it was Joab, not himself, who wanted to bring Absalom back to Jerusalem. At the time, David saw it as empty remorse. Besides, how might it look to the people of Israel to have his son return?

But now David was confused. Absalom had desired to see his father, but in his stubbornness, David would not let Joab arrange for his return. So Joab even cut off contact with Absalom (2 Samuel 14:23-24,28). "Joab was too good a commander," David mused. "He always was committed to carrying out my desires, even when they appeared to be wrong."

Another flash of insight hit David. "Oh, Lord, my stubbornness cost Joab a significant amount of money." Joab had lost an entire year's harvest because David would not see his son. Absalom must have finally realized that the only way to get David's and Joab's attention was by burning Joab's crops (2 Samuel 14:30).

Joab never mentioned the loss, but David heard about it soon after. David didn't remember ever compensating his commander for his losses! *This is too great for me to bear*, David thought. *I must do something about my feelings.*

He took out a pen and opened the papyrus scroll. Laying it on the plank of wood he had designed, he scripted, "A Psalm of David. When he fled from Absalom, his son."

David paused and looked up the river valley to where his men were camped. He caught the irony of the moment. *Mahanaim* means "encampment." This spot, some forty kilometers northeast of Jerusalem, was named by the patriarch Jacob after he had wrestled with an angel (Genesis 32:2).

He must have camped here and then named it Mahanaim, David thought. He looked at the camp and was again reminded of God's faithfulness toward him. He was alive and provided with a group of men who stood ready to give their lives for him.

But an arrow of grief again struck David. He was forced to put down his pen. He recalled how he had finally allowed Absalom to return, and how he was so glad to see him. But in his heart remained the lingering feelings of anger at what had happened in his home. Feelings that prevented David from embracing and accepting his returned son. David wondered if Absalom sensed that.

He must have, David thought. *Perhaps that's why he so deliberately stationed himself at the gates of the city and turned the people away from me*, he reasoned. *I should have been more aware of what was happening there, too. I should have gone down to the city gates myself to check out what was happening. Why didn't I?* David asked himself. *Was I too busy or too afraid to face the reality of what my own son was doing behind my back?* David couldn't answer those questions.

David recalled his emotionally charged retreat from Jerusalem. It was not easy to leave his own city. But how could he go to war against his own son? He would rather not be king than be in a position where he was forced to kill his own son. David was still questioning his decision to leave.

He was sure of one thing: he should not have left his ten concubines behind (2 Samuel 15:16). Who would have believed Absalom would do what he did with those women? David remembered receiving the report while still on his way to Jericho. A runner caught up to the procession and told David the news. Absalom had pitched a tent on the exact spot where David had first seen Bathsheba. He then lined up all the women David left behind and had intercourse with them. He did it in broad daylight and in public view of the entire city, just to humiliate his own father (2 Samuel 16:22). It was symbolic of what David had brought upon his own head. David was outraged by the act, but was helpless to do anything about it. Absalom, his son, had humiliated him in so many ways. "I am to blame," David confessed.

He picked up his pen and again began to write.

O LORD, how my adversaries have increased!
Many are rising up against me.
Many are saying of my soul,
"There is no deliverance for him in God." [Psalm 3:1-2]

A musical pause might be appropriate here, David thought. So he wrote "Selah."

As David looked down into the valley he saw his men sharpening their swords, building fires they could use to help in hammering out the many dents in their war-torn shields. David asked himself, *Is it really these men, by themselves, who protect me? No, they are but the agents God uses to be either my downfall or my success.*

David inscribed,

But Thou, O Lord, art a shield about me,
My glory, and the One who lifts my head.
I was crying to the Lord with my voice,
And He answered me from His holy mountain. Selah.
> [Psalm 3:3-4]

David humorously reminded himself of how many times he had run for his life. He thought, *It seems I've spent more time in the wilderness than in any permanent house.* "But the Lord has always lived in a tent since He first brought us out of the land of Egypt," David laughed. "If it's good enough for Him, it's good enough for me."

He also recalled the many times he had gone to bed not knowing how he would find provisions the following day for his men. But the Lord always allowed him to sleep, even when on rocky terrain. He had also seen how God worked in giving him the military advantage in his many battles. "God has indeed sustained me!" David added. His pen touched the tablet again and wrote,

I lay down and slept;
I awoke, for the Lord sustains me.
I will not be afraid of ten thousands of people
Who have set themselves against me round about.
Arise, O Lord; save me, O my God,
For Thou hast smitten all my enemies on the cheek;
Thou hast shattered the teeth of the wicked.
Salvation belongs to the Lord;
Thy blessing be upon Thy people! Selah. [Psalm 3:5-8]

David looked over the text he had written and said, "I wish Asaph were here. I would have him put this to music. But I *do* have my *kinnor* with me. Perhaps I can still work up a tune."

RECONNAISSANCE: PROTECTING ONE'S BORDERS
The four men climbed back into the jeep and started their slow, deliberate drive along the fence that separates Jordan from Israel. Although Falah had slept earlier, he was now awake and the most important person in the group.

As Sergeant Eyal drove the eight-hour shift from checkpoint to checkpoint, Falah walked ahead of the command car, sweeping his eagle eyes left and right, looking for any detail that did not fit the terrain.

After every sweep by the trackers, a truck following behind the jeeps would rake the sand, making it easier to detect new movement across this no man's land. Ari was also alert, because it was in the early morning hours, while the sun is rising in the east, that they were blinded by the sun's direct rays. Even against reflective goggles, the direct rays still inhibited normal vision.

This was the peak time for terrorists trying to sneak across the fence undetected. Falah and a fellow tracker from another jeep walked about ten meters in front of the two-car procession. Everyone was geared for action. All weapons were loaded and locked. Ari consistently swept the horizon with his field glasses while Private Yishai kept the mounted FN MAG light machine gun pointed toward the fence.

The only sounds heard were the hum of engines, an occasional squawking of radio chatter, and the beating of one's own heart. Their trek along the fence took them nearly five days. When they saw the modern high-rise buildings of Elat on the horizon, they all breathed a sigh of relief.

On this occasion, their 100-kilometer journey through the Arabah was uneventful. The only event of note came when Falah thought he might have found a carefully concealed terrorist track. They followed the tracks for several kilometers, but they turned out to be those of a wild donkey.

As they drove into Elat, they saw the port of Al Aqaba on the Jordan side of the Gulf of Aqaba, with Elat nestled on the edge of the beautiful Red Sea. Coming out of the "Valley of Salt," they had steadily risen in altitude from a thousand meters below sea level to two hundred meters above at their highest point. By the time one has driven through this barren valley, the sight of the deep blue waters of the "Red" Sea is quite refreshing. Needless to say, the entire caravan was more than ready for a shower, a real meal, and a bed with sheets.

A few kilometers north of Elat, the vehicles pulled into their IDF post. After obtaining their billets for the weekend, the soldiers got unpacked, showered, and put on some fresh clothes. Falah and the tracker from the other vehicle were going into Elat for dinner, while Sergeant Eyal and Haim just wanted to hit the mess hall and go to bed. Ari decided to hitch a ride with his Bedouin friends and check out the nightlife of Elat.

On their way to the city, the Red Sea took on the most unbelievable color of deep blue Ari could remember. Small sailboats darted here and there in the warm, clear waters. Ari had once gone snorkeling in the bay with his daughter and young son. They remembered the experience as one of their most significant family vacations. The children were fascinated with the sizes and shapes of the multicolored fish. The Red Sea teems with exotic aquatic life, and is one the best vacation spots in Israel.

This unusual trio of two Bedouins and one Israeli officer found an outdoor cafe overlooking the water. Most of the food was Moroccan, but the cafe also carried the standard Israeli fare. Ari tried something he couldn't even pronounce. It was so "hot" that he had to order pita and *hummus* to kill the "burning" feeling. He discovered he wasn't a fan of Moroccan food. The two trackers decided on traditional lamb and shiashlik.

After dining, Falah and his friend wanted to find a place for after-dinner drinks and dancing. Ari parted company with them, and they agreed on a time to meet back at the jeep.

Ari mingled with the tourists, shoppers, and sunbathers on their way back to their hotel rooms. While he was waiting for a light to change at a crosswalk, a poster caught Ari's attention. It read, "Ben Gurion Symphony in Concert." Ari looked more closely and realized the performance was the following evening. Ari smiled and thought, *What a coincidence. She might actually be in town.*

⌐

DAVID'S BATTLE WITH ABSALOM

As David descended from the heights overlooking the Jabbok River valley, he felt better for having put his feelings into prose. Music and prose had always been David's outlet for expressing both the joys and woes of his life.

When he arrived back at the Mahanaim gates, he went into the inner recess between the gates of the double walls. He sat down with some of his men who were repairing and sharpening their implements of war, and encouraged them in the Lord. The preparations for battle were meticulous and many. David still saw it as his responsibility to lead and encourage these men who had chosen to follow him into exile.

As David conversed with the men, two runners entered through the gates, almost collapsing into David's arms. "The army of Absalom is coming. We have seen them entering the forests of Ephraim only this afternoon."

David congratulated the men for their excellence. He knew it was time to make battle plans. He immediately summoned commanders Joab, Abishai, and Ittai and invited them to his personal quarters. He greeted and embraced the three and then had them recline. "It's time, my companions. Absalom is on his way. He has been seen by Ahimaaz and our Cushite spy. They have numbered his army at well over twenty thousand men, so we will be significantly outnumbered. But this is not the first time for us, is it?" David said with a little smile on his face.

Joab could tell David was not joking. He knew David well enough to know when he was distressed, even when no one else could see it. Joab asked, "My lord, this is your son. Are you sure you want to fight him?"

David paused for a moment, then answered, "We have no choice. We are trapped in this valley. We cannot allow Absalom's army to enter the valley and slaughter us along with the people of Mahanaim, who have given us food, lodging, and favor. The valley is not large enough to move around in and fight. There is no way of escape once Absalom has entered the valley. We must take the initiative.

"Once we are out of the valley, I want the army to divide into three flanks, each under one of your commands. Abishai will move around to Absalom's rear, while Ittai will maneuver his men to the high ground above the forests. Joab, once they have positioned their men on these two flanks, you will start the attack by challenging Absalom's main force on the open field. As soon as the attack begins, Ittai will lead a charge down from the hills. Absalom will be forced to fight on two fronts.

"Abishai will cut off any attempt they may make to retreat and return to Jerusalem. If God gives us good favor, we should have them trapped in the forest where they can no longer fight and move with freedom."

David concluded by saying, "I will ride with Joab and lead the attack with him."

The three commanders and David went out to the people to explain the battle plan. Almost in unison, the people pleaded with David to stay at Mahanaim. One in the crowd yelled, "You are worth ten thousand of us. Why don't you keep back a reserve force to be ready to come to our aid if needed?"

Because the plan sounded good to both the people and his commanders, David answered, "Whatever seems best to you I will do" (2 Samuel 18:4).

The next morning, as the army filed out the city gates, David shouted to his commanders, "Deal gently for my sake with the young man Absalom" (2 Samuel 18:5). All the people heard the charge and marched down the narrow valley toward the forests of Ephraim.

The city was empty except for the inhabitants and the small reserve force that remained with David. David positioned himself at the city gates, very near the stairs that led to the watchtower. Periodically, David would climb up to see if the watchman had seen anything. Disappointed, he would descend the stairs and try to sleep on the ground near the gates. Hours turned into a whole day, still without any news.

The following day, the sounds of shofars could be heard echoing through the valley, followed by the shouts of men and the clashing of iron. David knew the battle had begun. Once again he climbed the watchtower, but no runners could be seen. He waited several hours in the watchtower, but finally gave up. David began to think the worst had happened. Perhaps his entire army had been defeated.

"A runner is coming," the watchman announced. David waited impatiently at the gate. "Another runner is behind him," the watchman added.

David said to himself, *It must be good news since both my runners are coming.* As Ahimaaz entered the gate completely out of breath, he fell before David and said, "All is well."

"But what about Absalom?" David asked.

"I did not see," Ahimaaz answered. David waited for the Cushite to enter the gate.

He staggered through the gate and likewise fell at his feet. "Good news, my king, the Lord has vindicated you this day."

"But what about my son, Absalom?" David questioned. "Is it well with him?"

The Cushite finally answered by saying, "May all of David's enemies be as that young man."

David immediately knew what the message implied. Absalom had been killed (2 Samuel 18:28-32).

David could not get himself back to his own quarters. But he had to be alone. He ran up the stairs leading to the top of the walls and, finding an empty storage chamber, fell to the floor and wept (2 Samuel 18:33). "Absalom, Absalom, Absalom, my son, my son. Would that I had been taken in battle rather than you."

Joab and the army returned, celebrating their well-executed victory that took some twenty thousand men of Absalom's army. But as the army marched through the gates, they realized the city was in mourning. David had isolated himself in his private quarters and would not come out. The sound of his weeping for Absalom was relentless. It went on for days, to the point that the entire city was afraid to have any celebration at all.

Joab had finally had enough. He stormed into David's quarters and asked bluntly, "Why is it you hate those who love you and love those who hated you? You are showing that your commanders and servants in the army mean nothing to you; but if Absalom were still alive and we were all dead, it appears you would be pleased" (see 2 Samuel 19:5-6).

Joab waited for a reply, not knowing how David might respond. He was being frank with his king. He had never before spoken to David so directly.

David looked up at his commander and asked, "Then what do you recommend I do?"

Joab took a deep breath and, as bluntly as before, said, "Get up out of that bed and go out to your people and speak to them. Tell them how gallantly they fought and how appreciative you are of them for staying with you in exile. And, my lord, if you don't, I don't think they will be here tomorrow, for why should they continue with you if you are not pleased with them?" (see 2 Samuel 19:7).

As abruptly as Joab had entered the room, he left. David knew Joab was correct in his assessment. In those moments alone, David realized his great failure with Absalom. He could not relive the years or the events or bring Absalom back from the dead. Therefore, he must be the king. He must be a king to his people in spite of his failures as a father. He must not become a prisoner of his passions and withdraw into a cave of isolation so that his own people wanted nothing more to do with him.

David washed himself, put on his royal clothes, and went out to the gates of the city. One by one his people began to gather around him, offering their sympathy for Absalom, and he offered his praise for their faithfulness and courage (2 Samuel 19:8).

MICHELE'S STORY

As Ari walked around the shops, he tried to remember her name. "Let's see, was it Michal, Michele, or Machiel?" he muttered to himself. Ari had heard her name only once, and then she was gone. He wondered if she was already in town and where she might be staying.

He tried to recall what she looked like. She was probably about five-six, maybe about 130 pounds with shoulder-length, auburn hair and high cheekbones. He also remembered her perfume. Because most Israeli women don't wear perfume, the scent of perfume is easily remembered.

At any rate, Ari thought it interesting timing should this American violinist show at the concert. As the three soldiers met back at the jeep, Ari already knew where he was going the next evening.

Ari woke up excited. Excited about having some time to spend on the beach, to swim, relax, and, of course, take in a concert that night. By the time Ari and his companions got to the beach area, the tourists, students, and other soldiers on R and R had already staked out their areas. Ari wanted to try jet skiing. He walked down to the stand to inquire about rates. He was shocked. Almost fifty American dollars!

Ari walked away thinking, *Yeah, only an American could afford such things. I think I'll just enjoy the sun. At least it's free.* He rejoined his companions. He chatted with Falah about how the Bedouin life was disappearing. By day's end, everyone had taken a little too much sun and was ready to return to the base.

Ari had to fight for the jeep that night, almost to the point of pulling rank. No one wanted to stay at the base, but Ari wanted to go into Elat alone for reasons known only to himself. Sergeant Eyal finally called him on his intentions. "You have a date, don't you?"

"Uri, you know me too well. How can I keep any secrets?" Ari answered. "It's not a date. I'm not even sure of the girl's name, and I'm not even sure she's in town. I'm going to a concert, and I *know* how much my friends enjoy classical music." That closed the discussion. The other three agreed they would either take a bus or just do the Israeli army thing and hitchhike.

Ari arrived early at the auditorium to try to spot the woman he had met so briefly at the Beersheba music shop. As the orchestra wandered onto the stage to prepare for the concert, Ari looked intently for the American. Finally, three violinists came in and took their seats, followed by a viola player and a cellist. Then, there she was!

He immediately recognized her smiling face and outgoing personality. Her shoulder-length auburn hair was pulled back around her head and woven into a twist. She looked extremely attractive in the long, black dress with high collar. She had a simple strand of pearls around her neck. As Ari watched her innocent movements, he tried to estimate from her distant appearance how old she might be. *Maybe midthirties or early forties*, he thought.

No matter. She looked well cared for and stood out from the other women on stage. Israeli women always put down American women for wearing too much makeup, but Ari had grown to like it. His ex-wife, he felt, could have made herself look far more attractive had she been a little more fashion conscious.

But in Israel, feminine beauty too often gets hidden beneath olive drab uniforms. Most Israeli men, when honest, would admit they like the looks of American women. But they would never admit it to their fellow Israeli sisters who think American women are pampered weaklings.

The performance was about to begin, so Ari perused his copy of the program. On the back side were the names of the orchestra members. He ran his finger down the list until he found the violin section. "That's it," Ari said to himself excitedly, "Michele Anderson, Second Violin." Ari felt better now that he could call her by name. It might impress her that he had "remembered" her name. He leaned back in his chair to enjoy the concert and watch her every move.

When the orchestra took its intermission, Ari tried to find his way around to the stage door. He saw many orchestra members darting here and there, getting drinks, smoking cigarettes, and retuning their instruments. But he did not see the person for whom he was searching. Ari was about to return to his seat when he heard a feminine voice inquiring in English, "Major?"

Ari turned around and there she was, smiling at him with an intriguing look on her face. "Is that you . . . from the music shop? Ari, I believe, is that right?"

"Yes," Ari stuttered out. "You have a good memory."

"And how about yours?" she asked with a subtle gleam in her eye.

"Michele Anderson," Ari proudly answered.

"Wow, I'm impressed, Major. And you followed me all the way down here," she added.

Ari didn't quite know how to play this scene with the attractive American. Should he tell her the truth, or play as if he happened to be here tonight because of his love of music? Quickly considering the hour and his age, he decided to be honest.

"Well, I didn't follow you down here, but once I saw a poster on the street advertising the Ben Gurion Symphony, I remembered that Yonah had told me you played in it. I guess I came hoping I might find you here."

"Well, you did," Miss Anderson answered.

"Did what?" Ari returned.

"Find me here, Major."

Ari suddenly felt tongue-tied, like an adolescent kid on a first date. He didn't know where to go next in the conversation.

Fortunately, the American broke the silence, saying, "I must go, we are about ready to begin the second half. Will I see you afterward?" she asked.

"Yes, of course," Ari responded. "Maybe we could grab a bite somewhere?"

"That would be fine, Major." She disappeared behind the stage door, and Ari turned to go back to his seat.

Well, that was easy enough, he thought.

Ari was halfway to his seat before he realized that Michele had both carried the conversation and initiated the activity for after the concert. He was impressed with how easily she carried herself and made conversation with him.

As he found his place and sat down, he reasoned, *She must be attracted to me in some way. Why else would she want to go out with me?* But then another voice played in Ari's head. It was the voice of too many experiences in which he had completely misread a woman's feelings and interpreted far too much from a simple smile. After several of these experiences, he had just given up dating.

It was bad enough being single again, but having to reenter the dating game was more than Ari had time for. But here he was having those same feelings again.

Ari did enjoy the concert, but he enjoyed watching Michele even more. She played with an intense passion that radiated from her serious expressions. Between numbers she would make eye contact with Ari and smile. Each time she did, he felt a little more confident about this surprise meeting in the desert.

When the concert ended, Ari waited at the stage door until she came out. He took her violin, and they walked back to her hotel a few blocks away. A lounge next to the hotel was the only place still open, so they went in and sat down. Ari had eaten earlier, so he ordered a plate of olives and cheese with a glass of wine. Michele ordered a Greek salad and a cola.

While waiting for their order, they talked about the concert, her bus trip down to the Red Sea with the symphony, and what a nice Gentile girl was doing in Israel.

To Ari's surprise, he found she wasn't a "goy" at all but, in fact, very Jewish.

She explained, "Anderson is the married name I inherited from my ex-husband, but my maiden name was Katz. During our graduate school days, I was a real feminist and went by Michele Katz-Anderson."

"Was your husband Jewish?" Ari asked.

"Oh, heavens no. He was as Aryan as one could be. My mother loved him because he was a Harvard law school grad. My father never really accepted him, because he wasn't Jewish."

"Is your father religious?" Ari questioned.

"No, he's just culturally Jewish; your typical Philadelphia Main Line Jewish doctor. But he did believe that one should marry into the same culture. You know all that kosher stuff about not mixing species, dishes, or various materials. Mom was into the garden club, the country club, and all that. So I was your typical Jewish girl."

"Sounds like a real JAP (Jewish American Princess)," Ari laughed.

"Oh yes, Daddy spoiled me, and Mother played the yenta and made sure there was always something I needed to feel guilty about."

Ari added, "I've never understood that about American Jews. This guilt thing. Why?"

"I don't know," Michele said. "Maybe it's the Holocaust or something. We're supposed to feel guilty for being left alive, and then we are to feel guilty for having too much money or not having enough money. It's all very complicated, and I'm a sociologist!"

"Who has the salad?" the waiter asked.

"Right here," Michele answered.

"That leaves the veggie plate for you, sir."

"Yes, that's right." Ari held up his glass of wine and uttered, "Lehayim."

Michele touched his glass with her soda and returned, "Lehayim."

Ari got a little serious and said, "Do you mind if I ask about your divorce? What happened?"

"No, I don't mind," Michele replied. "It's ancient history now." She swallowed a bite of salad and continued, "We had the perfect Ivy League romance. Daddy had sent me to Middlesex Prep School outside Boston so that I might meet the right kind of people and be in a better position to get into an Ivy League school.

"My grades weren't that good out of prep school, so we had to settle for Boston College. There I majored in political science. Being the status-conscious Jewish girl I was, I studied most of the time in the Harvard Law Library. I was a paradoxical political activist party girl. But during my last year at Boston, I met the man of my dreams.

"He was from a good family, I was led to believe (which meant they had money), active in crew, and I liked his personality and physique. He swept me off my feet, and we were married after six months of high, passionate romance. My reward for this romantic intensity was that I got to put him through law school!

"Once married, I found out that there was little money, and he had not even qualified for the large scholarship money at Harvard. So I worked odd jobs at minimum wage for four years. Not bad for a political science major from Boston College. He finally graduated and got into a good law firm. Actually, it was too good. He got so many important cases, I rarely saw him. When he did come home, he was too exhausted to do anything—talk, shop, make love, or get away somewhere alone with me.

"Because he was making good money, I no longer had to work.

So I decided to return to school and get back on my career track. I applied and was accepted at Harvard to work toward my Ph.D. in sociology. It took me four long, hard years to complete the degree program. I was so proud of my accomplishment. On graduation day, when I walked across that stage, I actually thought my life was finally coming together.

"Not! My husband took me out to dinner that night and, over a candlelight dinner, laid out divorce papers in front of me. All he said was, 'Now that you got what you wanted, I'm going to get what I've wanted!' He'd had a girlfriend on the side for several years, and I never knew it.

"I was devastated. It took me by such complete surprise, I couldn't even work or look for work. I went back to Philadelphia and lived with my parents for almost two years, before I was healthy enough to look for a job. Finally, through connections of my father's, I was offered a faculty position at the University of Pennsylvania, where I've been the last six years.

"So we were married for seven years, legally separated for another year, with the divorce becoming final the following year. My husband remarried two days after the divorce was final. So here I am, a single thirty-seven-year-old professor in the middle of the desert, still trying to fill some of the holes in my soul. So enough about me.

"Now, tell me about Ari Ammud," Michele asked.

Before Ari could answer, the waiter came over and told them the lounge would be closing shortly.

"Saved by the waiter," Michele kidded him. "Did you have that planned?"

"Well, I'm sorry. We'll have to save that story for another day," Ari returned.

"I hope there will be another day, Major Ammud," she said with a smile that melted his damaged heart.

"There will be," Ari assured her.

⌒

SACRIFICE AND FORGIVENESS

David looked down upon his pitiful city. Everywhere he looked, there were bodies. It looked like a war-ravaged town, yet no sword had come upon these people. They were diseased, struck with an incurable plague that spread quickly from Dan in the north country to Beersheba in the south. Family members and friends were too sick to even bury their dead.

David began to wonder about the Lord's fairness in this. As he looked upon the site and smelled the stench of death, he questioned, "Lord, it is I who have sinned by wanting to know the exact strength of my army. Why do you punish these who had nothing to do with my wrong?" David received no answer.

Leaving the roof of his house, he came down the stairs, walked out of the house, and ascended farther up the slope of the mountain. He prayed and argued with God as he walked. A few meters from the top he saw what he thought was old Araunah, also called Ornan, the sole Jebusite left on the mountain. He ran a threshing business on the stony, flattened apex of the mountain.

As David neared the top, he realized the man he saw was not Araunah. *Why would anyone else be in such an obscure place?* he wondered. As he approached the summit, the man turned around with a raised sword pointed directly at David. David fell on his face before this well-armed, dazzling warrior.

David pleaded, "Is it not I who commanded the count of the people in my army? Indeed, it is I alone who have done this wicked thing. Please, let Your hand be against me and my house alone, but not against these, Your people" (see 1 Chronicles 21:17). The warrior lowered his sword and motioned for David to leave his presence.

David arose and descended the hill, stopping only once to look back at the sight. The warrior was gone. By the time David entered the door of his house, Gad, David's seer and oracle, was waiting for him. Without court pleasantries, Gad revealed to David that some seventy thousand had already died throughout Israel. God's judgment was about to fall on the entire city of Jerusalem—complete destruction. But God had also told him to tell David to build an altar of sacrifice on the threshing floor of Araunah.

David immediately ran back to the hilltop and, seeing Araunah emerge from his little lean-to, offered to buy his land to build an altar. Araunah, without a thought, said, "O king, all I have is yours. Take even my oxen to sacrifice, and their yokes for wood to start a fire."

David answered, "I appreciate your generosity, but I must pay you for them, for I cannot offer a sacrifice that costs me nothing. My sin has cost Israel seventy thousand of God's people. Therefore, I will pay you fifty shekels of silver, a vast sum of the king's money" (see 2 Samuel 24:18-25).

David brought stones and piled them up into a rustic altar. The animals were sacrificed, and the Lord withdrew the plague upon the nation. As the animals were consumed by the sacrificial fire, David thought about what had happened. He thought about how he had tried to hide his transgression with Bathsheba. He was reminded of the utter deceit with which he had dealt with Uriah, and of the denial and lack of fatherly presence he had in Absalom's life.

And, of course, he reflected on his sinful desire for knowing the strength of his own army. As he watched the flames rise toward the heavens, he thought, *How blessed is he whose transgression is forgiven* (Psalm 32:1).

When David returned from the place of sacrifice and reentered his palace, he took pen in hand and began to write.

> How blessed is the man to whom the Lord does not impute
> iniquity,
> And in whose spirit there is no deceit!
> When I kept silent about my sin, my body wasted away
> Through my groaning all day long.
> For day and night Thy hand was heavy upon me;
> My vitality was drained away as with the fever heat of
> summer. Selah.
> I acknowledged my sin to Thee,
> And my iniquity I did not hide;
> I said, "I will confess my transgressions to the LORD";
> And Thou didst forgive the guilt of my sin. Selah.
> Therefore, let everyone who is godly pray to Thee in a time
> when Thou mayest be found. [Psalm 32:2-6]

David could go no further. He put down the pen and began to sob uncontrollably. The outburst evidenced the confusing mixture of regret for his massive failures as man and king and the overwhelming gratitude that God could forgive such things.

MICHELE LEARNS OF KING DAVID'S FAILURES

Ari finished his desert patrol and then traveled to Jerusalem for briefings on the Intifada and other West Bank–Gaza Strip issues. It seemed that Israel's next war was the political war about what to do with the West Bank and Gaza Strip.

By the time Ari returned to Beersheba, a conspiracy had already taken place in Yonah's music shop. Amongst Ari's pile of mail was an invitation to dinner at Yonah's apartment, upstairs from the shop. Yonah had also invited another special guest from America, Michele Anderson.

It was good to see her radiant, smiling face again. Yonah loved to cook for people, but since the death of his wife, he didn't enjoy cooking for only one. So this was a real treat for him to have special guests. Besides, Ari gained the distinct impression Yonah derived a certain pleasure out of playing "matchmaker."

Most of the conversation over dinner centered on Yonah's fascinating life: how he had survived the labor camps in Germany and come to Israel with no other skills than that of music. The entire history of modern Israel was wrapped up in this little man who ran an instrument repair shop.

After dinner they moved into the front room of his apartment, where Yonah served coffee and tea. Ari sat next to Michele on the sofa while Yonah reclined on an antique rocker. "Yonah has been teaching me about King David," Ari explained, looking at Michele's face.

"Oh yes, King David," Yonah said. "A great man!"

"Why is that?" Michele questioned. "It seems to me David was no saint or Hasid."

"What makes you think a righteous man needs to be a Hasid?" Continuing, Yonah added, "David sinned in more ways than most of them could ever conceive. When you look at his life, he did it all. He and Jonathan lied to find out Saul's intentions toward David [1 Samuel 20:1-42]. He lied to Abimelech the priest, saying Saul had commissioned him with a special mission. In fact, he was already on the run from Saul at the time [21:2]. Then he lied about needing the holy bread of presence for his men, when in reality, David himself was hungry [verse 5].

"And then, of course, there's his little insanity trick he pulled on King Achish. Achish even believed it [1 Samuel 21:13-15]. David even wrote a psalm about it, apparently seeing the pretense before Achish as God's provision for his deliverance [Psalm 34:4,19,22].

"Later, when he returned to Achish for protection, he again lied to the king by telling him he was making war in Judah, when he was really killing the Geshurites and Amalekites [1 Samuel 27:6-12]. When David finally rode with the Philistine kings to destroy King Saul, apparently David was a little disappointed when told he would have to return to Ziklag [29:8]."

Yonah stopped momentarily then asked Michele, "I hope you don't mind our history lesson here."

"Oh, no, I haven't learned so much since Sabbath school. I've never heard about this side of David's life. I find it very interesting. Please continue," Michele answered.

"Well, then, we all know about David's wives and concubines [2 Samuel 5:13]. The longer he was king, the more wives, children, and concubines he accumulated."

Ari interrupted, "I guess the three of us are going the other direction. We are all spouseless!"

Michele laughed and Yonah nodded. "Of course, it was very clear in the Torah that kings were not to have multiple horses or wives [Deuteronomy 17:16-17]."

"Is there a relationship between the two?" asked Ari.

"Sure," Michele broke in, "they were both the property of men!"

"Ouch," Ari responded, appearing half shocked and half in agreement. "I can tell you *are* Ivy to the core."

Yonah continued, "I also think David had difficulty controlling his passions. He was very angered when God seemed to capriciously kill Uzzah for trying to keep the ark of the covenant on the oxcart [2 Samuel 6:8]. Of course, there was uncontrollable grief for the two sons who died [2 Samuel 12:16-20, 19:1-7].

"It didn't bother him to express whatever feelings he had, whether the joy he felt in being distinguished before the ladies of Israel [2 Samuel 6:22], or the laments he vented against his enemies [Psalm 43:1-2]. And, as a warrior, he was a man of blood, killing at one time some eighteen thousand Syrians."

Ari interjected, "We Israelis have never done that well against them."

Yonah laughed, saying, "Maybe we need more Davids."

"Or fewer politicians," Ari added.

"Well, it was through bloodshed that David made a name for himself [2 Samuel 8:13]. It was also what eventually cost him God's favor in building the first temple [1 Chronicles 22:8].

"David wasn't much better as father and husband."

"Now I'm beginning to identify," Ari laughed.

Michele smiled at him with a look of pained understanding, and nodded with a pleased expression at his honesty.

Yonah continued, "I think the chronicler of David's life suggested that David's great sin with Bathsheba lay in the cover-up of their affair, and not the adultery. Desiring and taking another man's wife was, of course, a moral evil for all [Exodus 20:14,17], but later history records that David 'did what was right in the sight of the LORD, . . . except in the case of Uriah the Hittite' [1 Kings 15:5]."

Michele got somewhat feisty at this point and said, "That's sexist! David's greater sin was in killing her husband rather than in taking advantage of her sexually when he was the king? Didn't he have all those concubines for that?"

Yonah looked surprised, but graciously answered, "There were many cultural differences between those times and ours."

Michele answered, "I'm sorry. You're right. It's probably wrong to compare David's culture to mainline Philadelphia."

"Well, he still had the same kind of family problems that we see today. David's son Amnon raped his own sister [2 Samuel 13:1-14], and then Absalom killed Amnon out of revenge [verses 24-29]. David was so angry at Absalom that he exiled his own son for two years [14:23-33].

"Absalom was your classic neglected son who finally turned against his father and drove him into exile. He had intercourse with David's concubines in full view of the city just to humiliate his father.

"Lastly, David committed what many consider his most serious sin, because of the extreme consequences God brought upon him and the entire nation because of it. In numbering the people—those who could bear arms—he had become the king Samuel had foretold: a king who raises a large standing army with massive expenditures on weapons of war [1 Samuel 8:10-22, 2 Samuel 24:10,17]."

"Sounds like Israel today," Ari commented.

"Does that mean Peres is king?" Michele humorously added.

"Oh, no, our king is still coming," Yonah said, then continued. "The entire numbering of the troops displeased the Lord greatly

[1 Chronicles 21:7]. That's a quick . . . well, not so quick catalogue of David's failures. What do you think of it, Michele?"

"I'm stunned by your knowledge of the Bible. How can you rattle off these accounts so easily?"

"Years of study and lots of pain," Yonah answered.

"But it seems you still haven't answered my question," Michele reminded Yonah. "With all the warts, wrinkles, and wrongs in David's life, how is it that he can be called 'a man after God's own heart'?"

"Ah, maybe that's for all of us to figure out on our own," Yonah concluded.

Michele stood, picked up all the cups and plates, and took them to the kitchen. She then joined Ari at the door and thanked Yonah for his hospitality.

Michele leaned over and kissed the precious little man on the cheek. "Shalom," she uttered with a fairly good accent.

"I think I like this American girl, Ari," Yonah responded with a smile.

"Laylah tov to you, also."

Ari walked Michele to her car and opened her door for her. Before getting in, she kissed him on the cheek and said, "Laylah tov, Ari. See you later."

"Lehitraot," Ari returned.

A Man of God:
Passion for the Lord
"A MAN AFTER HIS OWN HEART"

It was a fall afternoon, and Michele was lecturing one of her classes at the university. This particular lecture for her was both enjoyable and painful. It was enjoyable because she loved teaching sociology of the family. Getting students to think seriously about mate-selection theories—or why they are attracted to and marry the people they do—is always interesting material for both student and teacher.

But the material was equally painful for Michele because it brought up again the pain of her own marriage and divorce. As professional and well educated as she was, she could never completely separate her personal life from her educator's role. "Social-exchange theories," the "symbolic interactions between couples," the "conflictual frameworks in families," and other related concepts sounded like high academia to most people. But Michele never approached her subjects as purely academic. She was compelled to bring the material to life by sharing her own experiences. Most of her examples were negative and painful.

Most of her students were fascinated by the lecture. A few slept, wrote notes, or did homework assignments. But the careful listeners appeared very interested in the subject matter and liked their American

137

professor. Dr. Anderson walked around as she lectured, animated and free from her notes.

She lectured, "The issue of who has greater authority, the higher position in the family, or the more power, is very complex, because many factors are involved in determining who calls the shots in the family. Generally speaking, the one with greater authority. . . ."

In the middle of her sentence, Michele noticed a door opening in the back of the sunken lecture room. As she continued her lecture, she observed the figure of a uniformed man taking a seat in the darkened last row. She could gain only a glimpse of the figure—not enough for clear recognition.

Michele continued, "Generally speaking, the one with greater authority in the family is also the individual with more authority in society at large." As Dr. Anderson continued, she began to wonder who the visitor was. In Israel, even on campus, it was not uncommon to have students, male or female, attend class in uniform, with their ever-present Galils or M-16s as near as their textbooks.

But Michele secretly hoped the visitor might be Ari. She hadn't seen him for months and, in spite of their casual relationship, she unexplainably missed him. Since she had been giving special lectures at other Israeli universities, and Ari had been involved in counterterrorism activities on the West Bank, they hadn't been able to connect for months.

After Michele finished her lecture, most of her students filed out. The dark figure moved down the stair-stepped lecture hall and approached as the few students who remained surrounded Michele to ask questions. When Michele looked up and realized who was standing behind the students, she quickly lost her "educator" countenance and blurted out, "Ari."

She broke off her conservation, slipped through the circle of students, and gave Ari a big, American hug, followed by a kiss on the cheek.

"Shalom, Michele," Ari greeted her.

"What a surprise," Michele returned.

The students began whispering about the apparent "chemistry" between this striking IDF major and their professor.

Finally, one coed released her thinking: "Is this part of the mate-selection theory you presented?"

Dr. Anderson blushed, backed away from Ari, and apologized

for leaving her students in the midst of their questions. The students soon left, leaving Ari and Michele alone in the large hall.

"If you don't have dinner plans, I would like to take you to my favorite place in all of Israel," Ari said.

"Well, I don't have plans, but I'm not really dressed for dinner," Michele returned.

"Don't be an American for this evening," Ari kidded. "You don't have to 'dress' for dinner. Put on some casual clothes, and I will pick you up in one hour."

"How casual?" Michele asked.

"Casual casual," Ari responded, rolling his eyes a little.

"Jeans?"

By this point, Ari had become a bit impatient with her American-type questions and said finally, "Jeans will be fine."

DAVID'S CONTRADICTORY CHARGE TO SOLOMON

Realizing his health was rapidly declining, David called for Solomon. Having already been anointed king, Solomon awaited the formal, national coronation ceremony to make it official. David would be giving his public charge to the king the next day. But first David wanted to have a private conversation with his son.

Solomon entered David's private quarters, bowed, and reclined on the floor near David's bed. "Solomon, my son, it's good to see you. How are you?"

"I am well, my lord," Solomon answered.

"That is good, very good. I wanted to talk to you king to king and father to son," David continued. "You know I have had many sons, but of all the sons the Lord has given me, He has chosen you to sit on the throne of the kingdom of the Lord over all Israel [1 Chronicles 28:5].

"You are unique, for you are a son born both of my lust and of my love. Of lust, because I did a terrible thing in having your mother's first husband killed in battle—simply because I saw her beauty and wanted her for myself. As a penalty for my sin, the Lord took home your baby brother.

"But you are also the son of my love, because after your mother became my wife, I loved her above all my other wives. You are the offspring of our love. Therefore, it is fitting the Lord has chosen you to be king. You are king by the gracious, tender mercies of the Lord. The Lord has taken my sin and turned it into a man who would be king.

"You also know how the Lord denied my deepest passion, which was to see a house built for the complete service of the Lord. But the Lord said to me, 'You are a man of war and have shed blood. . . . [Therefore] your son Solomon is the one who shall build My house and My courts'" (1 Chronicles 28:3,6).

Solomon answered his father, "I am privileged and honored indeed to be king, my lord."

"I know you are, my son," David responded. "Therefore, here are some things I want to tell you before I go to my fathers and you assume the throne. Tomorrow I will give you a public charge in the presence of all Israel, but today I want to counsel you privately about some very important matters.

"In preparation for your building the Lord's house on Mount Zion, I have provided for all the materials you will need [1 Chronicles 29:1-9]. The Lord Himself has also provided in writing a pattern regarding all the details of the house [28:19]. You will find the instructions in my map case with the rest of my writing materials.

"But building this house will not be easy. You must be strong, courageous, and willing to act decisively. I'm sure many will oppose your decisions or try to thwart what God desires to build here. Therefore, do not fear what men may do or say about you. Rely on the Lord's promise that He will not fail you until all the work for the service of the Lord is finished [1 Chronicles 28:20].

"My son, all Israel knows of my failures and how I petitioned and pleaded with the Lord for my crimes to be forgiven. I pleaded on the basis of God's loving-kindness and compassion, which He has covenanted with His people and me [Psalm 51:1]. As I have reflected on my failures, I want to leave you with what I have learned from them.

"Be the kind of king the Lord desires. The first and foremost element of being a righteous king is to watch to whom you inquire. To be a man after God's own heart, you must inquire of the Lord in things great and small. I should have known this after watching my predecessor, Saul. He started out right before the Lord, but then made a wrong inquiry. Saul inquired of the Lord until he stopped hearing back from the Lord [1 Samuel 10:22, 14:37, 28:6].

"Apparently, when he no longer got an answer from the Lord, he went to a medium and inquired of her instead [1 Samuel 28]. Later, an evil spirit came upon Saul, which created the need for me to soothe his demonizing spirits with my *kinnor*. As soon as Saul quit inquiring of the Lord, his life and reign went downhill. I should have learned from Saul's experience, as I was there firsthand. But apparently I didn't take it to heart enough.

"Early on I tried to inquire of the Lord before every major battle and event. I didn't trust my own instincts or the advice of my counselors or commanders. As helpful as they have always been, it is only the Lord who can give the guidance kings need. All other advice is merely the counsel of men.

"When I didn't know whether the Lord wanted me to attack the Philistines the first time, I inquired of the Lord and He answered me [1 Samuel 23:2]. After Ziklag had been sacked, I was so consumed with anger at having my own city destroyed and my wives and children taken captive, I didn't know what to do. I was tempted to take events into my own hands, but I inquired of the Lord to confirm my desires. He said, 'Go up against the Amalekites' [see 30:8].

"As soon as I heard of Saul's death, I inquired of the Lord to see if He wanted me to go up to the cities of Judah. Again, He said 'go,' and I was anointed king by my own tribe [2 Samuel 2:1]. After my anointing, the Philistines gathered their armies together to come against me. I again inquired of the Lord, and He said, 'Go up, for I will certainly give the Philistines into your hand' [5:19]. After that I was able to consolidate the kingdom and secure all our boundaries. I was finally king over all Israel, with all our enemies defeated or subdued.

"In tribute to what God had done through my life, I wrote a song expressing my deep gratitude. I confessed for all the nation to sing how the Lord had proven to be our only rock, fortress, deliverer, and savior [1 Samuel 22:1-6,18]. Even in my deep distress, when I called and inquired of the Lord, He heard me and answered me [verse 7]. I confessed how God had rewarded me for my righteousness and purity of hands [verses 21-22]. How arrogant I must have been to write such things. That was before my failure in committing adultery and murder and, of course, before Absalom overthrew my rule.

"When I look back at this period of my life, it is clear that I ceased inquiring of the Lord. After I became king, I can't remember inquiring of the Lord for anything. I began to rely on my own wisdom and desires. The only thing I inquired about was Bathsheba, your mother [2 Samuel 11:3], and that, of course, was a terrible inquiry to make. After I was restored as king, I had learned my lesson and began to inquire of the Lord again [21:1].

"So, my son, do not make the same mistakes as your father. Inquire of the Lord for all your decisions, and He will guide you."

"So, what other advice do you give, my father?" Solomon asked.

David continued, "You must understand and live your life on the basis of God's covenantal loyalty. Do you remember the promise God made with me: that when my days were complete and I lay down with my fathers, that you will be raised up as my seed, whose kingdom will be established forever [2 Samuel 7:12-13]?

"The reason God gave you this right is not because of anything you have done or will ever do, but solely because of His *hesed*, or covenantal love [2 Samuel 7:15]. Of course, this is the way God has always dealt with Israel. He promises to show His *hesed* to all who love Him and keep His commandments [Exodus 20:6]. God is loyal to us because of the covenant He made with us. If this is the way God deals with us, then should we not deal with our fellow Israelites in like fashion?

"There were many times I wanted to kill King Saul, and many times I had the opportunity. But the Lord always reminded me of the covenants and oaths I had made to the house of Saul. After the first opportunity I had to kill Saul, Saul realized it and asked me to promise to the Lord to preserve his name and his descendants. As my lord and king, how could I do otherwise? So I swore to protect his household [1 Samuel 24:21]. I even showed kindness to those who showed kindness to Saul after he was killed [2 Samuel 2:5].

"Because of the covenant I made with Jonathan, I had to be loyal to his family throughout my lifetime [1 Samuel 20:16,42]. We covenanted to protect each other's families should either of us be killed. After Saul and Jonathan were killed by the Philistines, I took a covenantal revenge upon those who had put the spear to them [2 Samuel 4:11-12], and then showed *hesed* to the house of Saul by taking in his surviving, lame offspring, Mephibosheth. I allowed him to eat at my table as one of my own sons, along with Saul's servant Ziba [9:1-13].

"Although I had no formal covenantal relationship with the Ammonites, when their king died, I desired to show *hesed* to his son Hanun. Because the king of Ammon had shown me kindness, I desired, in return, to be loyal to his father's gesture. However, Hanun questioned my motives and rejected my offer by humiliating my messengers [2 Samuel 10:1-6]. I should have gone out and taken care of the Ammonites myself, instead of sending Joab alone. Instead, I stayed in Jerusalem, helping them right this horrible humiliation to Israel [10:14, 11:1].

"So, my son, a king after God's own heart will keep his promises and be loyal to the covenants before God and with men. Any man is only as good and righteous as the loyalty he demonstrates to his own family, his friend's family, and his God. My greatest failures were when I failed to be loyal to the Lord, by betraying the loyalty a king owes the men who fight for him and protect him. In killing Uriah, I was disloyal to my God, my army, and utterly disloyal to his house. I am thankful the Lord was not disloyal to the covenant He made with me. I deserved death, but He spared me.

"Lastly, as king you must demonstrate fidelity to the Torah, God's Law. Remember how God through Moses gave specific instructions to kings? It is written in the Law, 'Now it shall come about when he [the king] sits on the throne of his kingdom, he shall write for himself a copy of this law on a scroll in the presence of the Levitical priests. And it shall be with him, and he shall read it all the days of his life, that he may learn to fear the LORD his God, by carefully observing all the words of this law and these statutes' [Deuteronomy 17:18-19].

"Along with the many psalms and hymns I have written, you will find the copy of the law I wrote out for myself when I became king. I suggest you take it to the priests and in their presence make a copy for yourself so that you may become familiar with every aspect of the law.

"But merely making a copy is not what is important for a godly king. You must make it the source of your encouragement, direction, and guidance. It must be the object of your daily meditation for you to understand it and live it.

"I have written a long tribute to the role of Torah in my own life. I have written, 'How blessed are those who observe His testimonies,' and 'How can a young man keep his way pure? By keeping it according to Thy word,' and 'O how I love Thy law! It is my meditation all the day. Thy commandments make me wiser than my enemies' [Psalm 119:2,9,97-98].

"So, my son, love the law, and keep it, and you will be a well-instructed king . . . a king after the heart of God."

David slowly rose to his feet, embraced Solomon, and kissed him. "Now go, my son. Tomorrow is a big day. And remember, it is for kings and godly men to *inquire of the Lord, be loyal to God and men, and be faithful. To know and do God's Law!*"

Solomon was halfway out the door when David called to him. "Solomon, I have one more thing to say to you."

Solomon reentered the chamber. "What is it, Father?"

"Do you remember what Joab did to the two commanders of Israel's army; how he needlessly shed the blood of battle in peacetime, after I had made peace with Abner, Saul's chief commander?" (2 Samuel 3:1-21).

"Yes, I remember," Solomon answered.

"So act in accordance with your good wisdom, my son," David requested, "but do not let Joab's gray hair descend to the dead peacefully" (1 Kings 2:5-6).

Solomon was shocked. Joab was his father's army commander—one of the few who had stayed with David through both exiles. Solomon always thought they were good friends.

David continued, "Do you also remember what Shimei did to me when I was exiled from Absalom, and how he threw rocks at me and cursed me all the while we journeyed to Mahanaim?"

"Yes, I remember," Solomon returned. "Didn't you swear to him by the Lord that you would not put him to death?"

"Yes," David replied. "But now that my time is drawing near, I do not want him to go unpunished for what he did to me. After I am gone, my promise is no longer in force. Therefore, as a wise man, you know what you must do. Do not let his gray hair see sheol without bloodshed [1 Kings 2:8-9].

"Also take note that Barzillai, the Gileadite, provided for me and my men at Mahanaim when I was fleeing from Absalom [2 Samuel 19:31-39]. Therefore, show kindness to him, and let him be one who eats at your own table" (1 Kings 2:7).

As Solomon left the room, he was a little confused. First, David had charged him to be a man of God, one whose passions were directed godward at all times. Then, in the next breath he gave him a personal "hit list" to be taken care of after his departure.

Solomon wondered if his father lacked the courage to deal with those two while he was alive, or perhaps he was senile and revenge had taken over in his dying days. Or was David playing politics, eliminating all potential rivals and opposition to the new king? Solomon couldn't come up with an answer, but he knew what he had to do. He would keep all of his father's requests.

⌒

ARI'S MORAL FAILURE

As Ari pulled his vehicle to a stop, he noticed Michele sitting on a wall outside her campus apartment. She quickly jumped off and threw her purse around her shoulder. Ari noticed how classy she looked even when dressed down. Her blue jeans fit nicely on her long-limbed body, and her other clothing touches reflected good style. Her white blouse was tied at her midsection, and a pink scarf knotted around her neck matched a pair of pink flats. A straw hat with matching pink band rounded out the package.

As she opened the car door, Ari looked into her doelike brown eyes and said, "Not bad, not bad at all."

"Well, if we're going to your favorite eatery, I couldn't go looking like a tramp," Michele added.

"Quite impossible, I think," Ari answered back.

The car proceeded along the Hebron highway, past the industrial district, until the couple had almost left Beersheba proper.

"Are we going to another town?" Michele asked.

"Sort of," Ari answered.

"What do you have up your sleeve?" Michele questioned with a little smile.

"I don't have sleeves on this knit shirt," Ari returned jokingly. He then turned off the main highway onto a dirt road.

"Where are you taking me, Ari?" Michele asked with a little uncertainty now in her voice.

"Right here," Ari responded.

"This is a restaurant?" Michele questioned. "It looks more like a pile of dirt."

"I didn't say I was taking you to a restaurant. I said I wanted to take you to my favorite place to eat," Ari explained. "So, here it is, old Beersheba, the city of our father, Abraham."

Ari walked around to the rear of the car, opened the trunk, and took out a picnic basket and a couple of blankets.

Michele, still wondering what she had gotten herself into, got out of the car and proceeded up the embankment with Ari. Michele occasionally slipped on the loose rocks, so Ari took her by the arm and helped her up the pathway leading to the entrance of the tel. At the entrance they both stopped to look at the ancient well positioned outside the "city gates."

"Abraham himself may have dug this well with his own hands," Ari explained.

"I can't imagine," Michele said in amazement. Ari took her hand again and led her onto the flattened area of the tel.

"What a view," Michele exclaimed.

"It's the best view in Beersheba," Ari said. He laid out the blankets on the ground and opened the picnic basket. He took out a bottle of Carmel rosé wine and a well-prepared veggie-and-cheese plate complete with several dips. He took out plates, napkins, and even a candle. "When the wind dies down, I'll light it," he said.

"My, you've thought of everything," Michele answered.

Ari popped the cork, poured the wine, held his glass to Michele's, and said, "To life, and to Michele."

Michele smiled and said, "Oh, Ari, this is delightful. I couldn't think of a better place to eat, or with any better person."

Michele leaned over and kissed him—this time not on the cheek, but on the lips. They held the kiss for several moments, and then Michele pulled away, saying, "Well, what else do you have to eat in the basket?"

"Well, I hope you like these. I have some *bourekah*, turnovers filled with cheese and spinach. And this is called *mahshi*, a kind of dumpling made of ground lamb and minced onions. And here is some cracked wheat bread called *ubbeh*."

"Oh, it all looks and smells delightful," Michele answered. As the last few rays of the reddened sun shone across the Negev, the beauty of the moment was almost magical. The couple leaned back on a large rock, and Ari put his arm around Michele to warm her shoulders from the chill.

Michele looked into his soft, greenish eyes and said, "Ari, may I ask you something?"

"Of course," Ari replied.

"What happened to your marriage? I still know very little about that part of your life. I know something very painful happened to you, and since I do care about you, I would like to know all the details."

"You deserve to know, Michele," Ari answered. "I have only told one other person all the details, and I'm not sure he really understood everything. So, where shall I begin?" Ari asked.

"How about the beginning?" Michele said.

Ari poured himself another drink and placed the remnant of a *bourekah* into his mouth. "I was seventeen when my father died in the Six Day War, but I remember many of the times we were together, including being here on this tel. He always made the biblical stories come alive. Although he wasn't very religious, he did love the Bible. I have often wished I could have known him as an adult. But I'm getting off track, aren't I?

"I was married in 1976 to Noam Shimron, a fair-skinned Ashkenazi of Austrian descent. We met at a military reception for the Medal of Honor winners after the Yom Kippur War. I and my tank crew had held off the Syrian armor in the Golan Heights for several hours until help arrived. For our heroism, we were all awarded the IDF Medal of Honor.

"One of our regional commanders was Lieutenant Colonel Mordecai Shimron. He made several of the presentations at the reception. Because his wife was ill, he brought his daughter, Noam, to the reception. She looked stunning in her cocktail dress and immediately caught my attention. Before the reception was over, I had asked her for a date. We dated off and on for a couple of years, and then were married in June of '76, the same month I was promoted to the rank of captain.

"Our first year of marriage was great in every way. But then I was selected to go to the U.S. Army War College at Carlisle Barracks, Pennsylvania. It was a nine-month assignment and a real plum to be a 'Distinguished Foreign Officer and Lecturer on Tank Warfare.' It was one of those assignments one did not turn down. Since Noam was already a couple of months pregnant, we both agreed that she would stay in Israel to have the baby while I spent the year abroad. *Mistake number one!*

"Although she never said anything, I believe Noam deeply resented my being away while she was having our first child. Besides, while I was in Pennsylvania, I realized I really didn't miss her. I was so enjoying the formal study alongside the American military elite. It was also an ego trip being viewed as a tank warfare expert as a result of my heroism against the Syrians. I guess I let it all go to my head.

"In addition, because most of the officers at the war college were married and had their families in the area, my free time was spent with the few single guys. On weekends we would frequent the bar and club scenes, at least what little of it there was in Carlisle! Most of the time, I was quite a hit with the single ladies because of my being Israeli.

"My daughter, Dorit, was born while I was away. She was several months old when I first saw her. After my time at the war college, my career really began to take off. There were more training exercises, special assignments, and the wining and dining of other high-command officers. I think our marriage, during that time, had become one of mere convenience and acceptability.

"By this time, Noam's father had become a general officer, and we were often invited to formal state functions and receptions. I was viewed as a rising star in the IDF. But in terms of our marriage, the warmth, passion, and closeness had departed. I was promoted to major in '79, and Benjamin, my son, was born in '81. I was there for Noam when he was born and, for a few months, we enjoyed each other and the new blessing brought to our marriage. I even took some time off. We got a hotel room in Tel Aviv and did a real family vacation. It was probably our last time of feeling close."

"So, how did the divorce come about?" Michele probed.

"Not easily," Ari said. "Israel is not like America. It seems that in your country, all two people need to do to get a divorce is file some papers — what do you call it?"

"No-fault divorce," Michele answered.

"Yes, that's it. Well, in this country, all marriages and divorces are authorized by the regional rabbinical authorities. There are no purely civil marriages or civil divorces. There must be grounds based upon intensive investigation."

"So, what were your grounds?" Michele asked.

"Adultery, what else?" Ari replied. "But it wasn't what I would call 'simple adultery.' That was the only category in which they could place what I did."

Ari took out a lighter and lit the single candle.

"The warmth feels good," Michele said.

A little chilly himself, Ari took one of the blankets and wrapped it around both of their shoulders and continued. "The years 1981 to 1983 were the best and worst years of my life. Well, 1981 was good. Benjamin was born, and I met the most fascinating, captivating woman I had ever met—next to you, of course," Ari quickly added.

"Sure," Michele interjected.

"I met her at a mental health conference in Tel Aviv. She was an IDF mental health officer. She had a vivacious and exciting personality, loved to dance and disco, and even enjoyed the symphony. During the conference, we went out for drinks every night. By the end of the week, the chemistry between us was more than either of us could handle."

"So what did she look like? What was her name?" Michele questioned.

"Dali'ah," Ari returned. "Dali'ah Shavit, a Romanian in her late twenties; never married, with a sort of oval face and slightly pointed chin. Other than her five-five, hourglass shape, what really hit me were her roses-and-cream complexion and painted lips. Most Israeli women do not use makeup, so she stood out like the rose of Sharon."

"So, did you make passionate romance?" Michele inquired.

"By all means," Ari answered. "After the conference ended, I got tickets to a summer symphony concert at Caesarea. It was one of those perfect moonlit nights under which to enjoy Mozart by the sea. Afterwards, we took a side road that led to the ancient Roman aqueducts that run parallel with the coast.

"We took off our shoes, walked in the sand, and let the waves splash our feet. Suddenly Dali'ah took off her clothes and ran into the waves. She motioned for me to come on as well. Well, what was an Israeli male to do?"

"Leave her to drown, of course," Michele answered laughingly.

"I followed suit," Ari continued. "I took off my clothes and joined her. That night was the beginning of a yearlong, passionate affair, whereby every time I went to Tel Aviv, I would stay with her for a couple of days."

"And no one ever knew?" Michele questioned.

"No, no one. Not even my best friends."

"And Noam never suspected?"

"No, I don't think so," Ari responded, "not until the Lebanon disaster."

"What happened in Lebanon?"

"You really want to know? It's pretty gory stuff."

"I'm a big girl. I can handle it."

THE LEBANON FIASCO

Ari continued. "In early 1982 I was assigned to Brigadier General Yitzak Mordecai's command. He was a battle-hardened paratrooper of Iraqi descent. As things unfolded, it looked as if we were planning a deep operation into Lebanon to secure our northern boundaries. However, our defense minister's thinking was something else entirely.

"Since the civil war in '75, Lebanon had become unstable, with various factions vying for power. During that time, Prime Minister Rabin began secret meetings with the Phalangists who occupied southern Lebanon. Their leader, Bashir Gemayel, wanted Israel to intervene in the civil war and back him into power. In return, he would make peace with Israel.

"Between 1980 and 1981, the Phalange and Syrian forces began to clash over the control of the Beirut-Damascus road. At this point, both the Mossad, our foreign intelligence service, and Aman, our IDF intelligence agency, agreed that this was a plot by the Phalange to bring Israel into the war.

"In April of '81, a Likud prime minister, Menachem Begin, was reelected. He named Rafael Eitan as chief of staff, and the two of them approved air strikes against the Syrians. Two Syrian helicopters were shot down. The next day, the Syrians moved four SAM missile batteries into the Bekaa Valley. Then in May, the IAF hit PLO camps in southern Lebanon. It seemed at this point that both Eitan and Begin wanted a full-scale war with the PLO and perhaps also with the Syrians.

"Then, in a critically determinative move, Begin appointed Ariel Sharon as minister of defense. Sharon immediately invited the Phalange leadership to his ranch here in the Negev. Many of us now believe that this was when the war really began. Operation 'Little Pines' was what would be 'sold' to the cabinet. This involved an IDF advance into Lebanon as far as Sidon to protect Israel's northern borders. Operation 'Big Pines' was more secret and more aggressive. It involved moving the army to a line north of Beirut and cutting off the Beirut-Damascus highway, a move that would surely bring the Syrians into the conflict.

"Sharon presented the plan on December 20, 1981, but did not mention 'Big Pines.' The cabinet approved the concept in theory. By this time, the Americans were getting concerned, so our Aman chief, Yehoshua Saguy, was sent to Washington to meet with Alexander Haig, the U.S. secretary of state.

"Haig made it very clear that the American government would only support an invasion of Lebanon if the PLO violated the UN cease-fire agreement. At this point, there was not agreement within the intelligence community about this proposed action. The Mossad had fallen completely under the influence of the Phalange leader, Bashir. Aman was against any kind of invasion. Sharon and Begin pushed for a 'limited police action, not a war.' While the U.S. and the Israeli cabinet were sold the concept of 'Little Pines,' the IDF and IAF, through Sharon, were planning Operation 'Big Pines.'"

Michele interrupted. "Where were you in all this, Ari?"

"I was preparing with General Mordecai to be a part of the armored coastal force that would work its way up to Tyre and then eventually to Sidon. On June 3, 1982, a most opportune event took place. Our ambassador to Britain, Shlomo Argov, was assassinated outside a London hotel. The blame went immediately to Abu Nidal, a terrorist group with bases in Lebanon.

"Now the Israeli leadership had the needed rationale to begin overt hostilities. On June 4 Israeli jets bombed Beirut, and the PLO immediately returned fire on Galilee settlements with their katyusha rockets. One rocket came very near to where my wife and children were. Then on June 5 the cabinet authorized a forty-kilometer thrust into South Lebanon to silence the PLO guns and rocket launchers. There was no mention of going any farther.

"On the night of June 5 we made our final preparations for the Lebanon assault to take place the following day. On June 6 our armored columns began to roll into Lebanon and up the coastal plain. At the same time, unknown to many of us, a second division was cutting through the central axis of Lebanon through the Shouf Mountains to cut off the Beirut-Damascus highway. This brought the Syrians into the war.

"As soon as the IDF entered Lebanon, most of the PLO officers fled the scene, leaving the small towns and villages to be defended by local home guards of refugee camps. At first, when we entered the towns, the citizens came out of their houses, waving greetings to us in our tanks. Women threw rice on us in homage of a victorious army. But the celebration did not last long.

"Suddenly, men sprang from behind the civilians and opened fire with machine guns and rocket-propelled grenades. A good friend, a tank commander, was the first to go down. He was shot in the head as he waved back to the crowds. Quickly, the entire street was taking fire, and we had to open fire into the crowds to proceed. We sprayed houses on both sides of the street, killing many women and children.

"It was, for most of us, the first time we had ever fought in built-up areas, where civilians were used as 'cover.' Throughout our move northward, the PLO fighters blended with the civilian population. Their only distinguishing factor was the weapons they bore. By the time we took Sidon, most of my men had vacant, blank expressions on their faces, with tired bodies and empty eyes.

"Often the PLO fighters would have their command posts secured in the basements of schools, hospitals, and even mosques. When we had to destroy those bases of command and control, we would go in and find women, children, and the infirm slaughtered along with the PLO. We even found 'patients' with IVs still in their veins, being drained of all their blood to be used for PLO victims.

"Then the political process started. The UN negotiated a cease-fire and the U.S. sent in their Marines to help the PLO out. The PLO were evacuated on August 21. On August 23 Bashir Gemayel was elected president with the obvious help and backing of Israeli money and guns. But then things got even worse.

"Gemayel refused to sign a treaty with Begin, and the Mossad got blamed for not delivering on their promise. Sharon, Eitan, and the Mossad, however, still believed the Phalange could be trusted. As the story goes, Gemayel told Sharon that the refugee camps needed to be destroyed, without a contrary response from Sharon. By this time, because the cease-fire was in effect, I was assigned to the IDF divisional headquarters atop a building overlooking Sabra and Shatilla, two refugee camps. I was to monitor activities with my Phalange counterpart, Elie Hobeika, a man I should not have trusted.

"On September 14, a bomb set off in an apartment below that of Bashir Gemayel killed the newly elected Lebanese president. This worked the Phalange into a frenzied rage and sent the entire army looking for revenge. On September 15, IDF paratroopers moved into West Beirut to establish the peace. While they were moving through the axis of Sabra and Shatilla, they took potshots from Palestinians in the villages. Sharon supposedly gave an oral command stating that the Phalange would take the camps 'under IDF supervision.' Later, everyone denied the existence of the order.

"On September 16, I was monitoring the radio with my Phalange counterpart, when the Phalangists pushed into Sabra and Shatilla. The IDF provided cover from a distance. Aman officers, including Saguy and myself, were at the radio monitoring all the communications. Midway through the afternoon, Saguy asked me to accompany him to Jerusalem to report the situation to the cabinet. We boarded a helicopter that took us immediately to the prime minister's cabinet meeting.

"At the meeting, very little was mentioned about the Phalange. And because Saguy hadn't slept for days, Begin finally told him to leave and get some sleep. He asked me to leave with him. When we got outside, Saguy gave me the keys to his staff car and told me to go home and see my wife.

"That was the moment when my destiny changed. Instead of going home, I went to Tel Aviv. To see . . ." Ari sighed.

"Dali'ah. You went to see Dali'ah," Michele helped him.

"Yes, I was so disgusted with the war, the killing of civilians, and seeing my own men killed, I had to have a human touch, the passionate touch of a woman."

Ari began to wipe tears from his eyes. His voice broke, but he continued to speak. "While I spent time with Dali'ah that night, some five hundred to seven hundred people, including women and children, were slaughtered by the Phalange. And who led the operation? My counterpart, the good Lebanese Christian, Major Hobeika. During the night, reports about the atrocities began to surface over the radio—the radio post to which I was assigned!

"At one point a Phalange communiqué came over the radio reporting that about fifty civilians had been rounded up. The Phalange were asking their commander what to do with them. The answer given was, 'Do God's will.' Later, another transmission was heard. 'What shall we do with these women and children?' the same voice from the village requested. The answer given was, 'You know what to do. Stop asking me what to do with these people. Just do it.'

"By the time Saguy and I returned to the front, the Phalange had appropriated IDF bulldozers and were trying to 'cover up' the slaughter. Entire villages were razed, and they were trying to bulldoze the rubble over the slain bodies.

"It was my fault. I could have prevented it." Ari broke down completely at this point. "It was all my fault. I betrayed my people, my post, my wife, my family, and my nation. How could we as victims of a holocaust ever allow such things to take place?" Michele heard underneath the sobbing.

She embraced Ari and let him purge his feelings and granted him this long-overdue release for his soul. He seemed to sob for hours.

Finally he said, "It cost me my marriage, my family, the respect of my peers, my career, and my own self-respect. If I could only get back that one day, that one evening. I wish there existed some sense of forgiveness for what I've done."

"I forgive you, Ari," Michele assured him with a radiant, candlelight smile. "And I know God forgives you," she added.

"God forgives me? How can one know such things?"

"Well, I know He can. But it's gotten to be quite late, and I had better be going." Michele moved closer to him and planted her lips on his, pausing only to say, "Thank you, Ari. I know it wasn't easy for you to share your pain with me. I respect you even more for being so open and honest about everything."

Ari gathered the remains of the food, folded the blankets, and placed everything back into the basket. From his pocket an army-issue flashlight emerged, and the two proceeded down the embankment. Michele again slipped in her flat-bottom shoes. Ari picked her up and carried both the picnic basket and her 130 pounds in his arms.

"I'm impressed, Major," she jested as they slid down the rocky terrain.

"Nothing at all. We have to carry far more weight than this in our regular maneuvers," Ari boasted. "But I must say, I've never carried anyone I care about more!"

In spite of her jesting, Michele felt secure in both his arms and his honesty. Ari equally felt secure in her embrace and in the strange emotional safety he was beginning to feel with her. He began to wonder about her somewhat incongruent and cryptic statement about forgiveness. It seemed to come out of nowhere, without any connection or context.

Just the same, the thought struck Ari as intriguing and comforting. To know one is forgiven for shedding innocent blood . . . how could this be? How could forgiveness be found for passions gone astray?

CHAPTER TEN

A Lion of God:
Passion for Yeshua
"THE LORD SAID TO MY LORD"

It was late and the palace was dark, but David was feeling unusually lucid and clearheaded. He arose and went to his writing table to try to put his thoughts to melody. Knowing his days on the earth might be short, he began reviewing his life.

He remembered his youthful days in Bethlehem and thought, *My, how the Lord has taken a lowly shepherd boy and made him the anointed shepherd of Israel* [2 Samuel 23:1]. *Who would have thought that You, O Lord, would have brought me this far?* [7:18].

He recalled the day he was anointed by Samuel the prophet. What a surprise it had been to everyone, especially his brothers. There was the glorious defeat of Goliath and the Philistine army. "The first of much bloodshed," David murmured to himself.

Then he remembered the joy that flooded his spirit when he clothed himself with the linen ephod and brought the ark of the covenant to Mount Zion. David could still feel the emotion and sense of celebration that spontaneously moved him to sing and dance. *Enthroned in Zion*, he mused, *God allowed me to be His king, to be enthroned on His holy hill, at His right hand!* David sat in silence, amazed by his life's events.

His thoughts then turned to his time with Solomon earlier in the day. "My own son, the king, is now God's king on Zion," David

155

uttered. "That's hard to imagine. But of course, God made an oath with the house of David. One of my sons will be on the throne unto the ages."

Then a strange thought passed through David's mind. *If Solomon is king*, he pondered, *then he is my lord as well. If he is my lord, I should pay homage to him, for the king of Israel is the visible representative of Yahweh's throne. Solomon will be the first of many Davidic kings who will reign from Zion and the City of David*, David reminded himself.

A horrible thought suddenly shattered David's late-night remembrance. *What if his sons, as kings, did not live in accordance with the desires of Yahweh? What if they went after other gods and set aside the Law of the Lord? What would happen to the Davidic throne if those things came to pass?*

Knowing his own fallen propensities, David knew the answers to those questions. There was no guarantee that his sons would walk in ways of righteous kings. Even David, at times, had failed terribly. *So, what ensured that a son of David would be on the throne of Israel forever?* David asked himself. He was at a loss with that question.

David seated himself at his writing table, took pen in hand, and wrote, "A melody of David." No sooner had he written the words than he felt a strange stirring within himself. His mind was quickly alerted to a familiar Presence that seemed to utter and guide his thoughts as he wrote. He scratched on the page, "Yahweh utters to my Lord, sit at my right hand, until I make your enemies a footstool for your feet" (see Psalm 110:1 and Matthew 22:43).

As he looked at what he had written, at first he did not understand the words. He likened the experience to Balaam's oracle, when God spoke through the mouth of a very unlikely prophet without giving prior understanding (Numbers 24:3). David then received the sense that his words were also prophetic. Maybe God was answering the uncertainty of his questions in this scribbled oracle.

If David could call Solomon, his own son, Lord because he was the anointed king of Israel, could not One be coming from his Davidic line from whom the scepter would never depart? In a somewhat veiled manner, David remembered that a Coming One was promised in the Balaam oracle. One who would be the "star of Jacob" and "a scepter from Israel," who would crush all the surrounding enemies of Israel (Numbers 24:15-25).

David had tried to do that, but there were still enemies on Israel's borders, always waiting for the right opportunity to pounce on her like a lion. David could see the picture, though somewhat dimly. Solomon, since his anointing as king, had sat at David's right hand as anointed son, and was thus worthy to be called "lord." Perhaps a future One would come who would finally subdue the nations for all times. *The utterance Yahweh is giving me,* David reasoned, *regards the One yet to come, who, being at the royal place of honor, deserves to be called "divine Lord."*

⌒

MICHELE'S REVELATION

The drive back to Beersheba seemed longer than their afternoon trip. It may have been because Ari felt exhausted from the emotional release at the tel. The gas pedal merely reflected the sadness that had set into his heart. For the first few moments, neither Ari nor Michele said anything.

Finally, Michele broke the silence. "Ari, I haven't been totally honest with you!"

Ari looked over at her and slowed down even more. "Oh no, you've had some affairs like me?" Ari suggested.

"No, not that," Michele chuckled. "You may think it is much worse than that, though."

At this point Ari didn't know if he wanted to hear such things or not, but went ahead and urged, "Go ahead, tell me. This is not the night to hold back anything."

Michele took a deep breath and began her "revelation." "Remember when I told you that when my divorce took place, I was so devastated I couldn't work or do anything but move back in with my parents?" Michele asked.

"Yes, I remember," Ari said.

"Well, it's funny. My physician father never believed in psychiatrists because he felt they only pushed pills. Well, he had finally had it with me. He started encouraging me to go see a 'shrink' near the hospital where he worked. Eventually I went, and I found that Dad was right. All the psychiatrist did was put me on antidepressive medication. But I must say, it did make me feel better. At least I could envision a future again."

Michele continued, "If my father had gotten so desperate to help me that he recommended a shrink, my mother was equally trying to find things to make me feel better. Anything! One morning while I was sleeping in, she opened my bedroom door, peeked in her Jewish head, and said, 'Here, go to this . . . it might help you.' With that, she walked over to my dresser and placed a brochure next to my purse. Mother, bless her heart, was always trying to fix me.

"When I finally got up, I glanced at the brochure. It was for a 'Divorce Recovery Seminar.' That's all I saw on the cover. I quickly threw it across the room and forgot about it until my mother asked me about it sometime later. I told her the last thing I wanted to do was be around other people like myself, depressed losers and loners. In her Yiddish accent she could put on for such occasions, she said, 'Go, it might help you . . . besides, you might meet a nice man there.' To appease my mother, I promised to read the brochure and at least look into the seminar."

By this time Ari had almost reached the university, so he broke back into the conversation, questioning, "Are you going to get to the punch line, or am I going to have to wait for our next date?"

Michele smiled. "Does that mean we *are* going to have a next date?"

Ari was taken a little off guard, but quickly regained his composure. "Well, of course . . . I mean, why wouldn't we?"

"Good," Michele said. "I didn't know what your intentions were until now. Does this mean we are dating or having a relationship or something?"

"Yes," Ari blurted.

"Yes to which? Dating, a relationship, or something else?" Michele inquired.

Ari smiled and said with a chuckle, "Yes to all the above. Continue with your story. I haven't heard anything really juicy yet."

Michele continued, "When I finally looked more closely at the brochure, I saw that the divorce recovery seminar was to be held at a church."

"A church?" Ari responded somewhat alarmed.

"Yes, a Presbyterian church in Bryn Mawr, not far from our home. It was then I knew my mother was really desperate about me. If she wanted her Jewish daughter to go to a seminar held at a church, I knew I should at least go and check it out."

"So what happened?" Ari prompted.

"In the first session, the speaker took us through the 'slippery slope' of normal divorce emotions. They ranged from denial to anger to depression. All the examples the speaker gave seemed to be taken directly from my own life.

"At the end of the session, we divided into small groups where we all introduced ourselves. A facilitator asked us to identify which of the stages on the emotional slope fit us each the most. I, of course, was seriously stuck in the depression stage.

"What surprised me most about the group was that everyone was so much like me. Some were the innocent victims, like me, who never saw the divorce coming. Others were initiators of divorce, who had their own stuff to work through—things like guilt, regret, and relief."

Ari interrupted, "What is this 'working through' stuff all about? It seems so American. In Israel, where survival is the goal, we don't work through emotional 'things.' There is no time for such activity. It seems like a nice American luxury to talk so much about one's feelings."

"Well, we probably do overdo it," Michele explained. "But it was what I needed in my life. Like what you needed to get off your chest tonight."

"So, what is the gigantic confession you have to make?" Ari asked.

"One of the individuals in my small group was also Jewish, which surprised me. But he equally confused me. He explained that he was a Jew who believed in Yeshua, the Anointed One. When I discovered he was talking about Jesus, I came unglued. How could a Jew believe in Jesus? He still went to synagogue, had Jewish friends, but he also attended a congregation called Beth Shar Shalom.

"This congregation was almost entirely Jewish believers in Yeshua. I went to several services with him. Over time, I began to see something in their lives I hadn't seen elsewhere. They were so vulnerable about their problems, but more than that, I sensed in them a genuine degree of confidence, peace, and assurance about life.

"After several weeks of attending services, I got off my medication, and my mother even began to see a change in my countenance. She thought I had met another guy and attributed my change to being 'moonstruck' or 'in love.' I guess, in some way, she was right. I had met Someone I had never seriously considered before."

Ari again interrupted, "So, what are you saying? You got religion?"

"Oh, I hope not," Michele explained. "Religion kills, but relationships bring life. What I found was a relationship with a God who is alive through Yeshua, my Anointed One. I believe He is the Messiah who came and will come again."

Ari stopped in front of Michele's apartment, turned toward her to kiss her, but then stopped. "You really believe this stuff?" Ari summoned.

"Yes, I do," Michele conceded.

"And I was really starting to fall for you," Ari confessed.

"So this ended it?" Michele solicited.

"I don't know . . . I mean . . . no, of course not. Nothing has ended. It's just that this has taken me by surprise," Ari said.

"You'd probably rather I'd had some passionate fling like yourself," Michele suggested. "That would be easier for you to accept," she gently taunted him.

"Of course not. I hadn't pictured you this way. Who is this Yeshua, anyway? Wasn't Jesus a blue-eyed, longhaired blond goy?"

Michele laughed and said, "Oh, Ari, he was born right here in Israel, no more than a few miles from here. Yeshua is the son of David, the son of Abraham [Matthew 1:1]. You can't get any more Jewish than that, can you?"

"I'll kiss to that," Ari chuckled. He leaned over, pressed his lips to hers, and held a kiss for what seemed like several minutes. Michele immediately knew a relationship had been born. And besides, this was the best kiss she had had in years.

"I'll call you tomorrow," Ari ended.

"Good," Michele returned. "Shalom, Ari."

⁓

THE GREAT AND FUTURE PRIESTLY KING

"Zion is the imperial abode of a future great King," David excitedly reasoned. Yahweh will one day place all the enemies of Israel at this One's feet. Having come into the midst of their sphere, He shall reign, forcing all His enemies into submission. David grasped his pen again and began writing, "Yahweh, You will stretch forth Your strong scepter from Zion saying, 'Rule in the midst of Your enemies.'" David stopped and elaborated in his mind, *To have a true reign there must be a people over which to rule . . . and an army to protect the nation's boundaries.*

David quickly reviewed how he had supplemented his little Judean army with foreign mercenaries. Israel did not exactly volunteer to fight in David's army. Military strength had come to him largely through the sword of mercenaries. David penned another line, "In the day of Your strength, the people of Israel will volunteer freely. These people will be like young, vigorous men who are like the freshness of the mountain dew. When this One comes, each of these will be clothed in the vestments of priests" (see Psalm 110:3-4).

As David recalled his experience, he realized how he had always functioned as a king-priest. He wore the priestly ephod, he inquired of the Lord, ate the priestly shewbread, and led his people in making sacrifices to the Lord. After all, hadn't God told Moses that Israel, even with a set order of priests, would be characterized as a nation of priests (Exodus 19:6, Numbers 16:3)?

David had always considered himself a priest since he was king of a priestly people. As king, he had the responsibility of modeling the priesthood before the people. Besides, hadn't the king of Salem, a former occupant of Mount Zion, functioned as a king-priest and accepted Abraham's spoils of war (Genesis 14:18-24)?

As a king-priest, David saw himself functioning very much like the ancient king of righteousness, Melchizedek. David again felt the unique Presence upon him. Would there be an another Anointed One to come after the likeness of this king of Salem?

David continued his song, "Yahweh has made an oath and will not feel pity for making it, 'You are a priest unto the ages, after the manner of Melchizedek.'" David felt empowered with concepts and words flowing into his mind. He mulled over how this Anointed One, who was and now is in his son, Solomon, will also be his divine Lord to come. "The Lord [*adonai*] is at Your right hand, oh, Yahweh; He will shatter kings in the day of His wrath, He will judge among all the gentile nations" (see Psalm 110:5-6).

As David penned these words, he realized how his judicial decisions and administration were almost exclusively for the citizens of Israel. But this coming Son, who sits at the right hand of Yahweh, will rule and exercise justice over all the nations. Therefore, the nations of the entire world should humble themselves and do homage to this Anointed Son (Psalm 2:2,12).

David paused for a moment and pictured what this ultimate judgment might look like. Ungodly people would be slaughtered. Their corpses would be in open view without the benefit of burial, and their leaders shattered and scattered. David added to his prose, "He, the Anointed One, will fill them with corpses, He will scatter the chief men over a broad expanse" (see Psalm 110:6).

David's eyes began to feel weary, and his mouth was somewhat parched from the heat of the night. As he drank from a nearby pitcher, he was reminded how many times he had quenched his thirst while on the run. There was no time for filling pouches or drinking from his royal cups.

While on the run, even a king must learn how to drink quickly. David picked up his pen again and wrote, "He will drink from the brook while along the way" (see Psalm 110:7). This Anointed One will be so consumed with His king-priest mission, He will barely take time to stop for a drink. Therefore, His head will be lifted up above all men (verse 7).

David's strength was slipping again, so he slowly paced himself back to his bed and reclined to sleep. His last thoughts were of Solomon and the kind of future he and later kings would face. David mouthed quietly, "O kings, show discernment; take warning, O judges of the earth, kiss the Son, lest He be angry and you perish in the way. . . . How blessed are all who take refuge in Him!" (see Psalm 2:10-12).

A CONCLUSION TO THE LEBANON DEBACLE

"I can't believe it, you haven't been in the Old City yet?" Ari exclaimed.

"No, I haven't," Michele explained. "I've been to Hebrew University to lecture, but I didn't have time to see the Old City."

"That settles it," Ari asserted. "Over the Yom Kippur holiday break, I will show you Jerusalem, the city of shalom, which hasn't seen any shalom since Solomon reigned!"

"Is that a date?" Michele asked.

"Yes, that is a date. And you are my date," Ari proudly exclaimed.

Michele was filled with a kind of excitement she had not experienced since her wedding day. During the next two weeks, she waited expectantly for the Yom Kippur school break. She worked feverishly getting her papers graded and all her correspondence finished so that she could completely enjoy the holiday with a clear mind.

However, thoughts plagued her about where they might stay and what the sleeping arrangements would be. Ari had said, "Don't worry about it. I'll take care of everything." However, Michele already knew about the reputation of most Israeli men. They almost instinctively expected to go to bed with their partners on the first date. But Ari seemed different. Even though there is no Hebrew word for "gentleman," she thought Ari had conducted himself with both a genuine interest in her and with a "gentlemanly" respect. She finally set aside her concerns and decided to trust him.

When the day arrived, Ari wanted to give Michele a taste of Israel's modern military history, so they drove northward toward Qiryat Gat. As Ari drove he pointed out certain sites where major battles had been fought. But Michele soon became bored with all the details of obscure battles. She was more interested in hearing what the final outcome of Ari's Lebanon experience had been.

"What happened after the IDF found out where you had been the night of the massacre?" Michele probed.

"Oh, all the parties began developing their own scapegoats and making their 'plausible deniability' statements to the press. No one in the Phalange leadership ever admitted having any part in the massacre. The most that ever came out of 'our allies' was that it 'might' have been 'a Lebanese faction.' For the most part, the Phalange put the blame on us. In return, we blamed the Phalange, and particularly Major Hobeika. In one of the strangest silences, the PLO did not condemn the Phalange at all, even though Palestinians had been killed. Their silence left the sentence of responsibility directly on the Israelis."

Ari's voice began to rise as he continued. "We could never find out how many were actually killed. The first Phalange reports said no more than fifty. The Palestinian Red Crescent put the number at two thousand, while an in-house Lebanese investigation mentioned four hundred sixty. Israeli intelligence put the numbers between seven hundred and eight hundred. However, death certificates were issued for twelve hundred. So who knows."

Michele asked, "Shouldn't someone have been punished for the slaughter?"

"Oh, sure, many got punished, such as people like me, for not being where I should have been. Even though I left my post at the request of the Aman chief! After four hundred thousand Israelis protested in Tel Aviv, asking for resignations of the entire cabinet, Prime Minister Begin appointed the Kahan Commission to make an internal investigation. All the key players testified before Chief Justice Kahan, a retired general, Yonah Efrat, and Justice Aharon Barak.

"They even brought in Dali'ah and put her on the stand for two hours. I had to watch the whole thing. She was so furious at both the commission and me for being drawn into this fiasco, it took all the passion out of our relationship. I called her once after the commission's findings were released, but she didn't want to see me anymore. I heard later that she had married. The investigation continued from October 1982 to February 1983."

"And what did they conclude?" Michele inquired.

"A few slaps on the hands for the major players in the debacle," Ari fumed. "The commission held the IDF 'indirectly responsible,' saying the officers should have anticipated the slaughter and stepped in much earlier. Our defense minister, Ariel Sharon, was 'remiss in his duties,' and was removed from his position even though he stayed on Begin's cabinet as minister without portfolio. He lost nothing!

"General Eitan, our chief of staff, was found 'negligent,' while Saguy, the chief of Aman, who got me into this mess, was found 'grossly negligent.' They also gave the Mossad a little slap by saying that they were too influenced by the Phalange elite."

"And what about you?" Michele probed.

"If the IDF was indirectly responsible, and its officers should have known what was going to happen, then that implicated me as well. If Saguy was grossly negligent, and I was his liaison, then I was doubly negligent. Since there was no direct evidence of dereliction of duty, and I was following the request of my superior, they could not court-martial me. So, in typical military fashion, the slaps got passed down the chain of command. I was given a formal reprimand, and taken off the fast-track list for high command. I've been a major ever since. They can't get rid of me, but they won't promote me. This is my fate for one night of ridiculous pleasure!"

Upon reaching Qiryat Malakhi, Ari turned toward the northeast and took the road leading to Latrun. "I've got something to show you up here," Ari announced.

The two stopped at a tourist-type gas station, purchased a few snacks, drinks, and a bottle of the famous Latrun liqueur made at the nearby monastery.

"Now this is my kind of religion," Ari humorously blurted out, as he gave the clerk his shekels. "If I ever get out of the army, maybe I will come here and make liqueurs with the monks."

Michele shook her head, but was inwardly delighted to see Ari had at least regained his attractive sense of humor.

From the gas station Ari pulled around into the Israeli war memorial. Tanks from the different periods of Israel's warfare lined the security fence of the museum. Ari gave Michele a quick overview of the history and then had one of the young IDF guides take a photo of the two of them.

Back in the car Ari headed up the Sha'ar Hagay pass. This historic pass is still littered with the remains of armored trucks destroyed by the Jordanians, as the Jewish fighters were trying to take food and supplies to their fellow Jewish fighters in Jerusalem.

"The road to Jerusalem is always a reminder of the lives that have been lost to regain our ancient capital," Ari lamented.

A few kilometers later, Ari pulled off the main road and took a detour.

"Now where are we going?" Michele questioned.

"Here," said Ari. He pulled up to an entrance that read "Ma'ale Hahamisha."

"It's a kibbutz. This is where we will be staying. It's a lovely setting, complete with guest accommodations and a swimming pool. I have friends here. Besides, it's only about eight kilometers from Jerusalem. It will be a good base camp for us, and less expensive."

DAVID'S DEEP UNDERSTANDING, ARI'S SKEPTICISM

During the night David's fever began to take its toll on the aging monarch. Blankets were piled on him to warm his fever-induced chill. Abishag was once again summoned to help keep David warm. As David transitioned between consciousness and delirium, his only prayer was for God to give him one more day.

If Yahweh would grant him one more day of breath, he could be present for Solomon's coronation. Once when he was more lucid, he asked that he be buried somewhere in his beloved city. He wanted it to be without pomp or ceremony, and he wanted to be laid to rest in a simple grave or tomb. David wanted to leave this life as he entered, as a simple shepherd boy from an obscure village.

Early in the morning his fever broke, and he was again alert. David prayed to the Lord,

> My soul, wait in silence for God only,
> For my hope is from Him. . . .
> The rock of my strength, my refuge is in God. . . .
> Men of low degree are only vanity, and men of rank are a lie;
> In the balances they both go up;
> They are together lighter than breath. (Psalm 62:5,7,9)

David had been both a boy of low estate and a man of rank. But both die the same way, and their lives are weighted as upon a balance. David was glad his hope was in the loving-kindness of his Lord, who would recompense him according to his works (Psalm 62:12). David woke Abishag, who was next to him, and asked her to prepare his royal clothes for the coronation.

Michele was pleasantly surprised with the accommodations. Their separate rooms were each furnished with single beds, a private bath, and a lounging chair. By Israeli kibbutz standards, the guest rooms were extremely comfortable and private. After a brief swim in the pool, the couple caught the Egged bus into the city. As they boarded the bus, Michele realized the bus was three-quarters filled with black-garmented Hasids. Ari ushered them to the back of the bus, where they found seats side by side.

Michele whispered into Ari's ear, "Once, while in Beersheba, I sat next to one of those long-bearded, side-curled rabbis. As soon as I sat down, he quickly moved to another seat. The bus continued on, and at the next stop another rabbi got on with the same kind of hat, and wearing black clothes. He marched directly to the seat next to me, gave a word of greeting, sat down, and engaged me in delightful conversation.

"Why would one rabbi move away from me, and the other enjoy my company?"

Ari laughed and responded, "Because the first rabbi was a 'Hasid,' a holy man, and the second was a 'Hacham,' a wise man! I've always preferred the idea of being wise rather than being holy," Ari teased.

As the bus turned onto Jaffa Road leading to the Jaffa Gate, Michele caught her first glimpse of the Old City. Centuries of war and destruction have left no royal palaces and few magnificent buildings. Ruled from distant capitals for most of its history, the city had been rebuilt and destroyed many times.

Ari pointed out the Ottoman walls that surrounded the city. They have stood since the 1530s, but had been in disrepair until the late 1800s. Once inside the walls, the modern world becomes irrelevant. Walking through the Jaffa Gate propels one back into time in a multisensory way. A mosaic of people, images, colors, sounds, and smells all makes the city what it is.

Arab women carry baskets on their heads. Hasidic Jews, in their frozen-in-time eighteenth-century Polish garb, are on their way to the Wailing Wall to pray. Bareheaded Franciscan friars join the mix, walking barefoot in brown cassocks. Elderly Arab men wearing the traditional kaffiyeh sip their thick Turkish coffee, generating the sweet smell of the aromatic cardamom spice. And of course, the scene would not be complete without the ever-present green-bereted Israeli security forces, carrying their M-16s to provide a "calming" effect.

As Ari got off the bus, Michele became a bit agitated after seeing the handle of a pistol emerging from Ari's hip pocket. "Why do you carry a gun when you are out of uniform?" she asked somewhat naively.

Ari retorted, "No Israeli officer should ever be anywhere in Israel without a weapon close by, especially here and in the West Bank."

"But you didn't have one when we went to tel Beersheba!" she lashed back.

"Oh yes, I did," Ari swore. "It was in the picnic basket." Michele again shook her head in amazement.

"What a country," she replied.

"It's the city of peace, like I told you." Ari reached into his back trouser pocket, pulled out the 9-millimeter Beretta, then quickly added, "And this is the peacemaker!"

Ari took Michele by the arm and proceeded through the Christian quarter bazaar. "This is David Street," Ari said with a smile, "but it looks more like Abdul's street today."

Even the Christian quarter was mostly populated by Christian Arabs. "Being 'Christian' here means you are a non-Moslem Arab, that's all," Ari reported.

Michele was immediately taken with the energy and excitement she felt on these narrow, ancient streets. The city seemed to pulsate. She also liked the quick attention she received from every shopkeeper, especially when they found out she was American. Occasionally, Michele would stop and barter on a few items, and then move on.

Upon reaching an intersection, Ari tugged on her arm, pulling her toward Ha Jehudim Street. "This will take us to the Jewish quarter and the Wailing Wall," Ari explained.

Michele immediately noticed the change of appearance and smell. "My, how the complexion of the city changes so quickly," she noted.

"Sure," Ari agreed. "The Palestinians say it's because the Israeli government won't spend any money on the Arabs. The real answer is that most of the Jewish quarter was burned and destroyed by the Jordanians. The quarter looks better because it is newer. It's been entirely reconstructed, not with government money, but with Jewish money from all over the world."

Ari then showed her the destroyed Hurva Synagogue Memorial and the Cordo, an ancient Roman market, and finally they moved toward the most holy site, the Western Wall, the only remaining section of Solomon's temple mount.

Ari led Michele up some winding steps until they came to an open patio overlooking the worshipers.

"Oh, what a marvelous site," Michele voiced.

Ari didn't look all that impressed. "Sure, it's become God's mailbox for both Christians and Jews," Ari said. "Pilgrims come here to worship and pray, but they leave written notes and prayers stuck between the crevices in the stones. Do they think God can better read them here than elsewhere?" Ari noted skeptically. "Well, it's about time to meet your friend from the States. Let's go on down to the plaza and find him."

DAVID CROWNS HIS SON

David abruptly chased all the servants out of his room, leaving only Abishag with him. "They want to dress me in all those royal garments. Don't they know I am an old man, ready to die? Give me one of the simple, plain robes I wear every day. I will crown my son in peasant attire," David blurted out.

Abishag got him dressed and then asked the servants to return to help him to the coronation. By the time David arrived, everyone was in place waiting for the king and his son. All of Israel's officials were there. All the army commanders were present in dress uniforms, along with David's faithful *gibborim*. In addition, all of David's property and livestock managers were there (1 Chronicles 28:1). As David looked at the company gathered before him and Solomon, he asked the Lord for strength, and then rose to his feet.

"Listen to me, my brothers and my people. I fully intended to build a house of rest for Yahweh's ark of the covenant, but God told me I was 'a man of war and bloodshed.' Therefore, my son Solomon shall sit upon the Lord's throne, and he will build a house to the Lord our God [1 Chronicles 28:2-5].

"Because Solomon is still young and inexperienced, I have left most of my wealth for the building of God's house. Besides, all of you gathered here have offered your good fortune as well for the construction of this house [1 Chronicles 29:1-9]. Therefore, I want each of you to support Solomon as you have supported me.

"And now, in the sight of all Israel, I ask you to pledge before this company to observe and seek after the commandments of the Lord, our God. If you desire to maintain a good land and one to leave to your children, you will so pledge" (see 1 Chronicles 28:8).

David then looked at his son and asked him to come forward and kneel. Solomon came forward and reclined before his father. David took off the signet ring, looped around his neck, and placed it over the head of his son. Then, as his last act as king, David took off his regal crown and set it upon the head of Solomon. He then asked Solomon to face the assembled crowd.

"As for you, my son Solomon, will you pledge before this company to know personally the God of your father and to serve Him with the same kind of heart and soul as I have?"

Solomon simply answered, "I will."

As both David and Solomon faced the gathering, David said, "If you seek the Lord, He will let you find Him; but if you forsake Him, He will reject you forever; therefore, be courageous and do the things the Lord finds pleasure in [see 1 Chronicles 28:8-10]. Be strong as a warrior and take courage to act on the things you should. Do not let fear overtake you, for the Lord will not fail you until all the work on this house is completed."

David lifted up his hands toward heaven and prayed, "Blessed are You, the Lord God of Israel, our Father forever and ever. All riches and honor come from You, and in Your hand lies all power to make great. Therefore, we praise Your glorious name, for who are we to be able to offer You anything? We are but sojourners and tenants in Your land; our days on this earth are like a shadow, and without You there is no hope. Therefore, give to this, my son, a heart of peace, a heart wholly devoted to You, a heart desirous of keeping Your testimonies and statutes and the spirit to want to do them."

David asked the entire congregation to bless the Lord, their God, and to ascribe honor to their new king (1 Chronicles 29:12-19). In response, the gathering broke out in a simultaneous, "Blessed art Thou," and fell to their faces before their new king (verse 20).

David felt both exhausted and exhilarated. He felt as if the weight of a threshing stone had been taken from around his neck. But as he walked back to his quarters, with servants buttressing both of his arms, he knew his life was over. He wondered if he had been a good son to his earthly father, Jesse.

Likewise, he questioned whether his own heavenly Father would be pleased with his life. And like any father, he worried whether his son would be able to handle the pressures of being a ruler. Most of all, he worried about whether Solomon would keep the concerns of the Lord God of Israel, and be a true son to Him (1 Chronicles 28:6).

CHAPTER ELEVEN

A New Passion for
Ari ben David Ammud

Neal Johnston had already arrived at the Wall and was waiting to meet Michele and her "guest." Dr. Neal Johnston was a fellow faculty member of Michele's at the University of Pennsylvania. He taught in the area of biblical archaeology and served as assistant curator of the Biblical Archeology Museum at Penn.

He was in Jerusalem for a two-week lectureship at the Institute of Holy Land Studies, located adjacent to the Old City. It just happened that he was in Jerusalem the same time Michele was. They had gotten to know each other through casual lunches at the museum, and occasionally Michele would ask Dr. Johnston questions about biblical historiography. The University of Penn museum houses one of the earliest manuscripts of the New Testament gospels, and has many artifacts from biblical digs. Neal had become a fatherly friend and mentor to her during her first years at the university.

"How will we spot him?" Ari questioned.

"Not to worry," Michele answered. "I'd know him anywhere. Look for someone who looks bewildered in Main Line drab clothing."

"What in the world is Main Line drab?" Ari probed.

"Oh, I'm sorry. Philadelphia's Main Line (western suburbs) is where we both live, but the old-money people sort of dress down. Dress is not in their consciousness. He'll probably have on a frayed old jacket, walking shoes, maybe a bow tie, and a funny hat. In fact, there he is!"

Michele had almost described him perfectly. He did lack the bow tie, however, obviously showing a little cultural sensitivity, as no one in Israel wears such things!

"Michele," Dr. Johnston exploded as he gave Michele a hearty embrace. "It's so good to see you. We all miss you."

"Let me introduce you to my friend," Michele replied. "This is Major Ariel Ammud. Ari and I met in Beersheba, where we both live."

"It's nice to meet you, Major," the professor returned. The two men shook hands and began some superficial small talk about Israeli culture. Meanwhile, Michele kept eyeing the mass of people moving toward the Western Wall, saying their prayers.

"I think I would like to do that," Michele reported.

Ari took off his jacket and covered Michele's arms and pointed her in the direction of the women's section. In an area between an iron fence and the stone wall, men and women must pray separately. Here no heads are uncovered and no immodest dress is allowed. Dr. Johnston asked Ari if he wanted to pray, but Ari declined.

"I'm not an observant Jew, Dr. Johnston," Ari answered.

"Please call me Neal, Major," the slender, pale professor requested. As the two men continued to make small talk, Ari kept one eye on the woman he had so quickly grown to care about. Finally finding a place at the crowded wall, Michele reached out and put one of her hands on the huge monolith. She bowed her head for several moments, leaned forward to kiss the stone, and then turned around and walked back through the crowd.

"For what did you pray?" Ari asked.

Michele smiled with a certain gleam in her eye and answered, "Only the Holy One and I know such things."

Dr. Johnston reentered the conversation and offered to take his two guests to dinner. "How about the King David Hotel for a good American steak?" the professor suggested.

"Steak is a little heavy for me," Michele replied. "Besides, it's such a lovely evening, wouldn't it be nice to find someplace we could eat outside?"

"I know just the place," Ari claimed, "but it's a little distance from here. Are we up for a little walk?"

Everyone agreed, so Ari led the trio out the nearby Dung Gate and followed the old Turkish walls down the Ophel overlooking the descending slope where David's ancient city once sat. Professor Johnston noted in his scholarly lecture tone that this was the perfect place to build a city, as it was protected on three sides by the valleys of Kidron, Hinnon, and Tyropoen, with the only spring in the area, the Gihon, nearby.

David, as a sensible, strategic warrior, built his city on the easily defensible high ground. Ari, as a military man, could only concur with the scholar's assessment.

As they neared the Zion Gate, Michele asked where David was buried.

"Well, Professor?" Ari appealed.

"We do know he was buried in the City of David somewhere, because the Scriptures tell us so [1 Kings 2:10], but exactly where, no one really knows. His burial site wasn't like Absalom's, whose tomb was very elaborately carved into the side of the hill near the Mount of Olives. But we have unearthed some barrel-shaped burial vaults near the southern end of the Ophel slope. David may have been buried in one of those," Dr. Johnston expounded.

"Imagine that, Israel's greatest king, and we don't even know where he is buried," Michele uttered in amazement.

⌒

THE KING NEARS HIS LAST BREATH

"Sheol, the abode of the dead, the pit," David murmured. "All other enemies I have defeated, but this one is stronger than the Philistines and more real to me now than Goliath himself. Out of the depths I cry to You, O Yahweh. Lord, hear my voice! Let Your ears be attentive to the voice of my supplications [see Psalm 130:1-2].

"But I am fearful. Sheol is darkness, foreboding. Its appetite for humanity is never satisfied. What is really out there, the spirits of my fathers, or the bones of long-vacated flesh and blood? Who knows for sure?"

David knew his time was short. Every breath was becoming more difficult. He felt overwhelmingly tired. Not a physical tiredness, but a complete exhaustion of his humanity. He was wrestling both within himself and with the paradoxes of his own life.

"If You, O Yahweh, should mark iniquities, who could stand before Your scrutiny?" (see Psalm 130:3). David was suddenly overtaken with the horror of his own rebellion. He had connived with the Philistines, lied to the high priest, rode with the Philistines against his own king, stolen another man's wife, committed murder, covered up his crime, lost contact with his own children, seen his own son lead a rebellion against him, and finally numbered his army, which cost the lives of thousands of his people.

David's iniquities appeared before his face and seemed magnified by his fears and exhaustion. He was frightened to face sheol. Sheol's voice was calling, and its power over his faint heart was winning the battle.

For a moment, David breathed a little more freely and remembered, "But with You there is forgiveness in order that You may be feared. Therefore, I will wait for You, Yahweh; my soul awaits You, and in Your word do I place my hope; my soul exists for Yahweh" (see Psalm 130:4-6). David knew it was too late to resolve the irreconcilable tensions within his own heart. His breath was too short, his mind too feeble, and his sins too great.

As he threw the covers off his bed, he found a certain solace in knowing he had tried to be a godly king. He had fought for God's honor with all his strength, established safe boundaries for Israel in which God's people could live in safety and prosperity. He had conquered Israel's enemies and made treaties. He was leaving his legacy to finish what he could not finish. But he, at least, had provided all the resources necessary to accomplish the task. *I can die a satisfied old man*, David thought.

"O Israel," David muttered triumphantly. "O Israel, place your hope in Yahweh, because with Yahweh there is *hesed*, God's loving covenant mercy; the abundance of redemption is also with Him; He will redeem Israel from all her iniquities" (see Psalm 130:7-8).

A peaceful serenity flooded David's mind, a serenity he had never known before. It was as if everything was suddenly new, a vigorous empowering sweeping through his body, and then . . . the empowering departed and he with it.

Abishag tried to awaken him early the next morning, but David, the great king, the man of so many contrary passions, was gone. The swirling whirlwind of his passionate personality had taken wing during the night and left. The chronicler of David's life inscribed in his ledger, "He died a good, gray-headed, and gray-bearded man. His days were fully lived and he left a legacy of riches and honor to his son to rule in his place" (see 1 Chronicles 29:28).

LION OF GOD

As the three rounded the corner from the Jaffa Gate, Dr. Johnston asked Ari, "Your name, isn't that the Hebrew word for lion?"

"Yes, that's right, but my given name is Ariel. Everyone calls me Ari for short," the major returned.

"Ariel . . . Ariel . . . Ariel," the professor rolled over several times. "The lion of God!" the doctor finally blurted out.

"Right again," Ari complimented. "You know your Hebrew. Are you Jewish?"

"Oh, no, I've worked in the Semitic languages so long I know most of the vocabulary, but don't ask me to speak it," Johnston replied. Turning toward Ari, the doctor's warm smile reflected a mysterious pathos for the middle-aged major.

"So, are you a lion of God?" Dr. Johnston inquired.

Ari was about to cross over Hativat Hatzanhanim Street, so he didn't answer. He took Michele's hand and led her across the busy street with the professor trailing along behind, almost unaware of the horn-blowing traffic. They entered a security gate and walked into a lovely green grass compound bordered on three sides by a Jerusalem stone hotel.

"What is this?" Michele inquired.

"It's the Notre Dame of Jerusalem Center, to which the pope fled and lived during the last days of World War II. It's now a tourist hospice, and has an excellent restaurant with an outdoor cafe. The view of the Old City is exceptional at night," Ari replied.

As they took their seats on the outdoor veranda, Ari answered the professor's question. "I've certainly been a lion most of my life, tearing apart and devouring anything that got in my way, but I don't think I know what it means to be a 'lion of God.' That's foreign territory for me," Ari confessed.

"You know, 'Ariel' is the both the name and the official seal for the city of Jerusalem," Ari added.

"Yes, I know," Dr. Johnston returned. "The prophet Isaiah addressed the city with the name Ariel and warned all the nations to think twice before waging war against Jerusalem" (Isaiah 29:1-2,7).

"I guess the Arabs have never read that," Michele entered.

Ari quickly suggested, "We'd better not talk about the Arabs here, most of the service personnel are Arabs."

Michele blushed a little as a white-coated Arab waiter appeared over her shoulder and asked for her order. Ari spoke Arabic to the waiter, Hebrew to some other patrons, and English to his two American friends. Dr. Johnston was quite impressed with the major's linguistic abilities.

Over dinner, conversation appropriately turned to the upcoming preparations for Yom Kippur. Because the holiday begins with Rosh Hashanah, the Jewish New Year, and extends ten days to the Day of Atonement, Michele asked Ari if he was going to make any promises for the new year.

"Are you kidding?" Ari declared. "That's for observant Jews, and I'm not religious. Besides, you have to go one whole day without eating."

"You don't feel the need to ask forgiveness for your sins and the sins of others?" Michele probed, looking him firmly in the eye.

Ari knew exactly what she was getting at, but didn't like the direction the conversation was going—focused on him!

He turned to Dr. Johnston and asked, "What about you, are you religious?"

The professor looked at Michele and then back at Ari, and recounted, "Well, yes and no. I suppose if you followed me around, you would find me doing some things that could be looked upon as religious, like going to church, praying, reading the Bible, and such.

"But I don't believe those things are the essence of a true, religious faith. True faith is relational, a daily relationship with the living God and relationships with people. For me, I came to this concept of a personal faith quite apart from any organized religion. I was a young graduate student at Harvard when I got involved with a student study group. Two of the students and one of our professors were Christians. By the time I finished my Ph.D. studies, I held a personal commitment to Jesus Christ."

As soon as Dr. Johnston let the word *Christ* out of his mouth, the waiter arrived with the food. The professor held up his glass, pronounced some ancient cryptic blessing upon the food, and closed with "lehayim."

"Lehayim," the two others responded, and with the clink of their glasses, delighted in a sumptuous meal.

ARI'S DAY OF ATONEMENT?

Ari asked Michele, "Did you observe Yom Kippur in your Philadelphia home?"

"Yes," Michele answered, "but I don't think I really understood its significance. As a little Jewish girl, I was more caught up with the family aspects of it, like not eating or drinking, and then going to the synagogue and hearing the *Kol Nidre* sung by the cantor. I enjoyed the special majesty and beauty of it all, but missed its true meaning."

"Which is?" Ari questioned.

"The meaning is . . . ?" Michele mimicked with a little surprise in her inflection. "'Day of Atonement,' the day we come before God in humility and confess our sins, and receive His cleansing and forgiveness" (Leviticus 16:29-34).

Ari interrupted, "So, one day of the year, all the things we have done wrong for an entire year are wiped clean by God. If this is true, then why can't this God do it on any other day?"

"You have asked a very profound question, Ari," the professor interceded. "I'm sure you remember your history well, how there could be no atonement without the high priest offering the blood of a goat upon the mercy seat, and then confessing the sins of the people upon a live goat and sending it into the wilderness [Leviticus 16:15-22]. In other words," the doctor continued, "a sort of commercial ransom took place between God and mankind. The sins of men were paid for, ransomed, by the blood of innocent animals. The debt being paid, God, in turn, pardons His people and wipes the slate clean. That's what it means to be forgiven. So your question strikes at the heart of what is missing in every Yom Kippur.

"So, what is missing, Ari?"

By this time, Ari had moved into his comfort zone in talking about such things, and was growing in both interest and serious inquiry.

"Well, it is obvious," Ari replied. "There is no high priest, no temple, and no sacrifice. But isn't that what the Temple Institute is all about? Getting ready to rebuild the temple? You aren't connected with them, are you?" Ari bemoaned. "They don't exactly have the best reputation in this town, at least with the military and security forces."

"No, Ari, I am in no way connected with them. But I do believe they are trying to restore genuine worship based upon the Levitical instructions. They have, in my humble opinion, missed the One toward whom all those rituals point. When God delivered Israel from their servitude to Egypt, He did so at the price of the slaughter of all the firstborn in Egypt [Exodus 4:23, 12:29].

"In return, Israel became the firstborn of God [Exodus 4:22]. In most of the ancient Near Eastern writings, the firstborn son is the royal heir to the throne, the legitimate coequal successor to his father's kingdom. In Jewish theology, this idea begins with your name, Ari."

"You're kidding," Ari laughed.

"It's true. When Jacob gave his prophetic word and blessing to each of his sons, he called Judah a 'lion's whelp,' with the promise that the royal scepter will not depart from Judah until Shiloh comes. To this one will be the complete obedience of the peoples [Genesis 49:9-10]. Even though the meaning of Shiloh is hotly debated by both Jewish and Christian scholars, it is clear that the royal throne will remain in the tribe of Judah until someone brings about the people's subservience.

"Some take the fulfillment of the passage in David's lifetime, but the Qumran Jewish community, even before the Christian era, was interpreting the passage messianically. In the Christian Scriptures, this Lion from the tribe of Judah and the Root of David is also the one called the Lamb of God. It is this Lion-King-Lamb who was sacrificed and became the purchase price before God for every tribe, tongue, and nation on earth [Revelation 5:5-9]. In other words, in Yom Kippur language, He is the high priest, the sacrifice, and the place of mercy, all wrapped up in one person" (Hebrews 3:1; 10:10,19).

"Yeshua Hamashiach," Michele piped in.

"I can't believe I'm sitting here talking about this stuff," Ari said, surprising himself, as he ordered dessert and beverages for everyone.

"But if this Jesus, Yeshua, is all you say He is, then why was He not from the tribe of Levi, making Him qualified to be a priest?" Ari inquired.

"Simple, but not so simple," Dr. Johnston continued. "The early Jewish Christians saw Him as a priest after the kind Melchizedek was."

"Wait a minute. Jewish Christians? That's like a contradiction, like a Moslem Jew or Israeli intelligence!" Ari replied.

"Well, all the first Christians were Jewish, Ari, so it was a contradiction beginning in the first century. But it's no more a contradiction than referring to someone as an atheist Jew or a Chinese Christian. One term describes a national heritage, whereas the other a personal belief. The early Jewish Christians saw Jesus as a king-priest, likened after the king of Salem who probably first lived right here [Genesis 14:18, Hebrews 7:1-28].

"If this is true, then Yeshua is both the ruling high priest and the lion-king who is coming. As David functioned as a king-priest without being from the tribe of Levi, so this Yeshua functions as our high priest today. He truly is the ben David, son of David!"

Michele reentered the conversation, "That means there is daily forgiveness when we acknowledge Him as the ransom for our sins and claim Him as our King and Lord. When we confess our sins to Him, He can cleanse us in that moment because He has been our sacrifice and the payment price for our iniquities" (1 John 1:9, 2:2).

"Yeshua is ben David," Ari said in amazement. "I don't think I told you, Michele, that contrary to most Israelis, I have an added legal or middle name. Supposedly, my father named me Ariel ben David Ammud. I have never known why he put the 'ben David' in the middle. I only knew from my mother that King David was his prime example of a man. I always thought I was named in tribute to my father's love of David. Do you suppose there was more to it than that?" Ari asked.

"I'm sure none of us could answer that, Ari," Michele prompted.

"Maybe my father was not only looking back, but looking forward as well," Ari wondered.

A LOOK AT MESSIAH
THROUGH THE PARADOX OF DAVID
"Do you remember when King David wrote, 'The Lord says to my Lord, "Sit at My right hand, until I make Thine enemies a footstool for Thy feet"'?" the professor inquired.

"Vaguely," Ari responded.

"Well, it's in one of David's psalms [Psalm 110:1]. When Yeshua was somewhere in the temple compound, He proposed a question to His religious challengers. He asked, 'What do you think about the Messiah, the Christ? Whose son is He?' Everyone gave the right answer, 'ben David.'

"But then He added, 'How then could David in the Spirit call this one Lord?' He then quoted Psalm 110 and concluded by saying, 'If David calls Him "Lord," how is He his son?' The text says that no one was able to answer Him.

"Yeshua's argument is simply brilliant. If David called Yahweh's son 'Lord,' then His son must be a divine son. But if the Messiah is to be David's son, then He must be human. The Messiah must then be both human and divine. That is precisely where we are in history, still trying to reconcile how God could have a Son, and how a human could be divine. If you figure that one out Ari, please let me know. Understanding the Messiah's two natures is about as difficult as understanding your namesake, David."

"Please explain, Neal," Ari asked.

The professor took a sip of his drink and began to elaborate. "David is a paradox. He is by far Israel's greatest king because all other kings are measured by his performance [1 Kings 11:4, 15:3; 2 Kings 14:3, 16:2, 18:3, 22:2]. On numerous occasions, God declared that David walked before Him with integrity of heart [1 Kings 9:4]. The later prophets indicated that God spared Jerusalem for no other reason than for the sake of David [Isaiah 37:35; 55:3].

"Yet, it seems there was a dark side to David's life as well. When we look at the details of David's life, we find inconsistencies, bloody violence, murderous adultery, polygamy, concubines for sexual pleasures, and sometimes an outright disregard for the truth. At times David seems to only have God's agenda on his heart, whereas after he became king, it appears he becomes a political animal. Some scholars have maintained that David's downfall almost began when he became king. It seems his heart was most pure when he was running for his life in the wilderness.

"So David was a very complex man. But one thing I do know, he was a man of multiple passions and affections. When his passions were turned toward God, he was a man after God's own heart. But when men of passion set their affections on pleasures other than God, the dark side of their passions emerges. I have traced the lineage of

David and have concluded that the evil seen in later kings really has its beginnings in David. It's almost unthinkable that a man after God's own heart would have in his own heart the very seeds for later evil. But that is precisely the case.

"David was the first to build a mercenary army. Under Solomon, the army became huge, complete with Egyptian horses and chariots [2 Chronicles 1:14-17]. David collected concubines, but Solomon raised the practice to unbelievable heights [1 Kings 11:3, Ecclesiastes 2:8]. David took several wives for himself, but Solomon expanded the practice to seven hundred! [1 Kings 11:3]. David built himself a palace, and wanted to build a house for the Lord. Solomon built both, but his own palace was larger than the temple [1 Kings 6:2, 7:2]. David made a few foreign alliances and left a standing army, but Solomon established his whole kingdom on the practice [2 Chronicles 9:25].

"So I come back to my premise. David is a paradox. God said that David had a heart wholly devoted to Him, whereas the chronicler of his life records all the dark episodes. We see his heart for God in the Psalms, and his heart for other things in the narratives.

"So you ask, how can I put this together?" the doctor humorously pried. "I can't, but perhaps David's life gives me some hope. If God can look down upon David's horrible sins and failures and still call him a man after His own heart, maybe there is hope for me, too.

"Could God perhaps sift the barren darkness of my own heart and find a heart that desperately wants to do what is right and good? I believe the Bible calls that 'grace,' a sort of unmerited benediction and a mercy based solely in God's covenantal love for His people" (Deuteronomy 7:6-9, Titus 3:4-7).

With that long summary, the professor looked at his watch and realized that he must be on his way. "Let me take care of the bill here, and then I must go back to the Holy Land Institute. Besides, I sense some chemistry here between the two of you that says you might like to enjoy the rest of the evening here alone." Dr. Johnston stood up, extended his shalom, and went off to pay the bill.

"I like him," Ari affirmed as he looked deeply into Michele's moonlit eyes. "He doesn't come across like a lot of the tourists here who are always trying to get us Israelis into their religion. He seems very sincere and knowledgeable, with a healthy regard for my questioning spirit. I appreciate that. I wouldn't mind talking with him some more."

Dr. Johnston returned and placed a generous tip on the table. He then kissed Michele on the cheek and shook Ari's hand. "I hope we can meet again, Ari," the professor extended.

"Likewise, Neal," Ari countered.

"Laylay tov . . . lehit," Ari and Michele added.

Ari stood up and moved around to the side of the table facing David's city. A brilliant, golden moon hung over the Old City. It was one of those rare occurrences when the autumn moon literally lights up the ancient city from above.

Ari reached over and gently cuddled Michele to his shoulder. "The city of the Great King," Ari declared.

Michele looked up into his eyes, smiling. "Ariel Elohim, Lion of God."

FANFARE FOR THE PASSIONATE

David was buried without the royal fanfare and public procession due most kings. The great king had wanted it that way. He desired to go as he came—a simple shepherd pasturing his father's sheep. Asaph led a few simple choruses with the solitary sounds of the *kinnor* as the only instrument, David's instrument of choice. Solomon wept as he said a few words of tribute, and then turned the ceremony over to Asaph.

David's children and wives, Joab, and the *gibborim* were the only witnesses. Although most of the city's inhabitants didn't know where David's body was laid to rest, the entire city grieved. The Lion of Judah was gone, but his legacy was only beginning.

Asaph returned to the palace and immediately went to his writing table. He had already started work on a new pilgrim song in tribute to David. Now he knew he must finish it. Taking pen in hand, he wrote what has come to be known as Psalm 132.

Remember, O LORD, on David's behalf,
All his affliction;
How he swore to the LORD,
And vowed to the Mighty One of Jacob,
"Surely I will not enter my house,
Nor lie on my bed;

I will not give sleep to my eyes,
Or slumber to my eyelids;
Until I find a place for the LORD,
A dwelling place for the Mighty One of Jacob." . . .

For the sake of David Thy servant,
Do not turn away the face of Thine anointed.
The LORD has sworn to David,
A truth from which He will not turn back;
"Of the fruit of your body I will set upon your throne.
If your sons will keep My covenant,
And My testimony which I will teach them,
Their sons also shall sit upon your throne forever."

For the LORD has chosen Zion;
He has desired it for His habitation.
"This is My resting place forever;
Here I will dwell, for I have desired it. . . .
There I will cause the horn of David to spring forth;
I have prepared a lamp for Mine anointed,
His enemies I will clothe with shame;
But upon himself his crown shall shine."

Biography of Ari ben David Ammud

Born   June 1, 1949, at Dagnia Kibbutz, Galilee.

1967   Begins compulsory army service at age seventeen. Fights in Six-Day War as a tank driver in the Sinai campaign. His father, Yakov, is killed in Six-Day War.

1970   Selected for officer training at age twenty-one. First assignment is in a tank group in Upper Galilee.

1973   October. Fights in Yom Kippur War as first lieutenant. Is assigned as tank commander on Golan Heights. Is awarded IDF Medal of Honor for heroism.

        December. Long-time Arab friend, Hassan, is killed in terrorist attack.

1976   Promoted to rank of captain at age twenty-seven. Marries Noam Shimron, daughter of Lieutenant Colonel Mordecai Shimron.

1977   Selected to U.S. Army War College, Carlise Barracks,

Pennsylvania. Serves as visiting foreign officer and lecturer on tank warfare. First child, Dorit, is born in Israel while he is in United States.

1979   Promoted to major at age thirty.

1981   Son, Benjamin, is born.

1982   June. Serves in Lebanon War, assigned to Lieutenant General Yitzak Mordecai's coastal force.

September. Assigned to divisional command as liaison with the Lebanese Phalange.

1983   Israeli government investigates slaughter of Lebanese civilians; he is cleared and reassigned. Noam divorces him, taking Dorit and Benjamin, and moves to Kibbutz Mahagan (Galilee). He is reassigned to "Samson's Foxes" special forces.

1988   Intifada begins. At age forty-one, undergoes special training in local insurgencies and counterterrorism.

1990   Turned down for promotion to lieutenant colonel.

1990-91   Assigned to American and British forces as intelligence liaison during Gulf War.

1994   Age forty-five, divorced and living alone in a Beersheba apartment. Daughter Dorit is age seventeen; son Benjamin is thirteen.

1995   Meets Michele Anderson.

Biography of
David ben Yishay

Age	Date (B.C.)	Event
12	1026	Anointed by Nathan the prophet.
18	1020	Kills Goliath; becomes Saul's armorbearer.
26	1012	Flees from Saul and exiles in Ziklag.
28	1010	Named king of Judah in Hebron.
35	1003	Defeats Jebusites and captures Jerusalem.
48	990	Becomes king of Israel and moves capital to Jerusalem.
68	970	Dies in Jerusalem; son Solomon becomes king.

Resources Consulted

Air War College Military Studies Course, vol I. Montgomery, Ala.: Air University, United States Air Force, Maxwell AFB, 1993.

Alon, Azaria. *The Natural History of the Land of the Bible*. London, England: Hamlym Publishing Group Limited, 1969.

Author unknown. *Land of Our Heritage*. Jerusalem, Israel: Keter Publishing House, no date.

Beers, V. Gilbert. *The Victor Handbook of Bible Knowledge*. Wheaton, Ill.: Victor Books, 1981.

Black, Ian, and Benny Morris. *Israel's Secret Wars*. New York: Grove Weidenfeld, 1991.

Craigie, Peter C. *The Problem of War in the Old Testament*. Wm. B. Eerdmans Pub., 1978.

Dayan, Moshe. *Living with the Bible*. New York: Bantam Books, 1978.

Dunnigan, James, and Austin Bay. *A Quick and Dirty Guide to War*. New York: Quill William Morror, 1991.

Friedman, Thomas L. *From Beirut to Jerusalem*. New York: Anchor Books, Doubleday, 1989.

Hindson, Edward E. *The Philistines and the Old Testament*. Grand Rapids, Mich.: Baker Books, 1971.

Katz, Samuel M. *Israel's Army*. Novato, Calif.: Presidio Press, 1990.

————. *Israel's Special Forces*. Osceola, Wis.: Motorbooks International, 1993.

Keel, Othmar. *The Symbolism of the Biblical World*. Seabury Press, Crossroad Books, 1978.

Meyer, Lawrence. *Israel Now*. New York: Delacorte Press, 1982.

Negev, Avarham. *Archaelogical Encyclopedia of the Holy Land*. Jerusalem, Israel: SBS Publishing Inc., 1980.

Owen, Frederick G. *Jerusalem*. Grand Rapids, Mich.: Baker, 1972.

Rasmussen, Carl G. *NIV Atlas of the Bible*. Grand Rapids, Mich.: Zondervan, 1989.

Rosovsky, Nitza. *Jerusalem Walks*. New York: Holt, Rinehard and Winston, 1982.

Schiff, Ze'ev, and Ya'ari Ehud. *Israel's Lebanon War*. New York: Simon & Schuster, 1984.

Stewart, Steven. *The Spy-Masters of Israel*. New York: Macmillian Pub., 1980.

Taylor, W.M. *David, King of Israel*. New York: Harper and Brothers Publishers, 1898.

Tenny, Merrill C., General Editor. *The Zondervan Pictorial Encyclopedia of the Bible*, five volumes. Grand Rapids, Mich.: Zondervan, 1975.

Turner, George A. *Historical Geography of the Holy Land*. Grand Rapids, Mich.: Baker Book House, 1973.

Wight, Fred H. *Manners and Customs of Bible Lands*. Chicago, Ill.: Moody Press, 1970.

Author

Dr. Robert Hicks is an educator, communicator, chaplain, and writer. He has taught at three institutions of higher learning and founded a counseling center in the Philadelphia suburbs. He has studied in Israel and represented the United States Air Force at the first International conference on wartime stress held in Tel Aviv. As a chaplain in the international guard he serves an A-10 fighter group. A frequent speaker on men's issues, he has authored *The Masculine Journey* and *Uneasy Manhood*. He also co-authored with his wife Cynthia, *The Feminine Journey*. He lives in Berwyn, Pennsylvania, is a Philly's fan, and loves to ski. *Man of All Passions* is his seventh book.